BURNED BRIDGES

AJ STEWART

JACARANDA DRIVE

Jacaranda Drive Publishing

Los Angeles, California

www.jacarandadrive.com

Cover artwork by Streetlight Graphics

ISBN-10: 1-945741-11-2

ISBN-13: 978-1-945741-11-1

For my grandfather, John Stewart, and all the brave men and women who served in World War II.

And for Heather

NEITHER OF THE TWO MEN EXPECTED TO DIE THAT DAY.
Not that it wasn't a place for dying. The hard, hot landscape
had seen more than its share of war and more than its share of
death. And while both men were aware of the possibility, each
carried assumptions about the other that assured them that
today was not the day they would end. Both men had been
wrong before.

The clay structure worked like a convection oven. The rear
of the building had been consumed by the sand, or perhaps built
into the slight undulation in the ground on purpose. There were
only three openings—two glassless windows and an entrance
with no door, but the entrance faced the afternoon sun, and the
desert wind pushed the hot air into the building and circulated
it, roasting anything inside the dark space. The poor design was
probably part of the reason the building had been abandoned,
and part of the reason the man in the standard-issue army
combat uniform had selected it as his home base.

The man had served long enough to become a staff sergeant,
but he wasn't used to the full ACU, and the sweat had soaked
through the so-called moisture-wicking T-shirt he wore under-

neath. The T-shirt alone was his preferred dress, especially in the air-conditioned confines of the quartermaster's office, where he spent as much of his time as possible. But out in the middle of this hellhole, with insurgents still taking potshots at military vehicles, he couldn't be too careful.

He stood feet splayed, struggling to recall his training, his Beretta M9 aimed at the rectangle of bright light bursting through the doorway. His technique was poor and his thumb hurt when he tried to disengage the safety with his dominant hand, so he flicked the switch with his left and then held the weapon in a two-handed fashion. Then he waited. He gripped the gun tight and it quickly grew heavy. But he wasn't planning on being there all day.

THE SECOND MAN walked casually toward the door. He kept his cadence slow but steady. His hands by his side but away from his sidearm. He had no wish to alarm the staff sergeant inside with unnecessary movement. The man's heart rate was slightly raised, but his hands were dry. He had spent a decade in the heat, somewhere or other on the planet, and his body had become as used to it as it ever would. He wore a sand-colored coat and trousers, no camouflage pattern, and a US Army surplus advanced combat helmet.

He stopped on the road, a rough track barely discernible in the satellite images from the rest of the baked earth around it, and looked at the building ahead and the makeshift structure beside it. In another place and in better condition the side structure might have been called a carport—corrugated iron sheets covered in canvas and dirt to hide it from the prying eyes in the sky. The iron roof sloped from the edge of the clay building down into the ground. It was a hasty but effective ruse that not only prevented the building from casting shadows that could be picked up by satellites, but also served to hide the Navistar 5000-MV tractor-trailer and the sand-colored twenty-foot intermodal shipping container the truck carried.

The man stepped from the white light of day to the dark hole of the doorway. He lifted his hands further from his hips, an unnatural way to walk, but disarming for the man he knew to be watching him. He stepped into the darkness and then stopped. He was, as his father would have called it, a sitting duck. He was not a huge man—not in his army—but his frame filled the small doorway. He was blinded, his vision nothing but random smudges like paints on a palette. He felt softness underfoot, as if someone had laid a carpet of dried palm fronds on the bare earth, and he smelled the acrid tones of diesel fuel. There was nothing to do but wait. His eyes would adjust, in time. If there was time.

THE STAFF SERGEANT licked the sweat from his upper lip. The skin was rough and in need of shaving. He looked forward to it, the ritual of cleanliness. Such things separated him from the barbarians that inhabited this dusty platter of earth. He rolled one shoulder, feeling the tension from holding the gun. Then he watched the silhouette in the doorway, not moving, hands away from his body. Like a gunslinger from the movies, the man had watched as a child. Feeling his arm fatigue, the staff sergeant finally spoke.

"You have no business being here," he said.

"Nor you," said the second man. His accent sounded vaguely American, but the staff sergeant knew that the man was not wearing a Stars and Stripes patch on his shoulder.

"This is not your war," said the staff sergeant. "Your people chickened out, remember?"

"As far I know, it's no one's war. You won, didn't you? That's what I heard on TV. You won, and you're pulling out."

The sergeant licked his lip again and snarled. There was a mocking tone in the man's voice. "You're a traitor," he spat.

The man in the doorway took two paces. "You need to come with me."

"I said, you're a traitor."

"You'll need to do a lot better than that, Sergeant."

"You're a disgrace to your country." He felt the sweat seeping from every pore and longed for the air-conditioned comfort of the truck's cabin. "You turned your back on your people and fought for the enemy."

"I hunt the enemy. Now I hunt you."

"I am a soldier in the United States Army. You don't have the—"

"You're a shopkeeper. You work in supply, you run the canteen. And you deal drugs. And now you're supplying arms to insurgents. Guns that get fired against your own men. So don't talk to me about being a traitor."

"You don't have the authority."

The man in the sand-colored clothes swiftly drew his gun from his holster and aimed at the staff sergeant. "I have all the authority I need. Now drop your weapon, and let's take a little drive to Camp Victory."

The staff sergeant blinked hard. His eyes were well adjusted to the darkness, but the sweat burned them. The traitor had his gun out now, but he wasn't going to use it. He wasn't a real soldier, but he was wrapped up in the NATO web somehow, and that meant he had rules and procedures to follow. Rules that certainly prevented him shooting a US soldier. There would be hell to pay if he did. An international incident, like the

Gulf War all over again. But the staff sergeant knew the traitor would be true to his word to deliver him to the MPs at Camp Victory in Baghdad, so he ran the numbers. Running the numbers was something he was very good at. Playing the percentages. Looking at the angles. Risk versus reward. The staff sergeant knew this guy was connected. How and to whom he didn't know. But enough to make it risky. And he was a boy scout. Rights and wrongs, blacks and whites. The staff sergeant came to a conclusion and made his last play.

The staff sergeant said, "I'm going to need the money back."

"You're serious."

"Deadly. My people will want the money back."

"You try to set me up with a bribe, and when it doesn't work, you want it back?"

"They'll want it back."

"Well, *they* aren't getting it. The money will go into evidence, and you will go into the stockade. And if you're helpful, the army won't send you to Guantanamo, they'll just send you to Leavenworth. And whoever *they* are can go to hell."

The staff sergeant watched the frame in the doorway. The man didn't move. He was fit and used to the heat in a way the staff sergeant never wanted to be. But he was wrong. Wrong about the staff sergeant, wrong about the people directing him. Wrong about himself. He wore no uniform, no tags or badges, no rank. He looked like the thousands of other private security contractors marching around Iraq, getting fat and rich off the oil money. But he wasn't one of them. He was neither security nor private, neither official nor unofficial. Easily commanded and conveniently forgotten.

"My people won't go to hell," the staff sergeant said. "They own hell."

Then he fired.

The staff sergeant wasn't a combat soldier. He was a

wheeler-dealer in a combat zone. A very lucrative place to be for a man with his skill set. Finding things that his fellow soldiers wanted in an environment where such things were not so easily sourced. But the whole thing was predicated on understanding the risks. And driving all the way from Baghdad to Basra and back was a big risk. But the reward was big, too. As long as he kept his head down. Which he did. He was very good at keeping away from places where bullets were flying or bombs were exploding. Out of the sun and out of the heat and away from the fight.

Which meant he didn't spend as much time at the range as regulated. Truth was, he hadn't fired a gun since arriving in Iraq, and he had no plans to. Until now. But this guy was more trouble than he was worth. He was too close, and the pullout of troops too imminent. So he fired. But the first trigger pull on an M9 is long, and for the untrained user, the longer pull could affect accuracy. The staff sergeant pulled and the Beretta fired, but even at close range, the shot flew high and wide, just above and to the right of the traitor's shoulder.

Unlike the staff sergeant, the other man was trained, and trained hard. He seemed not to move a muscle, not in reaction to being fired upon, not as he pulled the trigger of his own weapon. The staff sergeant pulled the M9 down and across and fired again, and as he did he heard the explosion of the other man's weapon and the burst of flame that reached for him across the dark space like an angry dragon.

The impact knocked the staff sergeant backward. He hit the ground hard and his head spun for a moment. Instinctively he felt for the site of the pain and felt the thick blood oozing through his fingers. The pain was immense, and the staff sergeant was not built for pain. He dragged himself up onto one arm and looked toward the doorway. The bright light shone through, white and unrelenting. The silhouette was gone. He tried sitting, but vertigo swept through him. He felt the compulsion to vomit but nothing came.

On one side of his body, alarms were going off. It felt like half of him was shutting down. The muscles in his left leg were spasming as if he were receiving electric shocks. The sweat was pooling in his left eye, making it sting and close reflexively. He took a moment to breathe. He expected the pain to abate, but it did not. Was this what being shot felt like? Was this what death felt like?

The staff sergeant felt an immense desire to lie down and sleep. He was aware enough to know that it was a trick, that sleep with this much pain was surely impossible, and lying down meant giving up. And he wasn't giving up. He gingerly levered himself onto his right side, the functioning side, then straightened his arm to create a prop, under which he was able to place his foot. He moved his hand to his knee and used the lever motion again to raise himself to an unstable standing position. He was bent over, bolts of agony shooting across his chest and down the left side of his body. He realized that he had dropped his sidearm, but he didn't waste time looking for it. He knew guys in the ordnance corps who could replace a lost M9 for a little something of what the staff sergeant could supply.

He checked himself to confirm that his left arm was still attached, and found that despite the pain, it was. He looked in one piece, more or less. He stood upright in stages, each movement punctuated by pain and nausea. Once standing, he glanced again at the doorway. And then he saw the other man. The traitor. He was lying on the straw-covered earth. The lower half of his body was lit by the sun pulsing in through the doorway. His torso and head were in the shaded corner of the building. He wasn't moving, nor moaning. He wasn't doing anything.

The staff sergeant recalled getting two shots away. The first had missed, exploding into the wall in a burst of dried clay. The second was better, aimed somewhere near the target, before he was punched backward by the force of being shot himself. It seemed his second shot had hit. The traitor looked dead. But the staff sergeant wanted to make sure. Not by testing the guy's pulse. By finishing the job.

He couldn't be sure if the traitor had been alone. He had never been before. When he wasn't with his posse of misfits, he had been with the woman. But if she was with him, why hadn't she responded to the sound of gunshots? Had he told her to stay in the vehicle? She wasn't the type to listen to an order like that. So his best guess was that she wasn't around. The traitor was alone.

The staff sergeant shuffled into the back corner of the building, to the wall without an opening. There he found the drums. He had built his own stockpile of diesel and gasoline, and as usual, his foresight pleased him. The semitrailer had more than enough diesel to get back to Baghdad, so he could afford to lose what he left behind. He felt around in the dark for the lever ring he had left there. Finding it with his good hand, he wrapped the ring around the cap on the drum, tightened it, then pulled the lever. The pressure of the fuel inside gave a pop and the cap came away easily. The sweet tang of gasoline bit at his nostrils as fumes lifted up from the drum. But that was not the smell he wanted. He selected the next drum in line and repeated the process. This time he sniffed with less vigor and found the diesel fuel he was searching for. He found the hand pump in the corner of the building, which he grabbed up like a spear and thrust down into the drum.

He was a supply staff sergeant, so he knew enough to know that diesel was considerably less flammable than gasoline. That was why the army favored it. But he also knew that it was combustible enough to fire in an engine, so it did burn. He tried holding the end of the hose in one hand, but then he couldn't prime the pump, so he dropped the hose onto the straw matting and pumped the handle with as much force as he could muster. He felt like he had just woken from a deep sleep, dazed and unsure, time slipping away and then returning. When the fuel began running through the hose, he pulled it out to its full length, reaching the midpoint of the building. He sprayed the straw flooring like a gardener watering his flowers. He continued pouring the diesel out as he worked his way back toward the window on the side of the building where he had parked the truck. Once he reached the window, he threw the hose back into the darkness.

The staff sergeant took a matchbook from his pocket. He had heard that people didn't smoke much anymore. That wasn't his experience. Army guys spent a lot of time sitting around doing not much at all, and there was only so much make-work that the army could come up with. Lots of guys played video games. Some guys read. And plenty of guys smoked. So he always carried matches. He tried lighting a match with one hand but couldn't. Then he tried moving his left arm to hold the matchbook, but it offered nothing but stabbing pain.

He finally put the book between his teeth and struck the match with his good hand. After a few unsuccessful attempts, the match burst to life under his nose. He tossed the match into a pool of diesel and watched as it fizzled out on contact. He snarled and struck another, then bit down on the matchbook in his mouth as he crouched and set fire to the straw. The dry flooring took the flame and it crackled and spat as it heated the diesel into action. The staff sergeant watched it for a moment, the way people stare at newborn fire. It slowly ebbed across the floor in a line, separating the room into two spaces. One for the staff sergeant and one for the traitor, like it was protecting the staff sergeant from the dead man.

But then the fire turned on its master. It split from its line and spread out like points on a compass. The staff sergeant realized too late that the fire had cut off his route to the doorway. As the slow-burning diesel filled the room with black smoke, he felt his lungs tighten and his eyes burn more than from sweat alone. He stumbled to the window on the side of the building. Right outside he could see the truck and its cargo waiting in the shade, the air-conditioned cabin of the truck calling him.

The window was just below the midpoint of his chest, not an easy height to get through for a man who had put on a few pounds in the years since basic training. With his left side more hindrance than help, he decided to go through headfirst. He bent over the sill of the window—a thick, ragged clay ledge—and then squirmed like a pregnant lizard outward. Side to side, using his right hand to push himself out. Once he reached the tipping point, he reconsidered the plan, but it was too late, and he spun and dropped through the hole and onto the hard-packed earth under the makeshift canopy. He landed hard on his left side. More pain, so intense he felt consciousness come and go. He grimaced and swore under his breath and then repeated the process of levering himself into a sitting position. Even under the iron canopy, it was hot, and he felt the world tip side to side, fore and aft. Then the bright day ebbed away and his head fell back onto the clay wall with a crack.

The staff sergeant's eyes snapped open. He wasn't sure if he had been out for a second or for hours. The shadows looked vaguely similar, as if not much time had passed. He felt the pain stab at his left arm. Above him, a plume of black smoke billowed from the window. The staff sergeant wanted for nothing more than sleep, but the dinosaur part of his brain told him to sleep later. He edged up the wall, the clay scratching at him through his thick combat uniform, until he found himself leaning into the window space. There were no solid forms to see, just colors. Orange and red and black. The smoke choked at him and he closed his eyes and leaned his body through the window to lever himself up.

The diesel did its job well. It burned as it should. Less flammable as a liquid, it needed to be converted to a vapor to burn efficiently in an engine. In the clay building, it served to do no more than heat the room like a pizza oven. And it heated the contents of the space like a pizza. The oven gradually turned the liquid gasoline in the drum to vapor until it hit 232 degrees Celsius.

At which point the vapor ignited.

The blast erupted out of the three openings in the building. The staff sergeant was pushing himself away from his window when flame and heat exploded around him, propelling him like a missile across the space and into the side of the truck.

If death meant the absence of pain, then at that moment the staff sergeant was truly alive. It defied categorization. Not stabbing or shooting or numbing. It was as if the entire world were agony, a new state of being. The last coherent thought the staff sergeant had was that his face was on fire, and that self-preservation demanded he put it out. He plunged his face into the sandy ground, but before he could decipher the effect of that action, a new world of darkness opened up and swallowed him whole.

JOHN FLYNN SLIPPED HIS SNOW JACKET INTO HIS PACK AND zipped it closed. It was Tahoe wear, too heavy for the Bay Area in the fall, but a required item for a trip back East. Beth paced into the room wearing a blouse and tights that seemed utterly inadequate for DC. She wiggled into a skirt and threw a business jacket on top, and glanced at his backpack with a smile but said nothing. He knew the look. *We're flying first class and you're carrying a backpack.* He'd never gotten comfortable with luggage he couldn't carry on his back. He felt like his body had grown around the shape of a pack. His trapezius muscles were overdeveloped and his core was strong to bear the weight across his hips. He could feel as light as air walking with a properly fitted pack. Dragging a suitcase on wheels never felt that way.

Flynn hefted his pack onto his back, picked up Beth's suitcase, and headed into the living room. Beth already owned the townhouse when they had met, and he liked it fine. It was a new build, so under California law, it could not have a wood-burning fireplace, and Beth had not opted to install a gas fire, which had suited Flynn well. He took a look around the orderly room. It was all Beth. Flynn had no eye for design and was happy to defer to her on all such matters. It wasn't a large space, but it was more than enough. And it was home.

Beth swept in and pressed her hands against Flynn's chest. She looked at his crisp blue shirt and tan trousers and smiled up at him. He felt like a tech worker from Silicon Valley, wearing the company uniform. Not that he was against wearing a uniform—he had done so for a long time—but he wasn't sure what this particular uniform represented.

It was a short walk from their home near Mission San Rafael to the bus station, a massive open-air terminal shuttling people around Marin County and further afield. They waited in the cool morning air for the Marin Airporter. Beth put her arm around his waist and pressed herself into him. The air was clear and the sky azure, with barely a breath of wind. Weather conditions across the Rockies and the Midwest were good. Flynn expected a comfortable flight.

The airporter coach deposited them at SFO an hour and a half later, where they checked in, the woman at the first-class counter giving nothing more than a slight grin at Flynn's back-pack. Beth sipped a coffee in the first-class lounge and read the morning *Chronicle*. Flynn couldn't get used to the coffee of his homeland, so he took tea and found a copy of *Psychology Today* on a shelf.

The flight wasn't much different from the lounge. The aircraft was new, the service attentive, and the coffee undrink-able. Flynn watched what he thought of as the preflight briefing —exits, oxygen, life preservers—but he appeared to be the only one who cared. As the aircraft leveled out, the seat in front leaned back, but there was plenty of legroom. Flynn was not an unusually tall man—his driver's license said he was six foot, but he thought of himself as 183 centimeters—but their first-class seats provided plenty of space. Beth's feet couldn't reach the seat in front. She preferred to cross them under herself anyway, watching some news program on her tablet, one hand on the device, the other resting on top of Flynn's hand on the armrest.

Flynn had spent his fair share of time in the air. More than a family man who took annual vacations to Mexico or Florida, less than one of those software salesmen with the platinum frequent flyers and a king's ransom in hotel points. Very little of Flynn's airtime had been this comfortable. But regardless of how often he did it, or at which end of the aircraft he sat, he always felt the same disorientation when landing after a long-distance flight. The human body could handle sitting for five hours watching videos at 35,000 feet, but the human mind found the whole exercise disconcerting. They had left their home at 0600, boarded the flight at 0900 and landed five hours later at 1700, or 5:00 p.m. local time. All the passengers' habit-driven minds were ready for lunch and the push on through midafternoon, not a cab ride from Dulles just in time for dinner.

Washington, DC., itself was in a state of flux. It was difficult to ascertain whether the day was ramping down or ramping up. People were moving in great numbers—on the sidewalks, on the roads and beneath on the subway system—from one place to another. Office to bar, bar to restaurant, restaurant to home. Some were headed straight to suburbs clinging around the Beltway. The city was alive, the streetlights and flood lamps highlighting the vast buildings and giving the city dimension.

It wasn't a city that had grown to become grand. It had been designed that way from the ground up. The layout of the streets, the size and scope of what were for the most part nothing more than administrative buildings. Designed to inspire its people and intimidate everyone else, leaving them in no doubt that this was a young nation to be taken seriously. It still worked over a hundred years later. Flynn sat in the back of the cab, taking it all in with a sense that the city was watching him as much as he was watching it.

The Watergate was a plush hotel previously favored by a clientele a good thirty years older than Flynn. It had closed for many years and undergone refurbishment to pitch itself to a younger crowd. There was lots of low furniture and wood trim, and to Flynn, it all seemed to be trying too hard. But there was a bed and a light and a shower, and he didn't care for more. After checking in, he and Beth found their room and changed into running gear. Flynn pulled on a hoodie with *Giants* written across the front and then flipped the hood up over his head.

They ran down Virginia Avenue, past the evening traffic fleeing through Foggy Bottom, until they reached the Mall. Then they took to the path around the Washington Monument and onward toward the Capitol Building. The evening air was brisk and Flynn noted many other joggers were wearing gloves. Beth had pulled her Lycra sleeves down over her hands. Flynn liked the prickle of the cold on his skin. They ran past what might have been the greatest collection of museums in the world. When they reached the end of the National Gallery of Art, they crossed the Mall over to the National Museum of the American Indian and ran back along the other side, past the Smithsonian Castle, lit like a sentry over the whole strip, and on to the Lincoln Memorial.

There they stopped, gathering their breath in visible puffs. Flynn arched his back and stood at the foot of the memorial, looking up at Lincoln in repose. He had learned all there was to learn about the man, from American textbooks read in classrooms in faraway lands. The textbooks conveyed Lincoln as a man of conviction and certainty, absolute in his knowledge of right and wrong. History had judged him favorably, but Flynn knew, from reading beyond the prescribed texts, that Lincoln's views on such issues as slavery and emancipation and equal rights had developed and changed as he had progressed from a senator to become president. Things were not black and white, not in Lincoln's day and not in Flynn's.

They walked back to the hotel along the Potomac River, past the Kennedy Center and around the Watergate office complex that had forever given up its name to political scandal, and on which the hotel had traded ever since Nixon. Beth showered first and got dressed in a knee-length black dress and a silver necklace. Flynn sat on the bed and watched her.

"How does this look?" she asked him.

"You're fantastic," he said.

She frowned. "You always say that."

"It's always true."

"It can't always be true," she said, dabbing perfume on her wrists.

Flynn disagreed. It could always be true. He could never get his head around her lack of confidence about it. She was sophisticated in ways Flynn could never imagine in himself, but there was always an undercurrent of doubt, like everything she had achieved was the result of luck rather than hard work.

"I should only be about an hour," she said.

"Fine."

"We'll be in the rooftop bar. Why don't you come up and meet me? It'll give you a chance to meet the client. They want us to do some forensic digging on some financial instruments, and it sounded like there could be some work in it for you, too."

"What sort of instruments?"

"Don't know. They didn't say much. These people are always so hush-hush until a contract is signed, but it's usually bonds, or even just currency, something with a serial number."

"If it has a serial number, it can be found."

Beth wrapped her arms around Flynn's neck. "Even the bogeyman can't hide forever."

She smiled and kissed him. She smelled fresh, like the rose

garden she and Flynn had visited in Golden Gate Park during the summer. It had reminded him of Belgium, although he had kept the thought to himself. Beth grabbed her purse and tossed in her phone, winked at him and then walked out. He watched her go and then watched the door slowly close with a definitive thunk.

Flynn took his time showering and then turned on the television, which seemed preoccupied with the minutiae of Washington politics. He flicked around the channels and eventually gave up. He opened his backpack, fished around, and pulled out a plastic grocery bag, from which he took a small blue box. It was made from sturdy cardboard, and the lid fit tight, but he removed it with a good pull. Then he took the dark navy suede box from within and flipped it open. The ring was tasteful but elegant, so the associate had told him. The diamonds sparkled even in the dim hotel room light. Flynn stared at the gems for a moment, contemplating the jagged turns that his life had taken to get him to this point. He shrugged and closed the box and returned it to his pack. *Uncertainty is the only certainty there is, and knowing how to live with insecurity is the only security.* So said the mathematician John Allen Paulos. Flynn concurred. He got dressed in the same trousers and a fresh white shirt, and then he checked his watch.

THE ROOFTOP BAR swirled around the top of the hotel like the swell on an ocean. There were lots of low chairs and round manicured shrubs and glowing bottles of liquor. All the people were well dressed, somewhere between very smart casual and wedding ready. Flynn was at the far bottom end of the scale.

He stepped into the middle of the space and noted two things. The first was that the views were to die for, as people liked to say. He couldn't imagine putting his life on the line for a view, but he understood the sentiment. The city glowed below him—the Potomac, the Kennedy Center, the distant suburbs in Virginia. It looked a pleasant place to take a drink. Except for the second thing that he noted. The fall breeze had picked up, perhaps as a result of the altitude above the street, and the bar was only sparsely populated. Flynn barely noticed the temperature, but he knew Beth was perennially cold, even in California. It wasn't the kind of place she would stay without a damned good reason.

Flynn didn't think that a new client was such a reason, so he walked a lap of the rooftop, and then a second, just to make sure. The space was punctured by tall heaters with flames inside long tubes. He felt his pulse rise as he glanced at them and then away. He told himself they were enclosed and safe, but the prickle in the hairs on the back of his neck told him he wasn't buying his own story.

There was no Beth near any of the heaters. There was no solo man who might have been the client waiting for her to return from the restroom. Flynn thought to ask the bartender but discarded the idea just as quickly. *A woman, five-six, blond hair, black dress.* That described about two-thirds of the female population of Washington, DC. He took the elevator down to the lobby and checked his phone on the way. No message.

The lobby curled around like the rooftop bar, and resembled a swirling glass of cognac. There was a bar off the main desk, a showroom of whiskeys with a smattering of tables. The room was full of people dressed in the same style as the rooftop bar people, sans coats. The lively chatter bounced off the walls and formed a solid mass of noise such that no one conversation could be discerned from another. Flynn took in the space and then edged his way around the tables and the cliques of people standing around the room. He figured Beth and a client would want a table, so he focused on the groups standing around each table as he moved through the bar. A full circuit of the room drew a blank, as did a second. His third go-round saw him receive some frowns and looks of disapproval, as if to say whatever he was looking for wasn't there, and now he was ruining everyone's good time. He didn't stop to engage any of the protestors. Such actions only ever served to slow things down. But he came to the same conclusion himself anyway. What he was looking for wasn't there.

His preliminary alarms weren't quite going off, but they were warming up. There was usually a good reason for events, more often innocent than not, at least in civilian life. So Flynn did what he had always done. He put himself not in someone else's shoes, but inside their head. Beth had gotten cold, so they had left the rooftop. The whiskey bar had been packed full, no place for a casual business chat, so they had sought an alternative. Where would a couple of professionals go? The restaurant, perhaps. Always quieter than a bar, and people always sat. No one stood around in a restaurant.

Flynn asked at the concierge desk and was directed to the hotel restaurant overlooking the river. He asked the maître d' for Beth by name, and a cursory look at a monitor produced no result. Perhaps they had used the client's name, which he didn't know, or, being a walk-in, they might have used no name at all. Flynn told the maître d' he would take a quick look—in his experience, asking to look sometimes resulted in the answer Flynn didn't want. The maître d's mouth opened but no words came out, and Flynn strode into the space, marched to one end and then back. Nothing.

He checked the lobby one more time, and then his phone. Still nothing. His internal alarm set itself to ready. He pulled up Beth's number and called. He heard the distant buzz of ringing, a sound that no longer matched the tone that was heard on the phone at the other end. That could have been bleeps or harps or rap music. In Beth's case, it was the strumming of an acoustic guitar. But Flynn didn't hear guitar. All he heard was an electronic thunk and the fuzz of a disconnected line. No answer, no voicemail. An ended call.

He stood in the lobby watching his phone. If he was interrupting an important conversation, Beth would return the call or at least text back. He waited. Nothing happened. He waited some more. People walked around him through the lobby, as if he were a statue or an art installation. He didn't mind. Waiting was something John Flynn was very good at. He waited several more minutes for the call, at ease, hands by his side, breathing slow. Then his phone bleeped to let him know a text message had arrived as expected. He looked at the screen, and the alarm in his head went off like a Klaxon warning of a tornado. He didn't take his eyes from the phone. It was a message from Beth. Or at least from her phone.

We have your girl.

CHAPTER THREE_

THE OLD FLYNN WOULD HAVE MOVED INSTANTLY. THE version of him that had been known as Fontaine. He would have saved the questions, the processing, the analysis for later. Forward progress would have been his immediate response. He could think and move at the same time. He had done so plenty of times before. But he was rusty and he knew it. This new version of himself, this new life, didn't require that line of thinking. But now he needed to recall old skills.

Flynn gave himself the full sixty-second count to process the emotions. Misunderstanding, disbelief, denial, anger, acceptance. They weren't feelings that could be suppressed forever, but they could be managed, compressed, compartmentalized and then used to effect as and when. He stood in the lobby silently, breathlessly. He saw nothing around him, just let his mind do what it had to do. His jaw clenched and then relaxed.

Then he ran.

He glanced at the elevator bank, noting the floor that each of the cars was on and calculating the approximate arrival time, and then added the return trip to his floor. He tacked on a margin of error and concluded that the stairs would be faster.

He hit them three at a time, large lunges upward, like the starting sequence of a triple jumper. He dropped to two at a time as he hit the fourth floor, and completed the rest of the journey at that pace. Flynn ran to his room and used a card to get in the door. Then he froze. Only his eyes moved. He took in the space, as he had left it. Listened hard for a sense of biology, of someone in the room, and got nothing but the steady hum of the building.

Flynn grabbed Beth's work bag, a black leather item that looked like an oversized handbag. From it, he pulled her tablet computer, the same one she had been watching on the aircraft. Flynn pressed the little button to bring it to life, then typed in a numerical passcode that was supposed to keep the device secure. Beth was a cautious person. She didn't have a banking app on either her phone or her tablet. She didn't have a social media account. She said it was a professional thing. Her firm was conservative, and they wouldn't look kindly on seeing her private life splashed across the internet. Flynn thought them wise for such a policy. But Beth had told him the passcode to her tablet, the way people in relationships do. And Flynn knew there were certain applications that came with the tablet, put there by the manufacturer, that could work to his advantage.

He was constantly surprised that the citizenry, who had bought into the concept of individual rights so completely, who had become almost evangelical about personal privacy and freedom, had given up those freedoms so easily. No citizen would agree to the government tracking their communication, yet they happily emailed and texted and posted their most intimate details. No citizen would agree to the government videotaping their movements, yet cell phone video was part of every news bulletin. No citizen would agree to wear a transponder recording their location at all times, yet they all carried cell phones that did just that.

Flynn opened an application on Beth's tablet designed to find a lost phone. He stared at the tablet screen. It showed a map of the northeastern United States, and it dissolved and reformed as it closed in on its target. A blue dot, pulsing as if it were alive, centered on the map. Above the blue dot was a small image of a cell phone, and below the image were the words *Beth's phone*. Flynn watched the dot. It wasn't just pulsing, it was moving. Moving along a red line on the map. A red line that represented the Baltimore-Washington Parkway. The dot was moving through the greenbelt between the two cities, pulsing northeast toward Baltimore.

He grabbed his backpack and pulled out the things he wouldn't need. Extra clothes, stationery, file folders. He dropped Beth's laptop into the pack and zipped it closed and threw it over his shoulder, grabbing her tablet as he went. The blue dot was still pulsing toward Baltimore. He tossed the do not disturb sign on the handle and made for the elevators. This time he waited. It gave him time to think. The how, when, where, who and why. In ascending order of importance. The how was more or less irrelevant. Information for debriefing and implementation in the future. The when was obvious enough. No less than thirty minutes earlier, no more than an hour. Their time through DC. traffic and their position on the map, combined with the time Beth had left the room, told him all he needed to know. The where was his present location, some-where around the Watergate complex either by force or—more likely—subterfuge. Perhaps the rooftop bar was too cold, and the whiskey bar too full, and Beth's client had suggested another option, so she had willingly gotten into a car. A vehicle big enough to fit extra men, with darkened windows to keep out those prying Washington eyes.

The who was always the question people asked. *Who would do this to me? Who could do such a thing?* But the who was never the key. The key was always the why. Understand the why, and the who became infinitely easier to discover, and significantly easier to find.

Why had they kidnapped Beth?

Then his phone bleeped, and he found out why.

THE DRIVER WAS USED to the traffic. He lived in traffic. It was as natural to him as the flow of water is to a river otter. It was not something to cause anger or joy. It was what it was. His partner was more highly strung. He fidgeted and swore under his breath at other drivers for their obvious tactics designed to delay him and him alone. The driver could see him sitting in the third-row seat, full of constant tiny movements. It was a colossal waste of energy in the opinion of the driver, but his partner was one of those wiry guys who used a lot of energy performing even the most routine tasks. When he drank coffee, he sipped at it a thousand times, putting the cup down in the cup holder between sips, multiplying the effort required by a factor of ten. He picked at imaginary tufts of fabric on his shirt, and he tapped his toes inside his shoes constantly. Even when the traffic thinned as they pulled north beyond the Beltway, he sat in the back coiled and wary, as if the enemy were around every corner.

But the enemy wasn't around every corner. The enemy was in the back of the van, in the row between them. He didn't know why she was the enemy, but it wasn't the first time he hadn't been told everything. He never considered it part of his job to know. His job was the drive to the nation's capital, to collect the cargo, and to return. What his mission was beyond that, he didn't know and he didn't care to think about. All he knew was that driving a van was more fun than washing dishes, and the pay was generally better.

The driver aimed for downtown Baltimore but banked away before reaching the inner city, onto I-95 and across the harbor and on northward. He glanced in the rearview mirror at his partner, and his eyes fell on the woman. Her face was set hard. She said nothing and didn't look out the window at the city lights as they breezed by. Then she looked up at the rearview mirror and caught his gaze. Her eyes were cold and sent a shiver down him, but he found he couldn't look away. Then a horn from an adjacent vehicle grabbed his attention, and he jerked the wheel. The driver refocused his attention out the windshield, anything not to look in the rearview again. He had no desire to look into those eyes any more than he had to. He pushed a little harder on the accelerator and focused on getting to New York, and getting this thing done.

CHAPTER FOUR_

THE TAXI GUY DROVE FAST. PERHAPS HE FELT IMMUNE TO the radars and patrol cars of the United States Park Police. Perhaps it was the two hundred-dollar notes that Flynn pulled from a sewn-up compartment in his pack and gave him up front that stoked his fire. Either way, he wasted no time weaving his way through the surface streets and out onto the Washington-Baltimore Parkway. The southern section of the road was maintained by the National Park Service and patrolled by their own police force. It kept a lower speed limit than the section closer to Baltimore. There were no trucks allowed on this part of the parkway, which made for a pleasant drive through a tunnel of yellow and brown and red autumnal trees during the day. At night it was nothing more than a tunnel of darkness punctuated by on-coming headlights.

The taxi guy was a small olive-skinned man who paid no attention to the cars around him or the speed limit. Flynn let him walk the tightrope. If they were pulled over, it would not be Flynn who was fined or arrested, although they would lose time. As it was, the park police paid them no mind, and they hit the junction with State Route 175 in record time. Beyond the intersection, the parkway was maintained by the state of Maryland, and it opened up and the speed limit increased. The guy mashed down harder on the pedal and Flynn stared at his phone.

He had replied to the text. The expected response would have been *Who are you?* or *What do you want?* Flynn replied with one word: *Why?* He didn't expect a literal reply. But their response might tell him something about the why. From experience, his was the kind of response that put the asker of the question off-kilter. And putting alternative thoughts in their minds meant there was less time for thinking about what they might do to Beth. So he watched the screen and ignored the darkness outside his window. But no message came.

That was unusual. A knee-jerk reaction was common in such situations. People who believed they held all the cards were often easily upset by the line of questioning diverting from their expected plan, and they often responded from their subconscious. Traces of their personality might be uncovered. So the lack of immediate response led Flynn to two possible conclusions. Option one: they were very calm and, having expected such a question, they were letting him sweat, which suggested they were professionals. Alternatively, they couldn't figure a response and were arguing amongst themselves about how to proceed. That positioned them as not professional. Both options had their pros and cons. Flynn would focus on those when one path had shown itself more likely than the other. Until then it was wasted energy.

As long as he had a trace on Beth, he was content with the silence. Every fifteen minutes, he opened Beth's tablet and noted the position of the pulsing blue dot—heading out of Maryland and toward Delaware. His taxi slowed a little around Baltimore Harbor, and Flynn looked up to see they were approaching Fort McHenry, the site of the battle that became the basis for "The Star-Spangled Banner." It was a bittersweet song to him, an anthem of a time he had never known, about a place he had never been fully able to comprehend. He craned his head to catch a glimpse of the fort, but his view was jolted away as the taxi sped into the tunnel that took them under the harbor.

The taxi guy told Flynn they would need gas, and they stopped at a service center shortly after crossing over the Delaware River in New Jersey. Flynn handed another two hundred to the taxi guy, and he pumped the gas as Flynn stood in the harsh artificial light of the gas station forecourt and watched the pulsing blue dot race away up the New Jersey Turnpike. As he did so, his phone beeped again. A response. Whoever was sending the messages had taken their time to respond, but when they had, they had answered the question Flynn had asked.

Find the shipment.

THEY HAD CLOSED the gap to thirty minutes, give or take, by the time they reached the signs for Trenton. The taxi guy made noises about how long they were going to continue, and Flynn handed him another two hundred. He had a gut feeling about where they might stop, and he hoped his last few hundred would get them there. He always kept a thousand dollars in cash hidden in his pack, sewn into the base between the rubber outer and the nylon inner. He was prepared to blow it all to get wherever the blue dot stopped.

He mulled over the text he had received. He was fairly certain what the text referred to, but he also knew that clarification was a good delaying tactic. All the major hostage response teams around the world used it. If the captors wanted a vehicle, clarify what kind of vehicle. If they wanted cash, clarify what denomination of bills. Get them talking, keep them talking. He punched in his question. *What shipment?* Then he settled in to wait.

He waited about ten seconds. Long enough for them to read and respond. Not long enough for discussion. So not professional, but whoever held the phone held the power, however slightly. The response was fast because it was one word.

Iraq.

Further clarification was pointless. The single-word answer was definitive. There was no repetition, no *the shipment in Iraq.* The response was to the point and closed the matter. They knew that he knew exactly what they meant. So the why had led him to the who. Which was impossible.

Because the who was dead.

Flynn typed in a demand of his own and hit send. If clarification didn't work, then the next step was to request POL. He watched the speech bubble on his screen, his last text, *proof of life*, hanging like a line in an unfinished song. He waited for twenty minutes and twenty-six miles. But his phone didn't beep. It rang. It sounded like an old-fashioned rotary telephone bell. Urgent and unwilling to be dismissed. Flynn closed his eyes and took the call with a deep breath.

"Beth?"

For a moment, he heard nothing but white noise. He concentrated hard on it, seeing the spikes of sound in his mind. Sharp peaks and troughs, variations in pitch and decibel. Then a voice.

"John?" was all she said. A mix of uncertainty and fear. No discernible pain. No hapless sobbing. Clear with a hint of anger.

"John, what's happ—"

Then the phone went dead. No repeat of demands, no taunting or gloating. So not professional, but well drilled. Flynn dropped back into his seat and let out a long breath. The call told him that Beth was alive, at least for now. Which left him with one more question. Where the hell were they going?

He played with the idea as the taxi sped along the turnpike. There was only one rational reason for the kidnappers to run this far. They were running home. From the unknown to the known. To their turf. To cover. The animal kingdom proved it time and again. When preyed upon by a predator, animals would make for cover. Only if the predator got too close would they change tactics, to zig and zag. Which left Flynn with twin questions: If they felt the need for cover, then they considered him some kind of threat. A predator, even though they held the cards. And if they weren't zigging and zagging, then they didn't know he was close behind. They were heading for trees with a level of confidence. Confidence that wasn't due.

Flynn turned on the tablet and watched the pulsing blue dot approach the island of Manhattan from New Jersey. Then it stopped in place as if taking a break in Hamilton Park, just before the Hudson River. For a couple of minutes, the dot lay dormant as the taxi sped toward it. Then for a moment, it disappeared, reappearing on the other side of the river, having passed through the Holland Tunnel. The dot crept across lower Manhattan, first north on Broadway, then east along Houston. Flynn's taxi was in Jersey City, following signs for the same tunnel, when Flynn saw the dot head up Avenue D and come to a stop near the Con Edison plant at East 12th Street. He watched the dot pulse in place as the taxi dropped below the surface and hit the Holland Tunnel.

New York City. It was simultaneously the best and worst place to hide on the Eastern Seaboard. Even in the heavily populated tristate area, Manhattan was a forest, thick with man-made towers and the massive canyons that ran between them. A place where a person could be one of millions of faces, hidden by the constant ebb and flow of humanity. But a place that was itself such a target that it wore a matrix of technology that was designed to find those hiding among the faces.

The taxi headed down Houston. Even in the early hours, the thoroughfare was busy with traffic. Flynn directed the taxi toward the dot on the tablet's screen, which had turned from blue to gray. The gray solid dot told Flynn that the phone had been turned off, and the dot was its last known position.

Traffic on Avenue D was steady but lighter, mostly heading for FDR Drive. The taxi turned onto East 10th Street and pulled to the curb. Flynn took the remainder of his cash and handed it to the guy through the Plexiglass barrier. He counted it and waved it in the air with a smile.

Flynn stepped out into the cold night and the taxi pulled away. He was standing outside a self-storage facility. Across the street was a darkened asphalt playground in the shadows of the smokestacks of the power plant. To the east there were tall residential towers, the Riis Houses, project housing squeezed in between Avenue D and FDR Drive. Over a thousand families lived in the nineteen buildings, but few were out after midnight. Steam lifted from street vents, and the windows on the parked vehicles were already frosted. Flynn hooked his arms in and hoisted his pack onto his back. He rolled his shoulders from habit and then walked up Avenue D.

Flynn rounded the corner by the playground. Basketball hoops were held aloft by twin sets of hardy steel poles, chipped and rusted. He marched on toward the stacks of the Con Edison plant billowing steam into the cold night sky. He stopped at the corner of East 11th Street, which was more of a paved lane than a road. It cut the basketball courts off from another playground that was attached to Franklin Delano Roosevelt School. The school itself resembled a county lockup. It was gray and hard and squat. There was no grass and few windows, and painted gates made of thick bars closed off any access to it after hours.

It wasn't a building befitting one of the union's greatest leaders. Flynn recalled reading about him in battered secondhand textbooks, flown in for military brats to learn from. He had liked what he had read about FDR. Roosevelt was quoted as saying we have nothing to fear but fear itself. Polio, the Great Depression and the Second World War were the milestones of his life, and yet he was still regarded by many as one of the better presidents, maybe top three. Flynn concurred. He leaned against the cold brick wall of the school and watched the power plant.

He watched for twenty minutes. His breath was visible on the air, but he wasn't cold. He had lived a long time in the heat, but his training had seen him subjected to such cold that giants of men froze and shook without restraint. New York in the fall was pleasant by comparison. But there was nothing happening. There were no people about, not in this neighborhood. Even in the city that never sleeps, the apartments bunker down at night. Here people had jobs, kids went to school. He watched the corner where the blue dot had stopped and turned gray. A yellow streetlamp flickered as if on its last legs, covering parked vehicles in a sickly glow.

He could see three vehicles from his vantage point. On the corner was a white sedan—Japanese or Korean—behind which sat a dark-colored minivan. The kind of vehicle families used. Tucked in behind the van was a large black car that looked like an imitation of a Lincoln Town Car but with softer lines. He couldn't see if the black car had livery plates or if it was a private vehicle, but it had blacked-out windows. It was the kind of car that Beth might have gotten into without question in DC. The kind of vehicle that could hide anything and anyone behind its tinted windows.

Flynn wondered if Beth was in one of the thousand apartments adjacent. He glanced up at the nearest building, spanning out in four directions like a plus sign. Even in that one building, she was a needle in a haystack. And that one building was itself just one haystack in a field of haystacks. He had narrowed down the options, but from here it got exponentially harder. To go searching would be fruitless. The best way to find a needle in a haystack was to use a metal detector. Draw them out. But to do that, he needed resources and he needed help. He could find both of those things in this big city. He just had to wait for daylight.

Flynn wanted to stand watch all night, even if nothing happened. His gut told him that Beth was close and he should remain in place. But his head told him that nothing was going to happen tonight, and that his best move was a tactical retreat. Don't just live to fight another day. Get some sleep and live to fight well. He pushed away from the wall and huffed out a visible breath. Then he turned down East 12th, looking for the subway.

THE DRIVER LET out a breath of his own. He realized he had been holding his air, watching the guy across the road. The guy was the only one on the street, the cold having driven even the night owls into their nooks. He had arrived on foot, with some kind of backpack, like he had been on an expedition and gotten horribly lost. The driver had watched him disappear into the dark shadows by the school, and he hadn't seen him come out.

When they had stopped with the girl's phone to send their

last text, they had noticed a blue bar across the top of the screen telling them that location tracking was activated. On tapping the bar, an app had opened showing that the phone was being tracked by something called Beth's tablet, and the tablet was represented by a blue dot on a map. The map showed a close-up of lower Manhattan and the Hudson. The dot was pulsing in and out. It was in New Jersey and moving fast toward the river.

They were ordered not to engage the man. They had been told he was good—very good. Good at what, the driver didn't know. His information was not specific in that regard. But it was clear that the man had followed them. They turned off the phone and waited. His partner wanted to wait with him, to see if the guy actually turned up, but the driver told him to go. His partner was too twitchy for a stakeout. His constant movement might give them away, and if it didn't, the driver knew it would eventually drive him crazy anyway. His partner wasn't the most useful guy, but he was available and he worked cheap, and the driver didn't have the luxury of time in putting a team together. It wasn't Ocean's damn eleven. So the driver stayed in the stolen minivan alone and waited. He left the engine off and the cabin grew cold, but he waited.

And then the guy appeared. The driver couldn't see his features at all, but there was no doubt it was him. The guy stood in the shadows for almost half an hour. Then the driver saw him venture from the shadows and turn away and head down 12th. The driver pulled out his cell phone. It was a basic burner, not a smartphone. Untraceable.

"He's here."

"What's he doing?" asked the voice on the other end.

"He waited a while, now he's walking away. Down 12th."

"Can you follow him?"

"No, it's too quiet. He'll notice the van."

"You need to dump the van anyway."

"It's cold out," said the driver.

"Is that your final answer?"

The driver sniffed and shifted in his seat. "I'm on it."

He got out of the minivan, leaving the keys in the ignition, and then stuffed his hands in his jeans pockets. The wind was coming in off the East River, along the canyons of buildings. The driver stepped across the empty avenue and followed along 12th Street. He kept his pace up, not running, but moving quickly to catch up. He figured it was the kind of pace a cold person might keep late at night. He walked two blocks, seeing nothing. The guy could have gone anywhere. It was a big city. The driver slowed his pace but kept walking, his mind flip-flopping the options. He didn't see the point of chasing shadows, but he didn't want to report in that he had lost the guy.

He reached the halfway point between Avenue A and First Avenue. He stopped and watched the lights change at the intersection ahead. There he saw a man walking with the lights, turning north on First. A man with a pack on his back. The driver half walked, half jogged to the corner. There was some other foot traffic ahead, and he couldn't discern the guy from anyone else, so he dropped into his brisk walk and headed north.

He reached the intersection with 13th Street and saw people walking in each direction. He couldn't tell whether his guy was one of them. But people tended to walk in long straight lines in the city, rather than zigzag on diagonals. So the driver guessed his guy would be headed straight up First Avenue, so he crossed to the western side of First and headed across 13th Street to get a better look across the traffic.

First Avenue was a busier thoroughfare, and the wind swept down it and stole the feeling from the driver's nose. He picked up his pace and reached 14th Street, crossed it and stopped outside a hot dog joint. The smell of grease and fries made the driver realize he hadn't eaten since the previous morning, and his stomach voiced its displeasure. The hot dog joint was doing a roaring trade. Most of the stores around it were closed, but people strode along the sidewalk, preferring the well-lit and open First Avenue to the darker, tighter streets to the east. The driver looked back and surveyed the intersection. A large delivery truck drove by, pulling the cold wind along, and the driver shivered, tucking his neck down into his jacket.

Then he saw him. Kitty-corner, outside a closed-up bagel shop. He got the briefest glimpse of a man with something on his back. He caught just a fragment of it before the man disappeared down the steps and into the subway. The driver had marched past his quarry, and he thought to run diagonally back across the intersection, but even nearing 2:00 a.m. that was foolish. He crossed back over 14th Street and then dodged the blasts of taxi horns across First and dashed down the stairs of the subway.

The rush of air and the unmistakable clatter of accelerating carriages hit him halfway down. There was a small concourse but no ticket booth. Just a closed flower stand and the turnstiles. The driver jumped a turnstile and raced to the platform. He got there in time to see the train move away. The silver carriages yawed and groaned and gained speed, and the driver watched them disappear into the depths of the tunnel. He caught his breath and walked back, jumping the turnstile the other way. He stood outside the closed bagel store and took out his phone. He paused with his finger over the button. It wasn't a call he wanted to make, but he did.

"He got away."

There was no answer.

"He got on the subway. It took off before I could get there."

There was a pause, then, "Which subway?"

"L train. Rockaway Parkway."

"Brooklyn?"

"Aha."

"What's in Brooklyn?"

"Maybe he's looking for your thing," said the driver. His lips were getting cold. "Your shipment."

"I hope so. For your sake."

CHAPTER FIVE_

THE NEW YORK SUBWAY SYSTEM WAS THE CHEAPEST HOTEL in the city. It ran 24/7 and was more secure than people gave it credit for. Flynn waited until he heard the approaching train from the street and hustled down into the First Avenue station. He had put his East Coast cards in his wallet prior to the trip, so he pulled out an MTA MetroCard and slipped through the turnstiles as the train decelerated into the platform. It was a Brooklyn train, headed for Rockaway Parkway. The carriage was empty but for one guy snoozing at the other end. Flynn dropped his pack at his feet, checked the subway map and then sat down. He looped the strap of his pack around his foot and leaned back into the seat. It was no Four Seasons, but he had slept in worse places. It was warm and dry. The bright lights didn't stop him from grabbing a power nap, and he woke twenty-five minutes later, shortly before arriving at Broadway Junction in Brooklyn.

He jumped off and wandered to the A train platform for the return trip to Manhattan. The A line was the longest in the New York system at thirty-one miles and around two hours' duration between 207th Street and Far Rockaway. From

Broadway Junction, he figured he'd get a decent hour. Over the years he had developed a technique for sleeping deeply but lightly. Lots of REM, but close to the surface should trouble arise. He didn't expect any problems. The only people likely to rouse him from his slumber were the MTA police, who occasionally wandered through the carriages. If they were bored or otherwise so inclined, they would wake people sleeping on the train to check their tickets or to stop them from doing what Flynn was doing, using the subway as a hotel.

Sleep was a mixed blessing. His batteries were recharging, but his mind took him to places he didn't want to go. With a clear mission and actions to follow, he could control his thoughts during his waking hours. Compartmentalize. Keep focused. But in sleep he had no such control. He knew it would be so. He saw Beth. She was sitting on the grass at Crissy Field in the shadow of the Golden Gate Bridge. It was summer. Despite that, a cool breeze came through the gap in the coastline via the marine layer that blanketed the ocean beyond. Her blond hair was tied back under a blue ball cap. *Cal* in yellow script on the front. She was smiling at him, as if he were behind a video camera. She sat on a picnic rug. Red tartan. Beth blew him a kiss. The Golden Gate Bridge glowed orange behind her. Then the bridge began pulsing. Orange and yellow. Beth blew him another kiss. Then the bridge exploded in a ball of flame. Beth didn't seem to react at all. She looked at him, tilted her head, and smiled. Then she exploded. Like a bullet piercing an apple.

Flynn woke as the carriage shuddered to a stop at its terminus at 207th Street in Harlem. He rubbed his eyes and checked his watch. It was a little before 4:00 a.m. and well before banking hours, so he left the warmth of the carriage and ventured out onto Broadway. New York might be the city that never sleeps, but some parts stay up later than others, and the sidewalks had been well and truly rolled up this far north. He walked by shuttered stores and brickwork covered in bill posters. The only place open was McDonald's, which fit Flynn's budget. He had only a few dollars left in his wallet and no desire to use a credit card.

He sat on the hard plastic seat in the McDonald's over a cup of coffee that certainly wasn't good but wasn't as bad as expected. He thought about his situation. He had been involved in investigating a few kidnappings in his previous life, and he knew time was the critical factor. Every passing hour saw the percentages drop for the victim. There was usually little incentive for the kidnappers to keep their hostage alive. Hostages were baggage; they slowed things down. They had voices that could yell for help. They had eyes that could see and remember and report and testify. In Flynn's experience, there were only two reasons to keep a hostage alive: proof of life and propaganda.

Proof of life was tenuous and could be faked. And even if it wasn't, once the kidnappers had gotten what they wanted, the need for POL was gone, and so were the chances for the hostage. Propaganda was a different beast, an animal Flynn had more experience with. In such cases the hostage was a tool, a device to attract attention or instill fear. The time frame was still a huge factor. For propagandists, the hostage's death was often the whole point of the exercise.

Therein lay his dilemma. This was not a propaganda operation. It was an old-fashioned extortion. *Do this thing or we'll kill your girlfriend.* But the troubling factor was the time. This wasn't a case of extorting money that required a trip to the bank in the morning. This was bigger. This was asking Flynn to find something that he hadn't thought about in years, something that he had hoped was lost. Something that, even if he could locate it, would take a hell of an effort to find. And time. Time that Beth didn't have. It might take weeks or even months, if it could be found at all. And kidnappers who didn't want to use the hostage for propaganda wouldn't want to keep the hostage for that long. Weeks or months of food and water and risk of escape and discovery. Too much risk. The hostage would quickly become a liability. So Flynn knew the objective wasn't to find the shipment. The objective was to find Beth. And he had a talent for finding people.

THE A LINE made its way down the western spine of Manhattan before cutting to the southeast near the financial district. Then it banked east and headed off the island and onward to Queens. Flynn sat over his coffee for a good long time and then took the forty-minute ride and got off on the last stop before the river.

He walked up from the station onto Fulton. The street was busy with Wall Street workers charging to their desks like army ants. Their movements looked random, but a pattern quickly emerged. The flow favored the direction of Broadway. Flynn walked against it toward the sun rising in the distance over Brooklyn. The weak sunlight felt good on his face. Unlike the foot traffic around him, he kept a casual pace.

He knew exactly where he was going but took a circuitous route. He let the energy of one of the world's great cities seep into him. It didn't feel good to be back. Not under the circumstances. But it did feel energizing. He had spent time in Paris and walked its boulevards in the early morning and found it invigorating in a very different way. It was like a patchwork quilt, inspired and comfortable. New York wore a blanket that was electric. The city buzzed, even in cold autumnal light.

Flynn turned right down Water Street, using the chill and buzz and the people to clear his head. He walked as far as

Hanover Square, turned right, and then right again. Back-tracked up Pearl Street. Where Water Street was a main traffic thoroughfare, Pearl was not much more than an alley. Less pedestrian traffic. Easy to spot a tail. He didn't expect to see one, but it was time to recall old habits.

He walked past the Killarney Rose bar and stopped where Pearl crossed Wall Street. People bustled along the sidewalk. The smell of coffee, and salt from the river. He stood before a sandstone building. Not tall by Manhattan standards. Twenty floors. The financial district was lower than most of the island. Apart from the buildings around the new World Trade Center, the Wall Street firms mostly preferred squat and strong to tall and grand. The building before Flynn had shopfront windows along its Wall Street side. On Pearl, there was a solitary entrance. Brass handles on a plain wooden door. No name. Flynn looked at his palms. He had hoped he would never be here again. Back when Colonel Laporte had told him to prepare in such a way, he had said, *Hope for roses, prepare for thorns.* There were no roses in this building.

On the wall was a small, cheap-looking plastic intercom. Black with a single white button. Flynn pressed the button once. He heard a small metallic clunk. Not a buzz, not like an apartment building. He pulled the door open and stepped into the small lobby. White tile floor with yellow flecks in it. An old wooden chair with a high back and intricate carvings sat against the wall. Too wide to get through the door and too heavy for one man to lift. Opposite the entrance was a revolving door. The sort of thing one found in a fancy hotel, but very different. Black matte metal like a shotgun barrel.

The lobby looked old and a little beyond its prime. As if a low-level accountant or third-tier lawyer worked here and paid too much for location and had nothing left for the interior. Flynn knew better. The white tile was Italian marble. The flecks in it were pure gold. And the chair had belonged to Louis XIV.

Beside the revolving door was a small box. It looked like a speaker. It was the opposite. The box was placed at chest height and Flynn had to lean down to it.

"My voice is my key," he said. For a moment, nothing. Then the revolving door slid open and a green light came on above it. Flynn stepped through the door. It slid closed behind him. It was a tube rather than a revolving door. The other side remained closed. For the moment Flynn was fully enclosed in glass. Bulletproof. And then some.

The light inside the tube went red. Another small box was at hip height. It had a glass plate on top. Flynn placed his right palm on the glass. It was cool to the touch. A green LED lit up on the box. Flynn looked up. A small camera shot his face. For a few seconds, he waited while he was watched and checked and the protocols were passed. Then the light inside turned from red to green. The door on the far side slid open. Another small lobby. Or perhaps a continuation of the previous one, divided by the secure door. Flynn walked toward two elevators. One door opened. He stepped in and waited. Twenty floors were above him.

The elevator went down.

The doors opened to a much larger lobby. More marble. Softened by plush fabrics on the furniture. Reds and yellows. A tapestry on the wall. Not Flynn's area of expertise, but it looked old. Pictures of knights in armor and chain mail. A woman sat beneath the tapestry behind a dark wood desk. She was almost consumed by it. She did not look up. A man in a dark tailored suit approached.

"Monsieur Fontaine," said the man with a tight smile. His accent was mixed. Flynn guessed he was from Austria but had perfected his English in New England. Maybe Rhode Island.

He spent a lot of money on grooming and smelled like the ground floor of a department store.

"It is our pleasure to see you. How may we assist?"

"I'd like to access my box, please." Flynn found his accent softening as he spoke. Hints of Belgian French.

"Of course, sir. Follow me to the drawing room."

The man led Flynn to another room, designed to look like a library in an old European stately home. Long velvet drapes hung from ceiling to floor. Dark-stained shelves held leather volumes. A round teak table sat in the middle of the room. Candles were lit on it, long and thin. The light was muted. It seemed to emanate from one side of the room, as if streaming through a window on a cold cloudy day in Marseilles. Flynn knew they were underground, so there were no windows, but no lighting fixtures were visible. It was a well-executed effect.

Flynn sat on a long deep-green sofa. The man in the suit retreated. A grandfather clock ticked in the corner of the room. It reminded Flynn that he had better things to do than sit around in a Manhattan basement pretending to be in Europe. But he had learned long ago that these things had a cadence of their own. And it rarely worked to fight it. Colonel Laporte had taught him that as well. The man returned with a silver tray and a small white cup.

"Double espresso. No milk, no sugar. Yes?"

Flynn nodded. The man bowed and retreated again. The espresso alone was worth the time. It had been years between visits, but the institutional memory was good. Flynn assumed it was all linked to the biometric entry system. His name, his services with them. His beverage preference. He sipped from the quaint cup. Thick and dark and strong. The taste had little in common with American coffee. As if the beans weren't even related. It was tart on his palate. One step short of injecting the caffeine into his veins. He savored it. Despite his internal urgency, he remained patient. His box would be retrieved. He would be escorted to his own smaller room with a chair and a desk. He would not be offered another espresso. It wasn't done. All things in moderation. He would have the room for as long as he wanted it. He didn't want it for long.

It played out exactly that way. Two new men in tailored suits carried the silver box into the small room. Placed it on a heavy-looking side table. The box was one meter long by a half meter wide and a half meter tall. It filled the surface of the table. Which kept the desk free. The two men left. The man who smelled like a perfume department took a golden key from his jacket and unlocked one of two locks. Then he gave Flynn a small black box.

"Would sir like anything?"

"A backpack." The man didn't flinch. He ignored the backpack that Flynn held in his hand.

"What size, sir?"

"Daypack."

The man nodded and closed the door. Flynn waited. Looked at his Timex. It took two minutes. The man knocked and opened the door. Handed Flynn a black daypack wrapped in plastic. Flynn tore the plastic off and held the pack up. Victorinox. Like the Swiss Army knife.

"Perfect," he said. The man bowed and closed the door.

Flynn turned his attention to the small black box the man had left. It was heavy. Like the material that hotel room safes are made from. It had a slide up cover. The slide exposed a glass panel. Flynn placed his right thumb on the glass. The box clicked open. He took out the solitary key inside. It didn't have ragged teeth like a house key. The sides were smooth, and pinpricks of light shone from its length like tiny stars. Flynn used the key to unlock the second lock on the secure box. Then he took a deep breath and opened the box. He again remembered his commanding officer, Colonel Laporte, and one of his CO's many mottos. *Le seul moyen est en avant de l'avant.*

The only way onward is forward.

It was Laporte, as much as events themselves, that had set him on the course his life had taken. The colonel had taken him under his wing when Flynn had needed just that. Had given him knowledge and purpose. Had seen him develop as a soldier and a man. And then, when events had once again turned against him, Flynn had been ready because Laporte had made him prepare. Flynn could never have imagined such a place as that which he stood in now. He could never have imagined a need for it. Laporte had introduced him to a private bank in Paris and then recommended that Flynn make his own connections from there. It was safer that way, he said. And when the whole thing turned bad, the private bank in a basement in New York City was where his life had been deposited. Now things were bad again. It was time for a withdrawal.

The items in the box were all contained in plastic Ziploc bags. Cash in large bags. Dollars. Euros. Pounds. Yuan. Flynn dropped the one full of dollars on the desk. He flipped through other bags, checking the contents. Passports, credit cards, driver's licenses. Some had other papers. Birth certificates. Social Security cards. There were a variety of passport colors and driver's licenses issued by numerous states. Each with a name written on the front of the Ziploc bag. Flynn picked one up and looked at the name on it. Jacques Fontaine. The name didn't seem real to him, as if it was a different person. Which in a way it was. It was a different name from a different life. A life that, had the chips fallen another way, he would never have lived. But live it he had. Then he had left that life behind and found one that still didn't fit quite right, but felt good all the same. Like a pair of new boots that were only just starting to learn the contours of his feet. And now this old name, this name on the Ziploc bag, was back. Old life running head-on into new life.

Flynn tossed the Ziploc bag back into the secure box and turned his attention to a smaller black box within. It contained a selection of firearms. He selected a Glock 17. Felt the weight in his hand for a moment. It was black and boxy and finely crafted. He placed it on the desk and opened a large carton of 9mm Parabellums. The name Parabellum came from the Latin *si vis pacem, para bellum*. If you seek peace, prepare for war. Flynn was preparing.

He took out a smaller box of fifty rounds. Overkill. He sat at the desk and unclipped the magazine and loaded seventeen rounds into it. Pushed the magazine back into the weapon with a controlled but firm slap and pulled the slide, slotting a round into the chamber. He put the remaining rounds back into the larger box.

Then he removed a roll of duct tape and opened the new daypack and put the tape and cash in it. Fished around and found a Glauca B1 tactical knife. He slipped it from its plastic sheath. The knife was dull black like the Glock, but the cobalt stainless-steel blade shone in the officious light of the room. The blade had three sharpened edges and plastic cuff cutters along the spine. Flynn flicked the blade closed and put the knife in the daypack, and then dropped the sheath back in the security box. Then he emptied his pockets. His wallet with his driver's license and Visa card. He put everything except the MetroCard in a Ziploc bag and found a marker pen in the box and wrote John Flynn on the front of the bag. He took Beth's laptop and tablet from his backpack and slipped them into the new small daypack. Then he stuffed the big backpack into the secure box. For now, for however long, John Flynn would stay here.

He put the MetroCard in his pocket and slipped the Glock carefully down the back of his jeans. He would never carry some weapons that way, but the Glock had three passive safeties, so as long as he made sure the trigger didn't get snagged as he slid the gun in, it allowed him to carry the weapon ready for action without the risk of blowing a hole in his calf by accident.

Flynn hit the call button on a console on the desk. Locked the large box and returned the key to its own lockbox. Waited for the man who smelled like a department store lobby to return. The three men reappeared and two took the box away. Flynn used their bathroom. It had been a long night and a lot of coffee. More marble and gold fixtures and cotton hand towels. The man waited for him in the lobby and then walked him to the elevator. Wished him a good day.

When he stepped back onto Pearl Street, the city felt different. Clouds had drifted in over Queens. The scent of possible rain was on the air. And he could feel cold steel on his back. He slipped the small daypack over his shoulder and wandered down the street toward the subway to confront his past.

CHAPTER SIX_

FLYNN TOOK THE SUBWAY FROM WALL STREET STRAIGHT up the middle of Manhattan to 14th Street—Union Square. On the way, he practiced what he wanted to say. Nothing sounded right. He wanted to apologize, but wasn't sure an apology was necessary. They had been a long way from home and in need of companionship. It had started as a professional thing and become something more, for a short time. They had both known their orders could take them away at a moment's notice. And then Flynn had disappeared. He had thought long and hard over whether he should have gone to her. Trusted her. But he hadn't. He had done what had to be done. And now she was the only person in the lower forty-eight that he could trust.

Flynn walked up to street level and crossed into the park. He stopped by the statue of George Washington. It was an equestrian statue, Washington on horseback on November 25, 1783, the day he led his troops into New York after the British had evacuated. It was a European-style bronze, the likes of which Flynn had seen a thousand times in France. It was surrounded by small hedges. Washington looked triumphant. He knew he was living not just a great day but a day that would lead to greatness. A pack of small dogs yapped in a dog run on the side of the park, their owners each standing, staring at phones, arms crossed from the cold. He glanced back to the east, down 14th Street. A short mile away were the projects where Beth may or may not have been.

Flynn turned away from Washington on his horse, crossed the park and headed toward Park Ave. The building he wanted was a five-story sandstone just north of 15th. Commercial space ran along the street. Beauty products. A magazine shop. In the center of the block were some small steps that led to double doors. Brass-framed glass. The lobby was small with old floor tiles. A directory of white push-in letters stood near a vacant doorman's desk. Flynn found the listing he wanted and called the elevator. The elevator car was also small. Dark marble floor, and mirrors on the walls. He looked at himself in the mirror. He had flown across the country, driven for four hours, and then slept a couple of hours on the subway. Considering that, he thought he looked presentable. He ran his hand over his brown hair. He kept it short, but not quite as short as it had been. The old-fashioned ding of the elevator drew his eyes away from himself and signaled that he had reached the fifth floor. Another small lobby. No furniture. A small gold plaque next to a door: *Hutton Hedstrom Associates.* The door was locked. He picked up a telephone that hung on the wall. The phone rang itself as he lifted it from the cradle.

"Hutton Hedstrom Associates. How may I help you, sir?" It was a woman's voice. Young. He looked through the column window next to the door. A blond woman sat behind a standard-issue gray reception desk, phone to her ear.

"I'm here to see Laura Hutton."

"Do you have an appointment?" She said it in a way that meant *you do not have an appointment.*

"No. I'm an old friend."

"Your name, sir?"

"John—" He stopped himself. "Tell her it's Jacques Fontaine."

"One moment, please."

Flynn hung up the phone and stepped away from the door. He waited for five minutes. He walked tight circles around the small lobby. It was like a chicken run. He turned and went the other way to prevent getting dizzy. Then the door opened. A large man stepped out. He was about 190 centimeters or six-three, and pushing 110 kilograms. A big man. Buzz-cut hair, balding on top. He wore a black suit with a white shirt. He could have been an accountant. Or a wrestler. But he was every inch ex-military.

"Do you have a weapon, sir?" The voice was deep and vanilla.

"Yes."

"May I have it, sir?"

Flynn pulled the Glock out from his trousers. Slowly, by the butt. He slid his hand down so he held the barrel of the gun. Butt facing the man, barrel facing the floor. He handed it over.

"There's one in the chamber."

The man quickly ejected the magazine. Then he opened the slide and dropped the round from the chamber into his palm. Let the slide go and palmed the bullet. He didn't put the magazine back in.

"This will be held in our lockbox for the duration of your visit and will be available for collection from me when you leave. May I?" He gestured at Flynn. Flynn lifted his arms. Held them straight out from the shoulders. He held his daypack in his right hand. The man stepped forward and patted him all over. Front. Rear. Legs. He ran his hands across Flynn's crotch. The man was a professional, and he wasn't going to let some homophobic thought get in the way of doing his job. Flynn knew it was easy enough to hide a snub-nosed pistol in his shorts. The man stepped back and asked for the bag. Flynn handed it to him. The man opened it. Flicked through the contents. Didn't make any facial expressions at the cash inside. He handed the pack back to Flynn. Stepped to the phone and asked to be let in.

Inside it looked like a vanilla office. Gray cubicles. A water-cooler near a sofa, where Flynn sat. That morning's *New York Times* on the coffee table. Something about the Giants quarter-back on the front page. Fanned-out brochures for Hutton Hedstrom. Flynn picked one up. *Discerning Security Services. We keep a watchful eye on you.* The brochure talked about protective services, investigations, event security. There were photos of serious men in dark suits standing near people who were supposed to be celebrities. Flynn didn't recognize them.

The woman stepped from behind the reception desk. She smiled and asked him to follow her. He dropped the brochure on the table and they strode down a corridor between cubicles. Turned into a large boardroom. A table stretched its length. There were fourteen chairs. Six either side, one at each end. A large flatscreen was on the wall at the far end. A whiteboard on the wall where Flynn stood. A polycom phone shaped like a fat spider sat in the middle of the table. The woman offered him coffee, and he declined and she walked away. Flynn didn't sit. He wiped his palms down his trousers. The room was in the center of the building. There were taupe walls on three sides. The fourth was glass. Vertical drapes hung in a bunch at one end. He noted hand-drawn diagrams and notes on the white-board. He recognized both the handwriting and the thought process.

"They said you were dead."

Flynn spun from the whiteboard. Laura Hutton stood in the doorway. Her light brown hair was longer than he recalled. Just short of shoulder-length. Expensively styled. She wore a white blouse under a dark blue blazer. The blouse was buttoned to show the curve of her breasts and a platinum necklace. Her trousers were gray with a sharp crease down each leg. She hadn't gained any weight in six years. If anything her face was tighter. She held his gaze.

Hutton stood for a moment taking in Flynn, an unashamed up-and-down look, the way law enforcement types do. She moved toward him and a hint of a smile tore at the corner of her mouth. Flynn returned it with a smile of his own. She stepped to him and looked up into his eyes.

Then she punched him in the face.

Hard.

He wore the impact on his cheek, right on the bone. It wasn't hard enough to break anything, but it was shocking enough to send him staggering back into the boardroom table. He put his hand to his cheek and gathered his balance and watched her close the door and turn to face him again.

"It's good to know you're not," she said.

Flynn touched his hand to his cheek again. "It doesn't feel like you think it's good."

"Don't be a such a baby. You deserved that."

"I did?"

"And don't play dumb with me. Don't tell me you didn't look at every angle. You could have told me, whatever it was. But you chose not to."

Flynn stood and pushed away from the conference table.

"I'm sorry."

"And don't apologize. You did what you did because you had to do it—at least that's how you saw things. You can't absolve yourself of your choices with apologies."

"I'm not trying to absolve myself of anything. I made a call, and if I had my time again, I'd make the same call all over."

"All right, then. I thought you'd gone soft."

"I'm still sorry."

Hutton watched him but said nothing for a moment.

"You want some coffee?"

"I've had all the coffee I can take this morning."

"I mean real coffee."

Flynn frowned.

"Come on," Hutton said.

Flynn followed her through the thicket of cubicles, straight then right then left. They stopped in a large kitchen. There was a cream linoleum floor and gray cabinets and a stainless-steel refrigerator and dishwasher and microwave. And a massive espresso machine. It took up an entire countertop and looked like something from a cafe in Paris or Marseilles. There was a lot of steel and chrome, and pipes and taps and pressure gauges. Enough technology to fly a man to the moon.

"Impressive," Flynn said.

Hutton ran the faucet until it was steaming and took a demitasse from a cupboard and filled it with hot water. Then she brought the contraption to life, and Flynn watched her grind beans and tamp them into the portafilter, and then bang the portafilter into the machine. She moved with the assurance of someone who knew exactly what she was doing. She poured out the hot water from the demitasse and put it under the portafilter, and there was groaning and hissing and steam, and then dark brown liquid oozed down from the portafilter into the cup. Hutton was concentrating like her life depended on it. Her lips moved as if she were counting. He decided she might have gotten a more expensive haircut and much more expensive clothes, but she was still Hutton. And that confirmed his decision to come to her.

There was a final hiss and she slipped the demitasse onto a saucer and handed it to Flynn. She didn't offer sugar or milk. She watched him over the rim of the cup, waiting for his impression, completely confident that it would be great coffee. He sipped. It was better than great. It was thick but not sludge, creamy with a hint of bitterness on the back palate. It took him across oceans, to small villages and Gallic men and the smell of cigarettes and coffee mixed on the air, and then brought him right back to New York.

"As good as I've had," he said.

Hutton nodded as if she had expected nothing less, and then she turned back to the machine and pulled the portafilter out and discarded the grounds and repeated the process. As she worked, Flynn noticed a Bunn carafe on another counter, half-full of coffee. When Hutton turned back to him with her own drink he nodded at the carafe.

"You can lead a horse to water," she said. "Let's go to my office."

THE OFFICE WASN'T large but must have been worth a mint. A small round meeting table. Four chairs. A whiteboard on the wall. A large heavy desk covered in papers. A dark wood book-shelf. Pictures. Of Hutton and an older man. Maybe Hedstrom. Maybe not. Hutton in a blue FBI jacket at the firing range at Quantico. In a blue suit at the Capitol Building. In desert uniform and flak jacket in Iraq. Flynn's eyes swept past the photos to the window. The office overlooked Union Square Park. He'd once heard a Wall Street wannabe say that green makes green. A view of trees in Manhattan added to the value of any office or apartment. Hutton was obviously doing very well.

She closed the door and leaned against it. Flynn looked out the window at the park below.

"Who's Hedstrom?" said Flynn.

"Hedstrom is my partner."

"Partner?" Flynn asked, turning from the window.

"Business partner. Former US Marine and NYPD."

"Seems like a slick operation. I never pegged you for a bodyguard."

"I'm not." She walked past him and stood by the window. "I run the investigations division. Corporate theft, celebrity stalkers. That sort of thing. Hedstrom handles the events and personal protection side."

"How many bodies?"

"Full-time, about a hundred. That many again on the books for temp jobs."

"You've done well."

"Yes." She waited for him to speak again. He didn't. "So, you. Of all the gin joints in all the world, and all that."

"Yeah." He smiled. As quickly it was gone. "I need your help."

"What kind of trouble are you in?"

"I'm not in any. I'm about to make some."

"And what is it that I can do after all these years?"

"I need someone I can trust. To walk through some things."

"Are these things legal?"

"Someone I know has been kidnapped."

"Someone you know?"

"My girlfriend."

Hutton nodded but said nothing. Then she pushed off the windowsill and moved around the office and sat behind her desk.

"You call the cops?"

"No."

"Where did this take place?"

"DC."

"And you came all the way to New York to spitball with me?"

"I have reason to believe they brought her here."

"So they crossed state lines. Did you call the FBI?"

"No. I came to you."

"FBI is better resourced than me. If anyone can find her, they can."

"There's a complication."

"What do they want?"

"They want a shipment."

"A shipment of what?"

Flynn didn't answer. He just looked at Hutton. Her mouth fell open.

"Iraq?"

He nodded.

Hutton leaned back in her office chair and looked up at the ceiling. Her lips were moving again. Then she leaned forward.

"You better take a seat. Tell me what happened."

CHAPTER SEVEN

FLYNN TOLD HUTTON WHAT HE KNEW. ABOUT THE TRIP to DC. and the hotel meeting and the phone app and following the pulsing blue dot to New York. Hutton made some notes on a yellow pad. When he was done he waited as she played the information back through her mind. She tapped her pen on the pad and looked at her notes, and then up at Flynn.

"So, initial impressions," she said. "They're amateurs. No pro would let themselves be tracked by a phone app. They'd turn it off, or trash it altogether. After the first message. Getting the first message from her phone is a good move. It makes it real. It proves they have her, in a fashion."

"Unless it's a decoy. Leading me away from her."

"Doesn't make sense. They're gambling that you'd even think to look at the app to track the phone in the first place. They're gambling you even have the means to do that. Odds are against that, which makes the trek to New York pointless. No, they didn't know. Probably still don't."

"The trail went dead last night."

"Phone might have gone dead."

They sat in silence for a while with Hutton's last word reverberating around the room.

"So we wait until they call again," she said. "In the meantime, the question is, can you find the shipment?"

"You don't really think they'll keep her alive that long."

"No, I don't. But it's leverage you might need. You never know. And what else are you going to do?"

"Find them."

"But as of last night, that trail is dead, so until they call again, there's nothing there. You can't work what you don't know."

"So what do we know?" Flynn asked.

"We know it's linked to Iraq, so somewhere in the chain, someone knows what happened. And that someone was probably there."

"All right." Flynn stood and opened his new daypack and took out Beth's tablet. The battery had gone dead while sitting in the McDonald's. Flynn looked at it like it held state secrets.

"Do you have a charger for this? Just in case they come back online."

Hutton looked at the tablet and nodded and moved to a bureau on the other side of her office and pulled open a drawer. From inside, she selected a cable and plugged one end into the tablet and the other into the outlet. She gently placed the tablet on top of the bureau and turned to Flynn.

"So now what?" she asked.

"So now let's get another one of your espressos and you can tell me what happened after I died."

―――――――

THEY REFILLED their coffees with more hissing and gurgling and steam and then took them back to Hutton's office. Flynn paused again to look out at the cold light across the park. Hutton told her assistant to hold her calls, and they sat quietly at the round meeting table by the window. When Flynn's mind snapped back, he found her there.

"So tell me," he said.

"It was the strangest thing I ever saw." She sipped her coffee before continuing. "Last thing we did in Iraq—we went out to oil fields in Rumaila, you remember?"

Flynn nodded and tasted his coffee. It was as good as the first.

Hutton continued. "I had to wait for a couple of hours to get a ride back to Basra. When I arrived at the hotel, there were NATO MPs asking lots of questions about you."

"What did you tell them?"

"The truth. I told them I didn't know where you were. Beyond that, I wasn't in their chain of command, so I had nothing else to say."

"So what happened?"

"Nothing. You know what MPs are like. They don't give anything away. But they didn't get anything either. So I went out to search for you. After what happened to Babar, I was concerned. There was radio silence. I heard nothing. Not from you, not from your guys. Then it got weird."

"Weird?"

"I found nothing, so I went back to the hotel the next morning. The lobby was crawling with private security contractors."

"There weren't any PSCs staying in the hotel."

"No, there weren't. And these guys I'd never seen. They started throwing their weight around, demanding to know where you were."

"What did you say?"

"I didn't say anything. I didn't report to any private grunts, either, so I told them they could take their attitudes elsewhere."

Flynn smiled.

"So the PSCs left. I waited for a while in the lounge, and then I went to my room. Gorecki was waiting for me. He said the PSCs were still watching the place. He told me you had issued a get-out code and that the other guys had left. He wanted to let me know before he disappeared."

"He's very considerate."

"He said you'd want me to know."

"I would have."

Hutton looked at him. "But you didn't. You didn't let me know."

"Did you expect me to?"

"No. I guess what I didn't know couldn't hurt me."

"Right. So Gorecki disappeared?"

"Yes. The hotel manager said you had been there and that you'd met someone in the lounge. The description sounded like Staff Sergeant Dennison, but that's as far as I got."

"That's as far as you got?"

"You disappointed?"

"Surprised. I know you. You're dogged."

"Well, that's where things got really strange. I got a call. From my agent-in-charge in Baghdad. I got called back with urgency. When I got there, he told me Quantico was calling me back in. He didn't know why. First I spent twelve hours in a hot room with no windows, getting questions thrown at me by some guy who flew in just to talk to me."

"The FBI interrogated you?"

Hutton shook her head. "This guy wasn't FBI. I was ordered to offer full cooperation. You don't get ordered to cooperate with your superiors in the Bureau. You just do it. This guy was something else. CIA, NSA maybe."

"What did he want?"

"He wanted you."

She paused and sipped her coffee. It had gone cold, so she gave it a frown, and then she swallowed it down in one shot.

"More specifically, he wanted to know about the shipment."

"What did you tell him?"

"I told him what I knew. I had been ordered to cooperate. I said we suspected arms were being smuggled in, possibly from Afghanistan or Pakistan via Iran. That someone was arming insurgents. I told him we suspected a quartermaster from Camp Victory."

"Is that what we thought?"

"That's what I was investigating. That's what went in my report."

"Okay."

"I told him that you had disappeared. He told me that Dennison had also disappeared. Then the guy left, and nine hours later I was in Turkey. The next day I was back in Virginia. I was told it was part of the pullout. I was reassigned to Minneapolis-St. Paul."

"Minneapolis?"

"Uh-huh. You ever been?"

Flynn shook his head.

"Lovely in the spring. But you've got to be Nordic to enjoy the winter."

"That could be a shock after Iraq."

"Twin Cities is a big office, looks after a huge geographical area. But before Iraq, I was here in New York. A move from the New York City office to Minneapolis is no kind of career move. It was pretty clear that a black mark had been put on my file, and I didn't really know why." She glanced out the window. "Except that, I did know why."

Flynn said nothing.

Hutton turned back to him. "I ended up investigating irregularities in the fishing quotas on Lac La Croix with the state department of natural resources. You know where that is, Lac La Croix?"

"Canada?"

"On the border. Half Minnesota, half Ontario. In the middle of winter you leave Minneapolis, drive way the hell north to Duluth, get some gas and drive even more the hell north to a frozen lake where guys are cutting holes in the ice to fish."

"Sounds relaxing," Flynn said.

"You're not normal, you know that?"

"I was never working under that assumption."

"Well, whatever it was, it was my new Bureau career, writ large."

"You didn't see that coming after the interrogation in Baghdad?"

"Of course I did. The whole thing reeked of a cover-up. Not that I cared about a cover-up. Sometimes for national security we need to do these things. But I could see who they were lining up as the scapegoat. So I kept copies of every file I ever made of the case."

"Clever girl."

"Gee, thanks, Dad."

"But how did you get out of Minnesota?"

Hutton sat back in her chair. "Hedstrom."

"Now that sounds like a guy who would go ice fishing."

"He would. He's quite the outdoorsman. You remember back in Iraq, I had a New York PD contact, ran the ID of the Iranian guy that Dennison met?"

"That was Hedstrom?"

"Uh-huh. He left the NYPD and started doing personal security. Got a few jobs, nothing major. Then some Wall Street guy he's protecting gets a death threat. Nothing abnormal, but Hedstrom saw something in it, and he called me in Minnesota.

We worked it through together and he found the guy. Found him in the woods behind this Wall Street guy's estate in Pound Ridge, with an assault rifle and enough ammo to take Belgium."

Flynn frowned.

"So all of a sudden he's the flavor of the month. Lots of work. New York celebs started calling. Most of them don't need protecting, but it looks cool to have the suits around you like you're the president. But administration is not his strong suit. Like you say, he'd rather be fishing. So he called me again. He knew my situation. Asked me to help him. So I did. I left the Bureau, came back to New York, and did all the legwork to get this place up and running. Got a recruitment plan in place, and then when it was all done, I opened our investigation division."

"And got your name first on the letterhead."

"Hedstrom doesn't care about that stuff. We tossed a coin."

Flynn nodded.

"But you already knew all about my business," Hutton said.

Flynn nodded again.

"But you didn't call."

He shook his head.

"Better that way," she said.

"Until now."

"So you want to know what the rumor was?"

"Hit me."

She resettled herself in her seat. The pale light shone on one side of her face, making her features look angular and serious.

"The word from Quantico and Langley was that you were the link with the terrorists. They tried to position it that you hadn't been finding terrorists all that time, that you had actually been working with them."

"Nice theory. But we did catch some pretty big, bad fish."

"They tried to rewrite that. They started claiming they did

that. That's the downside of black ops. You're easily erased from the record because you weren't there to begin with."

"I wasn't asking for a parade."

"I know. But here's the thing. You were put on a watch list. I don't know how you entered the US, but it wasn't through a conventional channel."

"No, it wasn't. But they don't have anything on me. No fingerprints, almost no records."

"There's technology. It's not foolproof, but it's good. But that's moot."

"Why?"

"Because you were pulled. Just before I left the Bureau. One day Jacques Fontaine is on the list, the next day he's not. No reason given, just gone."

"That's interesting. Why would they do that?"

"I thought about that for a long time. There was only one explanation that made any sense."

"Which was?"

"They had reason to believe you were dead."

Flynn said, "And they'd be right. Jacques Fontaine is dead. He died in the Iraqi desert."

"So what do I call you?"

"My name is John. John Flynn."

"That's what you came up with? John Flynn?"

"That's what I was born with, more or less."

A small crease formed between Hutton's eyes, and she did her thing where she analyzed his face again. Not staring. Deeper.

"Is that the first real thing I know about you?"

Flynn didn't take his eyes from her. "No. Pretty much everything I told you back then was true. We didn't create intricate backstories. We just didn't talk about our pasts."

"In the French Foreign Legion."

Flynn nodded. "That's right."

"So that was true."

"Yes. We weren't under orders to lie about it, but we didn't make it public knowledge either. I knew you'd figure it out."

"Give me some credit, you guys did speak an awful lot of French. So how did you come up with Jacques Fontaine?"

"I didn't. When you sign up, you're asked if you want to use an assumed name. Most guys do. But you don't choose it. The guy doing the paperwork comes up with it."

"Wow, that must be fun. Did he come up with Babar?"

"Someone did. And only one guy ever brought up the cartoon elephant on the parade ground. He had to have his face reconstructed with steel pins."

"He was a good guy, Babar. I miss him."

"Me too."

She nodded, her analysis complete. "So, we have two problems. Both location problems."

"Where is the shipment, and where is Beth."

"Right."

"The shipment, I have no idea."

"Neither did your team. Gorecki went back to the truck. It disappeared."

"Yes, it did."

"You made it happen?"

Flynn nodded.

"Did you try to find it?"

"No," said Flynn. "It was gone and that was all that mattered. Trying to find it might raise red flags, and that could have endangered everyone."

"I could have told somebody you weren't dead."

"Yes. Or that someone else was investigating."

"Like me."

"Exactly."

"I think someone knows you're alive now."

"Yes."

Hutton nodded. "So, can you find it?"

"There's a guy I can call."

"Use the phone on my desk. I'll get more coffee."

Flynn sat in Hutton's chair. It was tight at the sides, as if it were designed for a woman. He had always assumed chairs were unisex, like desks or lamps or doors. He used Hutton's phone and made a series of calls.

The first link in the chain started across the pond. It was still morning in New York, but afternoon in London, so all the desks had bodies at them and all the phones were answered promptly. His inquiries were treated with suspicion, as he had expected they would be. But he knew the language and the cadence of these things, so he worked his way through the chain for an hour until he landed with a woman in personnel and records. It was an impersonal-sounding department for a private company, but exactly what Flynn expected from a company that was essentially a private army. Flynn told her all that he knew, which she matched against their records, and once she was convinced he knew what he claimed he knew, she broke the bad news. Flynn was watching the last of the leaves get blown from the branches of the trees out the window when Hutton came back in.

"Anything?"

"Dead end. Literally."

Hutton frowned.

"He was a military contractor. We had served together a few years before. He died in a car accident in Paris two years ago. No obvious connection to our thing."

"And he's the only one who knew?"

"No. I asked him to send it somewhere. Then someone else was going to make it truly lost."

"So make another call."

"That one's a bit tougher. Whoever answers the phone is not going to tell me what I need to know without me telling them who I am, and they think I'm dead."

"Is there another way to contact this person?"

"There is. But it's not as easy as a phone call. I need to leave a message. Someone may or may not get back."

"So one location problem is cold. That leaves your girl. Beth?"

Flynn nodded.

"And we're still waiting for contact, yes?"

"Yes."

"So in the meantime, let's refuel."

Flynn walked over to Hutton's bureau and tapped the button that lit up Beth's tablet. The dot representing her phone's last known location was still gray, and it was still in the East Village, near the Con Edison plant. He left the tablet and followed Hutton out of the building, the clock in his head still ticking.

The flight landed at Washington Executive Airpark at 0800. They saw the strip at Andrews Air Force Base on approach, but touched down at the private Hyde Field about eight miles away. The Gulfstream wasn't new, but it wasn't old, and it was a hell of a lot nicer than anything the men were used to flying in. They had received the message that the flag had been tripped, but after so long they doubted it. But then the flag was confirmed and the aircraft was routed out of Ankara, Turkey, to collect them.

The unit leader didn't like DC. It was one of those towns full of people who never said what they meant and never meant what they said. But it was better than where they had flown in from—there was going to be a big steak in his future, once he finished his business here. The unit rolled off the aircraft and into a waiting Suburban. There was no passport control, no TSA. That had been arranged.

The Suburban came to a stop under a building on L Street, a handful of blocks north of the White House. The building featured no corporate branding on its exterior, no tenant list in the lobby. The organizations in the building were the kind that preferred to keep a low profile, except in the circles in which they mixed. The unit leader got out and waited. A man in a bespoke suit came down in the elevator. He frowned when he saw the unit leader dressed in a black paramilitary uniform. The man had no idea who the unit leader was or why he had been asked to report to him. But he told the unit leader what he knew. The meeting was due for 8:30 a.m. The lawyer from San Francisco had not shown up. They had called her cell phone and her hotel and heard nothing. That was all he knew.

"You hear from her, I need to know," the team leader barked.

"I don't have contact details for you," replied the man in the suit, not impressed with the team leader's tone.

The team leader stepped forward so quickly that the man in the suit took an involuntary step back.

"Someone called your sorry carcass down here. That's my contact details."

The unit leader dismissed the man, who was not used to being dismissed, and then directed his driver to get back on the road, where his secure phone would work better. As the Suburban cruised out toward Dupont Circle, the unit leader called in. He heard what he had expected to hear. His contact had an appointment with the woman lawyer at the company's office and had no idea why she hadn't appeared. His contact told him to hang tight. The unit leader hung up. He had been hanging tight for a long time. Years, in fact. He was done hanging tight.

The unit leader directed everyone on his team to call in their favors. Do whatever they had to. Find the woman. Then he did the same. His first contact knew nothing. But he had others. The unit leader knew more than most about the powerful people he worked for. He knew that it wasn't a club. They didn't sit around a round table with cigars or have a secret handshake. They were like a cellular network. There might have been any number of them, but any one only knew two others. No more, no less. Terrorist organizations had often tried to replicate a similar structure with mixed success. The problem with terrorists was there was always a leader somewhere, an ideological or political head who had to know more than anyone else. The very presence of such a figurehead destined the system to failure. The unit leader knew this for a fact. He knew the network had no leader, and it was firmly agreed that no such leader should emerge. One had emerged, once. That member was no longer of this earth. The team leader knew that for a fact, too.

The nature of a cellular network was that each hub in the network gave birth to its own network. It was the secondary networks that the team leader tapped into. He was even part of one or more himself. It meant that he had people he could call. He knew the lawyer had booked into the Watergate Hotel. It took him ten minutes to learn that she had not slept in her bed. She had not checked out. She had not used her keycard for any in-house purchases.

"I need to see the hotel security video," he said.

The voice on the line said, "Our man doesn't work today."

"Get him in. This is priority."

"I'll do what I can."

The team leader ended his call and looked to his second-in-command—his 2IC—beside him. "We need a base."

"Done," said the man, dressed in the same black tactical gear. He leaned forward to the guy who was driving. "P Street, between Dupont and Logan."

He got a curt nod. The Suburban headed around Dupont Circle and east on P Street. The area was mixed residential—row houses, apartment buildings and retail—with a range of offices and smaller embassies. They pulled in behind a run of row houses and stopped behind one. It was vacant, a lockbox to which the 2IC had the code. Inside there were empty desks and a handful of chairs on casters. It looked like a failed dot-com had recently vacated. There was no power and no heat, but the team required neither.

The team leader said, "Keep on it. I don't need to tell you how much we need this done. Unless any of you feel like going back to Iraq?"

He got no answer.

CHAPTER EIGHT_

FLYNN AND HUTTON ATE PASTRAMI SANDWICHES AT A DELI
off Broadway. Combined it was a pound of meat, enough stores
for the winter. Flynn had learned to eat when food presented
itself. Hunger was always a distinct possibility later, so best to
get your calories in while you could. Flynn sipped an espresso
and Hutton took a regular coffee.

"You really don't like normal coffee, do you?" Hutton asked.

"Define normal."

She held up her cup. It was thick industrial-strength china.

"That was a point of contention when I was a kid."

"With who?"

Flynn sipped his coffee. "My dad. I grew up in an American
household with American traditions. Big carafes of coffee and
football on Sundays and Thanksgiving turkey. The only thing
was, none of it happened in America."

Hutton put her cup down. "You know, that's the first thing
you've ever told me about your past."

"It's our way. We don't talk about the past."

"You're not in, anymore."

Flynn shrugged.

"But you don't have to tell me. It's okay," she added.

"You know why I trusted you, back in Iraq."

"I was closer to the bomb."

"Right. That was proof. But I already trusted you before then. I trusted you because you were an investigator and you didn't hit me up with questions about who I was or where I came from."

"You didn't offer any information, and that told me you'd rather not talk about it. And it didn't feel relevant to solving the case."

"That's what I mean. Most people ask too many questions, as if that's the way to earn trust."

"So I earned your trust by keeping quiet?"

"No. Your silence was a by-product. You earned my trust by focusing on your job."

Hutton nodded and sipped her coffee.

Flynn reached for his cup but didn't pick it up. "But I never figured out why you trusted me."

"Was that important to you?" Hutton asked.

"No. Not initially. I've worked with plenty of people I didn't trust. But I guess it did eventually matter to me. We still could have gotten the job done, either way. But I thought about it. I had a lot of time to think about it later."

"And you want to know?"

Flynn shrugged.

"I didn't trust you. Not to start. But you were hell-bent on finding out what I wanted to know, so I went with it."

Flynn nodded again and sipped his coffee.

Hutton continued. "But then I did trust you. When the guy came. The French general. Clearly, someone wanted you gone. And you didn't care. None of you did. You all wanted to find that shipment of guns more than you wanted to keep on the right side of your superiors. Actions imply character."

"You sound like my old CO."

"He must have been wise." She smiled. "But you're right. I am an investigator. I do want to know things. I do like answers."

"About me?"

"Yes, about you."

"Ask me."

"You'll tell me?"

"Yes."

Hutton nodded. "Are you really American?"

"Born in Cincinnati, Ohio."

"So you said you had an American childhood but not in America?"

"Not an American childhood. An American household. We had the Stars and Stripes in the front garden. From the age of five, I was taught to raise the flag first thing every morning and take it down at sunset."

"Sounds more American than Mayberry."

"It was. All of it. Except for the fact that most of it was in Belgium."

"Belgium?"

"My father was a Marine. He was based in South Carolina when I was born. But my mother wanted to have me among her family, so I was born in Ohio. Then my dad got posted to Germany, when I was a couple of months old. We went with him. My brother was born in Stuttgart. We did stints in Darwin, Australia, and in Japan. Later my dad got assigned to a role as liaison with NATO, and we moved to Brussels. That's where I went to school."

"And learned to drink coffee," said Hutton.

"That was later, but, yes. It was a bipolar way to grow up. We watched the Bengals play American football on the Armed Forces Network, but on the streets, we played soccer. We went to international schools and studied a US curriculum, but we spoke French around town."

"That would be weird."

"At the time it was normal. What you do is what you do. You don't know that it's different. It was only later, when compared to other people, that it looked different."

Hutton nodded and finished her coffee. Flynn paid the bill with cash. They stepped out onto the street and braced against the cold wind funneling down Broadway.

"So what now?" Hutton asked.

"I need internet access."

"I have computers at my office."

"I want one not associated with us."

"Like an internet cafe? I don't even know if they still exist. Everyone has the internet on their phone."

But internet cafes came in all shapes and sizes. Flynn wandered back toward the East River. With each block, the apparent wealth of the residents dropped. Million-dollar properties on Broadway gave way to tenements. Groups of youths sat on stoops whiling their time away.

The storefront Flynn chose was filled with posters for low-cost cell phone providers. Inside, a range of dummy phones and tablets, their insides removed, hung from white pegboard that was most commonly found in garage workshops. Worn gray carpet covered the floors. Ancient fluorescent tubes gave the store an institutional quality. At the far end, a counter separated the shop floor from the rear office. A young guy with a dark complexion sat behind the counter. He was slouched over, tapping the screen of a phone. Playing some sort of game, if the sounds it was emitting were any guide. He didn't look up. Flynn crossed the room and stood before him. He glanced at Flynn, and then back at his phone. Then he looked up again.

"You lost?"

The guy was of Middle Eastern heritage of some description. He could have been anything from Palestinian to Iranian. His accent was all New York.

"I need a computer," said Flynn.

"Look around. Phone store." The guy's phone bleeped and he looked down at it, annoyed. Clearly, he had lost the game.

"I don't want to buy one. Just use it. For a couple of minutes."

"This look like the New York Public Library to you?"

Flynn assessed the guy. He was young and tough. But more young than tough. He had the false sense of bravado that young men have the world over. Especially those that grew up somewhere that offered the veneer of menace, like the Lower East Side of New York. But this guy had seen nothing. He hadn't been to Africa. He hadn't seen tribal warlords enter villages with machetes and leave a trail of limbs in their wake. So Flynn had two options. The easy way, or the hard way. The hard way would be fast and cheap. Smash the guy's head into the counter once, twice, three times. Then use the computer that sat on the counter.

He chose the easy way. Easier for the guy. Flynn remembered young and stupid. It wasn't the guy's fault. Not the first time.

"Five minutes." He slammed a hundred-dollar bill down on the counter and slid it toward the guy. It got his attention. He sat up. Looked at the bill and then looked at Flynn.

"Two hundred," he said.

Flynn withdrew the bill and returned it to his pocket.

"How about I break your nose with your phone and use the computer for free?"

The guy snarled and began to say something but stopped. He was smarter than the average bear. He saw the look in Flynn's eyes and made the right choice.

"A hundred. Five minutes."

Flynn pulled the bill out again and slammed it back on the counter. He kept his hand on it. "You got a machine in the back?"

The guy nodded.

Flynn lifted his hand. The guy slipped the bill away with practiced skill and spun off his stool. He flipped the end of the countertop over itself on small hinges to let Flynn and Hutton through. Then he dropped the countertop down and led them back to a small room. It was part office and part storeroom. Boxes of all kinds of phones and SIM cards and cables and cases. There was a flatscreen monitor on a desk attached to a tower system that sat underneath. The guy leaned down and hit a button, and the machine whirred and clunked and then offered a proprietary arpeggio, and the screen came to life. The guy stood back and Flynn dropped into the seat.

"Five minutes," said Flynn.

"You're on the clock," said the guy as he leaned back against the shelving behind him.

Flynn spun in the chair. "A little privacy."

The guy frowned and then looked at Hutton. He bumped his hips away from the shelves and stepped out of the office. Hutton closed the door.

Flynn opened a browser. Typed in an address and waited for a page to load. It was some kind of message board. He selected a private board and typed in a password, and the board opened up. There were numerous threads. Each thread was like a separate conversation, starting with an initial question. Below each question, a number told him how many replies there were to each thread. All of the questions seemed to be related to the collection in the Musée du Louvre in Paris.

With a click, Flynn opened a new dialog box to begin his own thread. He titled it *African collection*. Then he typed in his message. Hutton watched him ask something about ancient warrior masks. Then he hit enter and the screen refreshed with his question at the top. Zero replies.

Flynn closed the browser window and then opened the computer settings. He deleted the session history and the browser history and the cookies. Then he deleted the browser application itself. He clicked on the wastebasket icon and clicked Empty Trash. Then he typed in a command, and a black window appeared on the screen. It looked like an old-fashioned computer terminal. The on-screen font looked like a typewriter. Flynn entered an FTP command and the computer told him it was downloading. He waited sixty seconds and then closed the black screen. He clicked again and the screen told him it was installing a new browser application. Replacing the one he had deleted. It took a couple of minutes and the computer restarted and a screen appeared that said *Welcome!* as if they had landed at a resort in Hawaii.

Flynn stood and left the welcome for someone else. Hutton opened the door and led Flynn out. She flipped the countertop over itself and walked out. As he passed through the counter, Flynn glanced at the young guy.

"Thanks, kid."

"You better not have given me a virus."

"No such luck."

Flynn left the countertop open and strode back onto the street.

Hutton was waiting. "You're cautious."

"It pays to be, don't you think?"

"You know NSA tracks all internet traffic."

"No, they don't. They track some. There's too much traffic in the world, even for them. So they look for suspicious sources, which, I grant you, this place might be. Cell phones get used by terrorists, so this store would be on the hot list. But then they look for trigger words. I didn't use any."

"They can crack codes. They do work pretty hard on it."

"The secret to cracking a code is in knowing the key. The secret to knowing the key is in the repetition. Reading the patterns. Computers are good at that. But I don't repeat, so there's no pattern."

"Okay. When will you hear?"

"Maybe tonight, maybe tomorrow. Maybe never."

They walked back to Hutton's office. Flynn sat at the conference table and looked at his phone and then out the window at the leaves blowing from the trees. He thought about Iraq and France and the United States and Beth. Hutton answered emails. The sun decided its short winter day was done and started its descent toward the horizon.

Flynn dropped into low power mode. He was awake, aware of his surroundings but not using any energy on processing any of it. He was absently looking out the window at the park when his phone rang. He looked at the screen. It was a number he didn't recognize. Area code 917. He looked at Hutton.

"New York number," he said.

"Listen hard," she told him.

He hit the button to take the call on speaker. "Yes?"

There was little ambient noise, bar an electronic hum. The phone was most likely a burner and the microphone in it cheap. Manufactured for price, not clarity.

"I can only guess you don't want to see your girl again."

"I want to talk to Beth."

"You need to concentrate. Find the shipment. Focus on the girl you lost."

"I want to talk to Beth. I need to know she's safe."

There was no response. Just the electronic hum. Then the

sound changed. A higher pitch, like the difference between the sound of a tunnel before and after you enter it. Then a voice.

"John?"

Flynn glanced at Hutton. It was Beth's voice. The unmistakable sound of fear. Flynn listened not just to her words but the sounds in between the words.

"John, what's happ—"

Flynn said nothing. Her voice was suddenly ripped away. Replaced by the electronic hum, and then a male voice.

"That's it, pal. That's all you're getting. Now find that shipment."

Flynn set his jaw and stared at the phone as if willing it to throw a punch at him.

"I'm looking. It'll take time. Maybe forty-eight hours."

"Work faster. She doesn't have forty-eight hours."

The clunk of the call ending reverberated around Hutton's office. Hutton didn't move from her desk. She just watched Flynn. He hit the phone to kill the call from his end.

She asked, "Can you really find the shipment in forty-eight hours?"

Flynn shook his head. "No, but I can find them."

"That's a risk. What about Beth?"

"Beth is no longer the objective. They are the objective."

"How can you say that?"

"Because Beth is dead."

CHAPTER NINE

HUTTON STOOD AND WALKED OUT OF HER OFFICE. FLYNN waited. She returned with a man. He was older than her by a good two decades, but they had the same eyes—calculating and piercing. He was solid but fit, thick through the neck, with a bald head and a heavy salt-and-pepper mustache covering his top lip. His features were simultaneously hard and soft, like a granite boulder worn by the passing of time.

"This is Nils Hedstrom," Hutton said. "My business partner."

Flynn and Hedstrom looked at each other.

"I'd prefer to keep this operation tight," said Flynn.

"Do you trust me?" she asked.

"I wouldn't be here if I didn't."

"Well, I trust Hedstrom more than any person on this planet. Including you. And he knows this city better than you and better than me. He can help. And if this thing is at the point you think it is, you need the help."

"All right. We'll see."

Hutton and Hedstrom took seats at the meeting table with Flynn.

"You said you think Beth's dead. Why?" Hutton asked.

"When you were with the FBI, how many kidnapping cases ended with the death of the victim?"

"Very few. Most kidnapping victims are rescued."

"How many ended with death where the assailant was not family or known to the victim?"

"More."

"How many where proof of life was faked?"

"Faked? What do you mean?"

"How many?"

"I don't know. Most, I would guess. But why do you think POL was faked?"

"You said listen hard. I listened hard."

"It didn't sound like her?"

"It was her. But from yesterday. She said exactly the same thing. My name. Then she asked what was happening, but she was cut off and she didn't get the whole word out."

"That's not conclusive. It stands to reason she would say your name."

"That's the first thing. But there's a second thing."

"What second thing?"

"The ambient noise. When the guy was talking, there was none. He was somewhere relatively quiet. Maybe indoors, maybe in a stationary vehicle."

"So?"

"So, yesterday the sound was different. They were moving. They were driving to New York, so the ambient noise reflected that. It was higher pitched. The sound of tires on road. And that's what I just heard. A completely different sound. High-speed road noise. Either side of Beth's voice. But not around the guy's voice."

Hutton said nothing.

"They recorded her voice," said Flynn. "After they took her.

Possibly when I asked to speak to her. Maybe even before that. Maybe they told her I was on the phone to get the recording and then they killed her. She might still be in DC. I might have followed a ghost here. I might have even heard a recording yesterday. But I definitely heard one today."

Hutton flopped back in her chair and ran her hands through her hair. She hadn't done that in Iraq. She had longer hair now. She glanced at Hedstrom, but he was watching Flynn.

Hutton said, "We should call the FBI."

"No."

"I'm serious. I still know a lot of people there. Good people."

"As good as you?"

"Yes."

"Then, no. I'm not calling the FBI."

"Why? This is what they do."

"I know it is. And who would you consider the number one suspect in any missing persons case?"

"Family."

"Specifically?"

"The partner," said Hedstrom. His voice was like New York City gravel. "Husband, wife, boyfriend, girlfriend."

Flynn watched him. "Exactly. Statistically, the most likely person to cause Beth harm is me. And I know that isn't the case. But the FBI doesn't. They're going to waste a lot of time looking at me. Time I don't have to waste. I don't want these guys getting away. I want them where I can find them."

"But we can't find them," said Hutton. "Isn't that the point? No leads on the shipment, no leads on Beth."

"That was before. Now we know something about them."

"What do we know?"

"We know they're in New York."

"It's a big town, in case you hadn't noticed."

"They're in the Union Square area."

"How do you know that?"

"The guy more or less told me. He said I needed to concentrate. He said I needed to find the shipment. And then he said *focus on the girl you lost*. He didn't say focus on *your* girl. He said *the* girl. The one I lost. As opposed to the one I found."

"The one you found?"

"You. He meant you. He's seen us together. Maybe when we got lunch. He's watching us."

Hutton played the words through her mind. "Maybe."

"I'm sure of it."

"So what do we do?" asked Hutton. "Nils?"

Hedstrom said nothing. He moved his eyes from Flynn to Hutton and then back. He made no move to say anything. Then Hutton's desk phone beeped. She stepped to her desk. Flynn watched her. Hedstrom watched Flynn. Hutton hit a button on the console.

"Yes?"

"Boss, you in the daily brief?" asked a male voice.

Hutton shot a look at the men at the meeting table.

Hedstrom nodded.

"I'll be right there," she said.

Hutton picked a notepad and pen off her desk and turned for the door.

"Daily team update," she said to Flynn. "Give me a few," she said.

"Take all the time you need," he replied.

Hutton gave Hedstrom another glance and then walked out of her office. Flynn watched her go. Hedstrom watched Flynn. For a moment neither man spoke.

"You don't want her to help me," said Flynn.

"What makes you say that?" replied Hedstrom.

"You have doubts."

"Wouldn't you?"

Flynn took a deep breath. "Ask your questions."

Hedstrom's expression didn't change. "She trusts you."

"I know."

"Why is that?"

"You'd have to ask her."

"I did. Now I'm asking you."

"I don't know. Maybe because I was honest about how honest I could really be."

"Or because she cares about you more than she'd like to admit."

"I can't speak to that."

"I'd hate for someone to take advantage of her."

"She's not easily taken advantage of," Flynn said.

"No. But it is possible. For all of us."

Flynn said nothing.

"She looked for you, you know," said Hedstrom. "For years."

"I thought it was safer for everyone if I didn't make contact."

"Is that what you thought?"

Flynn leaned into the table. "What is it you want from me?"

"I want to know why an American boy joins a foreign army."

Flynn leaned back and let out a long breath. It was a question he had asked himself more times than there had been sunrises in his life.

"Hutton said you were a Marine?"

"Semper Fi," said Hedstrom.

"So was my dad. I was a military brat. Mostly outside of the US. I grew up an American, just not in America. And let's just say that something happened to change the way I felt about things."

"Not even close to good enough."

"My dad was killed. The government disowned him. It was politically convenient. They tried to make him a scapegoat for something that he didn't do. I was a kid, and I was threatened by our government with spending the rest of my life in Guantanamo, or somewhere worse. My dad's CO found me and got me out before they could make that happen."

"Go on."

"I was raised in service. I wanted to serve. I was supposed to go military college stateside. And my country turned its back on me. I found myself just out of high school, in a foreign country. I was alone, confused. But I still wanted to serve. And I met someone, an officer, who took me in and offered me a chance to do just that. He taught me that service is about ideals, beliefs. Not random lines on a map."

"So the French Foreign Legion?"

"Hutton told you."

"I joined the dots."

"Yes. I was told I could serve. They offered me a place to go and something to fight for."

"But not the Stars and Stripes."

"No. Just what the Stars and Stripes stand for. Liberty. Freedom. Justice."

"You sound like a recruitment poster," said Hedstrom.

Flynn crossed his arms but said nothing.

"Did you ever fire on Americans?"

"No. And I wouldn't have if I had been asked. And they know that. They don't send guys in against their own. They understand the conflict in that. They understand that asking men to make that choice could backfire on them. Besides, the US and modern France are born of the same cloth. We've been on the same side since the Revolutionary War. France was our first ally. We're different politically, and we've had our disagreements. But if you want a reminder of what we share in common, just look out in New York Harbor."

Hedstrom glanced out the window in the general direction

of the Battery. He couldn't see the water from his seat, but he knew what was out there.

"Statue of Liberty," said Flynn.

"What about her?"

"She's French."

Hedstrom looked long and hard out the window and then returned to Flynn.

"Tell me about the kidnapping."

Flynn explained everything from their arrival in Washington, DC., until he had gotten to the offices of Hutton Hedstrom Associates.

"Why take her?" Hedstrom asked. "Why not just go for you?"

"Leverage. If they want me to do something, they can't hold me, so they took someone they could hold."

"But then they kill her? What's the motivation?"

Flynn let Hedstrom's blunt assessment slide. "Less risk. They need the leverage. They don't specifically need Beth."

"But to use a recording, the same recording. What do you make of that?"

"Amateurs. A pro would assume I would figure it out."

"If they're amateurs, how did they track you here?"

"They got lucky the way I got lucky. I tracked Beth's phone. It went offline near the Con Ed plant. I figure they charged it and used the same tracking app on the phone to find Beth's tablet."

Flynn pointed over his shoulder at the bureau where the tablet lay attached to Hutton's charger. Hedstrom looked at the charger and then back at Flynn.

"They didn't get lucky. You wanted them to find you," he said.

"Narrows down the area I have to search to find them."

Hedstrom looked back out the window. This time he ran his eyes along the street and across at Union Square.

"So you think they're out there."

"Somewhere."

Hedstrom stood. "Let's take a look."

THE UNIT LEADER WAS PACING. He wasn't good at waiting despite having done so much of it. He was a man of action, of decisive gestures. Not waiting. So he paced. He watched his men tap at keyboards and make calls. He marched to the window overlooking the street. Leaves blew along the sidewalk, reminding him of a home he had left long ago. He clenched his fists and drove the thought from his mind. His phone rang as he turned from the window.

"Our guy is on his way in."

"Good," said the team leader.

"He'll want some kind of incentive. It's his day off."

"Do what you gotta do."

"I thought you might offer something."

"I could put a gun in his mouth."

"Never mind. I'll take care of it."

"You do that."

"Be here at six. Come to the loading dock."

CHAPTER TEN

Hedstrom strode to his office. It was similar to Hutton's—a view, a desk, a meeting table. Less paperwork. He opened a file drawer and pulled out a cylindrical bag with a single carry strap. He pushed the drawer home hard and walked out. He led Flynn into the fire escape—cold, raw concrete—and up onto the roof of the building.

It was cold on the roof. The breeze might have dropped at street level, but five stories up it broke between the taller skyscrapers and funneled through the two men. But Flynn had been colder and so had Hedstrom. The roof was flat and open. Tar and pebble covered the surface. A hutch with a fire door gave them access from the stairs below. There was a block of air conditioning units that sat quietly waiting for the summer heat, deferring the winter months to the furnace in the basement. An eighteen-inch parapet ran around the perimeter of the roof.

Hedstrom nestled in behind the parapet. Flynn got as comfortable as he could. Hedstrom pulled a spotting scope out of the bag, put his elbow on top of the small wall, and then positioned the spotting scope across the street. He ran the scope along the street, north to south, and then handed it to Flynn.

The scope was a Leupold Golden Ring model, an excellent piece of equipment. Flynn could see the stubble starting to grow on the shaved faces of men walking through the park on the other side of the street. He could practically see the pores in their skin. He adjusted the scope and slowly panned along Union Square East from south to north. Reached the north end of the park, where the road became Park Avenue. His vantage point gave him a view uptown another block on the west side, about a quarter block on the east side. No watcher would be on the east side. That gave them too limited a line of sight of Hutton's building. He focused on the west side. There were no cars parked on Union Square East. He moved the scope north to Park Avenue. West side, just north of East 17th.

He focused the scope in on that spot. There was a vehicle parked there. A basic blue sedan. A Chevrolet. Not the kind of Chevy that anyone would write a song about. The driver's seat was filled by a woman with a beehive of blond hair. She appeared to be waiting on someone. Looking over her shoulder toward the sidewalk, as if she was nervous that she would be shifted along by the NYPD. Flynn could see she was wearing earrings that hung heavy from her lobes, encrusted with blue gems. Perhaps aquamarine. He wasn't sure. Gemstones weren't his area of expertise.

He pulled the view out some and slowly panned back along the street to the south. Lots of people moving in various directions. In and out of the park, to and from the subway. Fast, slow. More fast than slow. Two individuals caught his eye because they were stationary in a river of movement, but both proved to be waiting for someone to arrive from the subway station. He reached the southeast corner of the park and kept going as far down Broadway as his angle would allow, which wasn't far. Broadway turned to the southeast itself rather than continuing in a straight line from Park Avenue, so his view only progressed a couple of buildings down. But if he couldn't see further down the street, then no watcher could see Hutton's building, so he panned back and kept sweeping the street.

Flynn knew a good team could keep eyes on Hutton's office around the clock without detection. They could pose as road maintenance workers, but there were none on the block. They could act as park gardeners. They could dig all day and not raise suspicion. They could pace up and down the street in turn, one watcher and then another. Dressed in suits, they could keep the rotation going for hours before someone might suspect they had seen one of those faces previously. But such techniques weren't random. They developed a pattern. Eventually, the same people followed the same path. And within his field of observation, a pattern would quickly develop.

He saw no patterns. He saw no repeat faces. No road works, no park maintenance. He scanned back to the north end and saw the blue sedan. The woman driver with the beehive of hair was talking. Agitated. She said something in the direction of the sidewalk, away from Flynn. He moved his scope slightly and saw the officer. NYPD. She was getting moved on. No lingering on the streets of Manhattan during the day. Parking was like clogging the arteries, and the cop was like a statin drug clearing the way. The woman looked flushed and annoyed, but she started her car and pulled out into traffic without the bother of a turn signal. The cop turned his attention to a large dark truck behind. Maybe a Yukon. An older model that you didn't normally see downtown. Black paint baked a dark purple on the hood by years of sun and snow and a lack of oil changes. The cop waved his arms at the Yukon. Flynn couldn't see the driver. He was behind tinted windows. But he didn't require a chat with the cop. He just signaled and pulled out, freeing up the lane for through traffic.

Flynn pulled the scope back and sat with his back against the parapet. Hedstrom was already there.

"Nothing?" asked Hedstrom.

"If they're pros, we could take all day to find them. If ever. They could be in a building opposite, with a chase car down the street out of view."

"But you don't think they're pros."

"Which means they could be limited in manpower. Maybe they can't do full-time surveillance. Maybe they're tracking the tablet, not watching the building."

Hedstrom considered this but was interrupted before responding by a call from the hutch leading to the stairwell.

"What are you boys doing up here?" called Hutton.

"It's a great day for fishing," said Hedstrom.

"It's a great day to curl up under a blanket with a good book," she said, crouching down.

Hedstrom grunted. "There's something I don't get." He glanced at Flynn. "You say this all leads back to Iraq. But the French weren't involved in Iraq. They were against the whole thing. Remember freedom fries?"

"Sure. The Legion is handy that way. It's French, but not really. That leaves a lot of wiggle room. The government can claim that France is not involved in something, or French lives are not in danger, because the soldiers they are sending in are technically foreign. My team was tasked with tracking down what you might call *ennemis de l'etat*. Enemies of the state."

"Terrorists," said Hutton.

"If you prefer," said Flynn. "Like the Legion in general, we mostly operated in places like North Africa and South America."

"Mostly," said Hedstrom.

"The Legion had a unit in Afghanistan, coordinating with NATO command."

"That was you?"

"No. We flew a little further under the radar."

"Black ops."

"Something like that. We were in Afghanistan, and we were ordered into Iraq to trace a network that was believed to be arming insurgents in both Iraq and Afghanistan."

"Was that unusual?"

"Yes and no. Going into territories where France had no footprint was nothing new. And we figured the network would lead to some bad guys, and that's what we did. But in hindsight, it was odd. Our remit was to find those committing acts of terror against France, not allies. In Iraq, we seemed to be cracking a small-time gun runner, and one who was in the US Army."

"Your guy," Hedstrom said to Hutton.

"Dennison," she said. "That's where our paths crossed. As you know, I was with the FBI in-country, training local law enforcement. We got wind of a movement of arms. As much as anything, I saw it as a training op. Teaching the locals how we investigate such things. But when I got closer, I realized that army personnel were involved. We didn't like showing our ugly side to the Iraqis, so I followed it up alone."

"And found a quartermaster dealing in everything from M9s to heroin," said Flynn.

"Right," said Hutton. "But he also seemed to be getting into some bigger shipments. It was the drawdown. The military was shipping a lot of stuff home and leaving a lot of stuff behind."

"The military is pretty good about keeping track of its stuff," said Hedstrom.

"But a crate here, a container there?" Hutton said. "It was a massive undertaking, logistically speaking. So we—John's team and I—witnessed a meet between Staff Sergeant Dennison and the man you later identified as Iranian military, Ahmad Kirmani."

"I remember," said Hedstrom.

Hutton continued. "The Iranian left a container on a truck and then crossed back into Iran."

"And you said you intercepted the container?" asked Hedstrom. "What happened to it?"

Hedstrom and Hutton looked at Flynn.

"My guys placed a decoy on the truck and then took the target container to a rendezvous near the airport. I then made it disappear."

"Why? What was in it?"

"I don't know," said Flynn. "The whole place went to hell. NATO MPs, an officer from the regular French Army, the US Army, CIA. Everybody got really interested and we were the ones left holding the bag. So I made it lost."

"But it was evidence," said Hedstrom.

"Against who? Dennison was dead."

"How do you know?"

"He shot me, but I shot him too. His hideout was a disused building in the desert outside of Baghdad. The sand had covered most of it, so the US sats couldn't see it. Dennison used it as a stockpile for fuel and who knows what else. But it was the fuel that blew up."

"You got out," said Hedstrom. "How do you know he didn't?"

"My driver pulled me out. No one was there to do Dennison any such favors."

"All right."

"And now someone has taken your lady. But the guy is dead."

"Clearly he wasn't the only one involved," said Hutton. "What about the guy who drove the general?"

"Who?" asked Hedstrom.

Flynn said, "A general not in my chain of command came to

Iraq to order me out. He had a driver who told me he was a private."

"He wasn't?"

"What's the first thing you learn at basic training?"

"To shoot," said Hedstrom.

"Before that."

"That your drill sergeant works for a living but his word is gospel."

"Right. You get a hard lesson in manners. This guy never once referred to me by my rank. He was no private."

"And he was still there after the general left," said Hutton. "You saw him, remember?"

"I remember," said Flynn.

"Was the dead sergeant an amateur or a professional?" asked Hedstrom.

"He was a professional hustler," Flynn said, "but in every other way he was an amateur."

"And the fake private?"

"Professional."

"But you're sure the amateur is dead."

"I believe so."

"And the private?"

"Dead."

"You sure?"

"Absolutely," said Flynn.

"Well, someone took your girl," said Hedstrom. "And they're down there somewhere."

"What do you suggest?"

Hedstrom held up the spotting scope. "I think you kids should go grab some dinner."

THE WHOLE OPERATION was amateur hour. The driver knew it. They needed a team; even four guys would have done. But he had two. Himself, and his twitchy little friend. Not that they were really friends. More work colleagues. Former roommates, of a sort. And the driver knew the twitchy little guy was good for some things, but not for others. Like watching. He couldn't sit still. Even his eyes didn't work that way. They bounced around in his head. Side to side, up and down and back again. Always moving. Which might have been useful if they were actually watching. But they weren't. Looking was not the same as watching. Most people didn't pay attention. And most people fell in the normal part of a bell curve when it came to attention. His twitchy little friend was firmly at the far end of the attention curve. An outlier. Probably ADHD or ADD or one of those things that kids got diagnosed with these days. Back in his day, those kids were just dumb or lacked discipline. They ended up at the back of the room, where they caused the least grief to their teachers, and they slid down the curve until they dropped out of school altogether. Unskilled and untrainable, they found legitimate work difficult to find and more difficult to hold down. So that left them with illegitimate work.

The driver knew a lot of guys like that. Useful to a point. But not for surveillance. His twitchy friend was driving him crazy. His constant tapping and squiggling and shifting in his seat made it hard to watch and harder to think. It was like being a one-man team. But a one-man team didn't work. Not without advance notice. If he'd known ahead of time, he might have secured a post in an unused office opposite the target's location. Or found a studio apartment left vacant while its tenant was away working in Europe or Asia or somewhere. But he'd had no such notice. So he was left watching while his partner tapped and squiggled and shifted and talked constantly.

He had made a mistake. Or more precisely, he had taken a

gamble and lost. It was cold, too cold to sit on a park bench or don a green vest and pretend to dig in the park gardens. So he had brought the Yukon. It wasn't the most inconspicuous vehicle in Manhattan. A stretch limo would hide easier. But he didn't want to sit downtown in a stolen vehicle. That was asking for trouble. So he stopped on Park Avenue in his own ride, and as he suspected, he was moved on by the NYPD. Nothing for it but to drive around the block.

He could drive around the block all day. But that would give him line of sight for about ten percent of the time. Close to useless. So he left his twitchy little friend on the sidewalk. It was a gamble. The guy would see almost nothing. His head and eyes and body were moving in place, but it would be a miracle if he actually saw the target, and an even bigger miracle if he could follow him without being spotted himself. But it was a better option than giving him the wheel of the Yukon. New York City driving was not for the likes of his twitchy little friend.

Manhattan was a good place to hide in plain sight, however, even for a twitchy guy. A needle in a constantly moving haystack. It was even better at night. He knew from experience. People searched for the light and shied from the shadows. And that left a lot of scope for a guy like him. And, he figured, a guy like the target. The target knew how to fall back into the shadows. The target liked the dark.

The whole thing was amateur hour anyway, and a lottery at best. So he drove a series of right-hand turns and came back down Park Ave, pulling up where his twitchy little friend stood with his hands in his pockets, swaying to a beat that only he could hear.

The driver liked being right. He was smart, he knew that. He saw things, figured things. Getting caught in the act by the cops—twice—had been bad luck, not bad judgment. He was confident of that. So as the sun fell behind the columns of towers and evening rush hour gushed by, he collected his twitchy little friend, and as they paused on Park Avenue, just north and east of Union Square Park, the target came out of the building with the woman. Under the cover of darkness. Just as he had predicted. The driver smiled to himself and pulled away from the curb.

CHAPTER ELEVEN

THE SUN FELL QUICKLY AND THE COLD AIR GOT COLDER. The wind dropped and then picked up again, a change in direction, now crossing the island from the Hudson River. They walked with their collars up, Flynn's hands deep in his pockets, Hutton with thick gloves. The streetlights played an orange glow over the city as people rushed from one warm bunker to another. Hutton led Flynn along the northeast side of Union Square Park, west along East 17th Street. At Fifth Avenue it changed to West 17th, and they walked on four more blocks into the teeth of the wind, before cutting down a block to Chelsea Market.

Inside the historic old building wasn't much warmer than outside, but the break in the wind made it feel almost tropical. They walked along the aisles of food stalls and restaurants. Through old brick arches and along thick plank hardwood floors. The market was busy with the after-work crowd, taking refuge from the cold before braving a dash to the subway and the long trip to Queens or Long Island or New Jersey.

They selected a seafood place and both ordered chowder

and bread. Hutton ordered a dark beer and Flynn took tap water.

"So do your guys know that you're alive?" asked Hutton.

"Yes. My CO told them."

"Do they know where you are?"

"No. Why do you ask?"

"Because someone found you. Someone from back then."

"You think it was my men?"

"No, I don't. But I'd want to check them off the list, all the same."

"They don't know. That was important. People were going to ask. Maybe they were going to ask hard. It was better they didn't know."

"Okay, so who else is on the list?"

"I don't know," said Flynn as their chowder arrived. It was thick and creamy and smelled faintly of the sea.

Flynn watched her eat. She did it analytically. She looked at the food as if calculating its calories and nutrients and assessing its value to her body, and then she took a spoonful and ate it as if it were the last meal she would ever have. She chewed and put her spoon down on her napkin.

"Who knew what you were doing back then?" she asked.

"My unit, my CO. You. Dennison clearly knew. I got orders to leave from a general not in my chain of command, so that suggests the list is bigger than the known players. Could be a few, could be thousands."

"Okay, but who could link to you now? It's been years. It's hard to believe they're still after a shipment of guns."

"I dumped the gun theory a long time ago."

"So what, then?"

"I don't know. Something bigger. Something more important. The container had biological waste placards. That might have been a ruse to keep anyone from looking inside. But it might have been a double bluff."

"Biological weapons?"

Flynn shrugged and ate. "But even something like that, you give it up, after a while. What do companies call them? Bad and doubtful debts? Surely after a few years something like that drops from the doubtful column to the bad column and you write it off and move on. Especially since most of the players would have left anyway. The US Army pulled out only a few months after we were there. Anyone who replaced Dennison would have been temporary."

"So there's something more. Tell me. I know you've thought about it."

"I have. In the beginning that's all I thought about. What about you? You didn't win out of this. You must have worked it through."

"Of course. Best I could come up with was there was something that could be traced. Somehow whatever was in the container could have been linked back to them. I figured it wasn't the thing in the container they were worried about. It was the link back that they were worried about."

"Exactly. That's where I landed too. But you're right, there is more. Dennison mentioned something about a clandestine group, as if they operated as a unit."

"Like a country or a company?"

"I don't know."

"Or a unit of individuals?"

"I never came up with a solid answer."

"I've heard rumors over the years, of a network of the rich and powerful. One theory was that it was a group of bureaucrats from the G8 countries. The US is part of that. So is France."

"But most of the G8 countries weren't in Iraq. Just the US and Britain."

"It all sounded like fairytales, anyway."

"Fairytales didn't kill Babar."

Hutton said nothing. She ate some chowder and stared at her bowl.

"From the way Dennison said it, I got the impression he thought there were interested people," said Flynn. "Individuals."

"Unless Dennison was making it up."

"He wasn't. The way he said it, it was deferential. Like he was even scared of them."

"All right. It makes sense that any organization ends with one person at the top. The army does, the FBI does. So does the United States."

"The United States has three points at the top, not one. Checks and balances."

"Well, whether it's one or three or five at the top, somehow they found you."

Flynn nodded and glanced away. The wind was howling now, filling the streets outside the window with flying paper and trash, like a ticker-tape parade.

"I think Beth was the link. Everything about this went through her. I think somehow they linked her to me."

"What did she do?"

"She was a lawyer. Sort of. In practice she was more like a forensic accountant. If a company wanted to put money offshore, she could advise on how to do it. How to keep it legal but keep it away from the tax man, or whomever else they wanted to keep it away from."

"Sounds shady."

"It was a law firm." Flynn shrugged.

"So how does that relate to you?"

Flynn stirred a chunk of clam around his bowl. "I don't know. Yet. But they're going to tell me. You can bet on that."

Hutton put her spoon down and crossed her hands on the table. "Are you okay?"

"Okay? Sure. Why not?"

"Why not? Because you just learned your girlfriend was killed, that's why not."

For the first time since he'd left the hotel room in DC., he thought about the little box in his pack that held the ring that he no longer had any need for. He wondered if he should return it. He wondered if he could do such a thing.

Hutton's face didn't change, as if she were holding it in place on purpose. "I'm sorry."

"Not your fault."

"That's not what I meant."

They finished their meal and hovered over the table for a while. The wind beat against the windows. It sounded like rain, but the sky was clear and cold. Then they retraced their steps back toward the office, watching the streets for anyone out of place. Flynn saw a hundred possibles. People waiting on street corners, huddled at the top of stoops in doorways. Cars driving slowly and vans parked on the roadside. New York was a great place to hide. If you were watching someone, it made it hard to be discovered. If you were being watched, it made it easy to melt away. It all depended on what you knew, and what you assumed the other guy knew.

They stopped at a convenience store. Not a chain, or at least not a brand recognizable to Flynn. The aisles were packed with everything from toiletries to hardware. Boxes of products were shelved right to the ceiling. A long pole with a hook sat behind the counter to hoist the boxes down when a customer needed a less common item, like toddlers' rain boots or plastic cutlery. Flynn didn't want any such items. What he wanted was behind the counter. A young Chinese man was on the phone, firing truncated syllables like machine-gun fire. He didn't stop talking, but he nodded to Flynn. Flynn nodded back at the collection of bottles behind the man.

"Wild Turkey," he said.

The man turned and grabbed the bottle and dropped it into a purpose-sized paper sack. He put the sack on the counter and continued his one-way phone conversation. He looked at Flynn but didn't offer a price. Flynn handed him a fifty. That would cover it, and then some. Maybe it was enough for two bottles. But he didn't want two bottles. He wanted one, and only one. The Chinese guy looked at the bill with suspicion. Felt it between his fingers like that was the defining characteristic of counterfeit money. He wasn't wrong. The paper was the most difficult part of US currency to copy. But it must have felt right because the guy dropped the bill in the register and handed Flynn his change and turned his eye to the next customer in turn, still talking into his phone.

Flynn stepped out onto the street, and Hutton eyed the paper sack in his hand.

"Is this the time for that?" Hutton asked.

"To be determined."

They arrived back at Hutton's office. The cubicles were mostly empty. Mostly, but not completely. A number of staff burned the late-evening oil.

"We're a twenty-four-hour kind of place," Hutton said as they reached her office.

"In a twenty-four-hour kind of town," said Flynn.

Hutton smiled. Then she called Hedstrom.

THE DRIVER HAD GAMBLED AGAIN. And he'd won again. Or perhaps he wasn't giving himself enough credit. It was an educated guess. The target and the woman had walked along the north end of Union Square, and he had followed in the Yukon. They had walked to Chelsea Market, which presented a problem. Parking was scarce. Parking enforcement was plentiful. And he preferred to deploy his twitchy little friend only when absolutely necessary. He bet on them coming back out the way they had gone in. He figured he could pick up the trail then. They hadn't walked a crazy route to get there, so they showed no signs of suspecting a tail. So he sat and waited, got told to move on a couple of times by parking inspectors, but they didn't have arrest powers, so he paid them little mind.

His partner was squirming in his seat and complaining that they had lost them and there would be hell to pay if they had, so the driver gave a satisfied grin when the target and the woman walked out of the market via the same door they had entered, jogged across the street, and then dropped into a steady pace for the return to the office. They made one stop at a convenience store, but only the target went inside. The woman stayed on the street looking around, and the driver thought he might have been made, but she was just killing time, waiting for the target to come out. Then they had walked along 17th which was one way east to west, so he couldn't follow. He cut up onto 18th and continued along until he turned right onto Park Avenue, and he was again parked kitty-corner across from the woman's building when she and the target wandered past and went inside.

He had earlier checked the tenant board for the building and found eleven listings. The building was a low five floors: a large retail space on street level topped by four mixed-use levels. In the city, they could be offices or loft apartments or a mix of the two. The tenant board suggested they were all offices. He didn't know who she was, or what her relationship to the target was. The driver looked up and saw lights in the window of just one floor. The top floor. He checked his personal phone. The photograph he had taken showed the tenant board. The retail space was not listed. The next three floors were denoted 2, 3 and 4. The fourth of the office floors was denoted PH—penthouse. There was a single tenant. Hutton Hedstrom Associates.

He opened his phone's web browser and typed that name in and found multiple listings for a security and private investigation firm. He tapped through to the company's website and found a listing of the principals. The woman might be an office drone working late to impress the boss. Or she might be something more. She might be Hedstrom.

Definitely not Hedstrom. The page that opened on his phone showed a bald, broad-shouldered Nordic-looking guy with a heavy mustache. Nils Hedstrom. The driver scrolled down some. And saw the woman. It was a professional shot. She was wearing makeup that he hadn't noticed on her in real life. Not blush and gaudy colors. Subtle. Like TV makeup. Designed to stop the skin from shining in the bright camera flash. He looked the photo over. She wasn't his type. She was one of those women who looked like a hawk. All angles and a beak nose and eyes that bored into their prey from a thousand yards. He preferred women who didn't seem to be reading his every thought, every moment of the day. Which this woman seemed to be doing from the screen of his phone.

He shut it off and pulled the other phone from his pocket. Hit the button to call one of only two numbers stored in it.

"She just returned to the office," he said.

"Who is she?"

"It looks like she's a private eye or something."

"Maybe he's hired her. Maybe he's looking for our thing."

"What is this thing?"

"Nothing of value to you."

"Do you know this woman?"

"Don't worry about the woman. Stay on the guy."

The call ended in his ear. He shook his head. He was

starting to think the job was more work than it was worth. But once engaged, there was no begging off. He knew that. He knew how his contact could react when displeased. Had seen it first-hand. It wasn't pretty. But his confidence in the contact wasn't high. How was it he knew who this woman was but they didn't? The whole thing felt like it had been thrown together on the run. He'd been involved in jobs like that before. They never ended well for the guy in his position.

HEDSTROM DIDN'T LOOK cold despite having spent close to two hours on the roof of the building. He was built for the conditions. He strode into Hutton's office and closed the door but didn't sit.

"You had a tail," he said.

"Black Yukon," said Flynn.

"With a sun-bleached hood," said Hutton. "They followed us to Chelsea."

Hedstrom grunted. "They were here earlier too. They just took up their post on Park Avenue." He gestured out the window with the spotting scope, which he had returned to its bag.

"What do you think?" Hutton asked.

Hedstrom glanced at the meeting table where Flynn sat. His eyes lingered on the plain paper sack in the middle of the table.

"No hurry," said Hedstrom. "You know they're there, they know you're inside."

"Time to plan," said Hutton.

Flynn said nothing.

Hedstrom placed his spotting scope on the table by the

paper sack and turned to Hutton. "I gotta get going though," he said. "The Russian oil guys."

"I know. Be safe."

"Call if you need anything. We'll be done around two, unless they decide to hit the bars."

Hutton nodded and Hedstrom walked out. She turned her attention to Flynn. She was concerned. She had seen a paper sack like the one on the table before. In Iraq. Flynn had gone out walking alone. She had seen him from the stairs, closing the door to his room, a fifth of bourbon in his hand. She had figured it for a coping mechanism. Everyone had one, at least everyone who coped. And in the scheme of things, there were worse ways to handle it, but there were also better ways. Especially years after they had returned. At the time it hadn't seemed to affect his performance. He had been sharp the following day, and she hadn't smelled anything on his breath. But it had worried her all the same. The second time he had gone walking and returned with a bottle, he hadn't needed it. He had found solace with her. That couldn't happen now.

"Is there a back way out of your building?" he asked, pulling her from her thoughts.

"Of course. Going somewhere?"

"Need to check something. Might help decide what the next step is. Don't want an audience."

CHAPTER TWELVE_

FLYNN MARCHED THE COLD STREETS WITH PURPOSE. Amber light spotted his way and the city pulsed around him. He felt alive. It wasn't a good feeling. Not this way. The woman who would be his wife was dead. His only link to a family, to a normal kind of life, was gone. He should have been inconsolable. He should have taken the bottle that was in the paper sack in Hutton's office and found a vacant, darkened room, and he should have exorcized his demons. But as he hit the cold Manhattan street and his walk dropped into that familiar cadence of a march, he realized that his regular process wasn't required right now. Right now he felt alive. More alive than he had in years.

It wasn't about Beth. He loved her. He knew that. He wasn't so alien that he didn't understand love. He had loved his mother, and he had been infatuated with girls back in school. And there had been Hutton. He wasn't sure how to classify that feeling. He had never found an adequate pigeonhole for it. But with Beth, he'd had someone to call home. Somewhere to be. Someone to be there with. A woman who didn't understand his background because she could never know everything about it, but who gave him her love anyway. Convention said he should be grieving that loss right now. Instead he felt alive in pursuit of her killers. He shivered. He told himself it was the cold wind heaving down the canyons of buildings. But he knew better. Shivers from the cold didn't emanate from within.

HEDSTROM STOPPED by on his way out. He had changed into his black suit and black tie. He looked like a Secret Service agent, which was what many of the clients wanted. Not just security, but visible security. And in their minds, security had a certain look. Someone could start a clothing line: *The Secret Service Collection*. Hutton thought he looked good in a suit, but she knew he would struggle all night not to keep pulling at the collar.

"Where is he?" Hedstrom asked.

"Wanted to check something, he said. I think I know what."

"You okay with this whole thing?"

"Are you asking do I trust him?"

"That's in there somewhere."

"Yes, I trust him."

"Why?"

"You know why."

"Because of the French general?"

"That's just an example. He could have—hell, he should have followed orders. He should have stood down and given it up. But he didn't, knowing that it might go as bad as it did. And that counts for something."

"It counts for something, not everything."

"You know the rest. He's giving me a chance to find out why it all went down the way it did. I'm never going back to the

Bureau, you know that. But it's still eating at me. I don't like not knowing."

"I don't have to go to this thing tonight."

"Yes, you do. You can't leave a client hanging."

Hedstrom growled a sigh. "Call me. Anything."

"Go. Do your job."

HUTTON HAD KILLED the lights and was watching the Yukon through the scope when Flynn arrived back.

"He's still there," he said.

"Yes. Traffic cops aren't so vigilant after rush hour." She dropped the scope from her eye. "What do you know?"

"Good news and bad news."

"Bad news," she said.

"I heard back about my contact."

"The phone store was still open?"

"Probably. This is the city that never sleeps. But I went elsewhere. No pattern, remember?"

"Where?"

"Not important. But as I say, the news isn't good."

"Tell me."

"He's dead."

"That isn't good. How?"

"He was in the Legion. Training accident in Algeria. Eighteen months ago. Helicopter went down. Six guys lost."

"Suspicious?"

"Not on the face of it. But one dead contact can be explained away. Two dead contacts gets harder to do."

"I agree," she said, closing the blinds. Flynn flicked the lights on.

"What's the good news?"

"It's dark."

"I noticed. So?"

"So my options for finding whatever it is they want me to find are played out. I'm done."

"What are you saying?"

"Time to go on the offensive."

"Can I remind you this isn't Iraq? There are rules."

"I agree. But they made the rules. Not me. They killed Beth. Now they get to play by those rules."

"I don't know if I can be a party to that."

"And I'm not asking you to. I needed your help to find Beth. That's not the objective now. I don't want to cause you trouble, Hutton. I wouldn't have come to you if I thought it would cause you harm. I'll just take my gun back and go."

"Go where? What do you plan to do?"

"I plan to get in their faces. There's no way the guys watching me are the top of the tree. From little things, big things grow. They're the first link in the chain. They'll tell me where to go next."

"What are you going to do? Attack a vehicle in the middle of Park Avenue?"

"No, not on Park Avenue."

Hutton leaned against her desk and looked at him. She was looking at Flynn, not Fontaine—the guy she had known in Iraq. He was different now. Still the same man in a way, but also changed.

"What can I do?"

"Nothing. I told you, I'm leaving."

"Flynn, this was my career. I loved being in the FBI, and this thing killed that. Don't get me wrong, I love what I do now, maybe even more. It's good being the boss. But the FBI is unfinished business for me. I didn't leave it on my terms. Someone screwed me over. I want to know who."

Flynn walked to the window. The wind had dropped, but it was still cold. There were people around despite the late hour. The Yukon was down there. It was the first thread in a much bigger blanket. It was time to start pulling the blanket apart.

THE BLACK SUBURBAN pulled into the loading dock of the Watergate Hotel. It would raise no eyebrows. People in this town were used to seeing large black SUVs discreetly pull into the rear of hotel complexes. It could be a senator or a governor or a self-important lobbyist. It wasn't any of these people. The team leader stepped out first, and his contact met him on the loading dock and ushered him inside. The rest of the team leader's men were hard at work in the vacant office, replenishing their energy on delivery pizza and Gatorade.

The team leader was led through the kitchen and down a corridor to the security office. The on-duty security officer had been told to take a hundred bucks and go relax somewhere for an hour. The large bearded man sitting before the monitors barely acknowledged the two men as they entered the small room.

"What do you have?"

The security guy hit a few keys on his keyboard with a force that suggested he wasn't impressed about being dragged in on his day off.

"This is her checking in," he said, starting the video.

The image came from a camera on the ceiling behind the desk. The team leader watched an attractive blond woman at the front desk. The woman looked professional and at ease with her surroundings. Staying in an expensive hotel was nothing new for her. But the team leader wasn't that interested in the woman. He didn't know her, other than having read her dossier.

"Is she with someone?" he asked.

"Not obviously," said the security guy. He fast-forwarded the video to another shot, this one looking at the elevator. The woman sped into shot, followed by a man. They stood at the elevator with their backs to the camera.

"Maybe that guy?"

"Got a facial shot?"

The couple got into the elevator.

"Elevator shot?" asked the team leader.

"That's car two. Video's on the fritz."

The security guy scratched at his beard and then tapped at the keys. The video on the monitor changed to a shot of an elevator lobby on one of the room floors. The couple got out, but the man was readjusting what looked like a backpack, and his arm covered his face. The couple entered one of the rooms.

"Room surveillance?" asked the team leader.

The team leader's contact shook his head. "Not at the Watergate. Could you imagine?"

The team leader didn't care about the history. The security guy fast-forwarded the video and then slowed it as the couple came back out of the room. They were dressed differently, in running gear. The man wore a hoodie, masking his face. The couple stepped out the front doors and ran away. It only took seconds for the security guy to have them back, heavy breath visible in the clear air. They made their way to the room again, and then the woman left alone.

"You wanna see where she goes?"

"I didn't come here for the sparkling company."

The security guy frowned and scratched his beard again and used his keyboard to follow the woman. She entered the elevator and took it up to the bar on the roof. The rooftop space was sparsely populated, and the woman appeared to shrug her shoulders against the chill on the air. She looked around the bar and was then approached.

"Who is that?" asked the team leader's contact from the rear of the room.

The team leader wasn't sure, but he knew the new person looked out of place in that environment. He watched them speak on the screen and a look of recognition sweep across the face of the blond woman. The team leader saw it in her eyes. She knew the name but not the face. They spoke some more and then turned back for the elevator.

"Too cold," said the security guard.

The video captured them getting back in the elevator, and then the security guy switched to the lobby camera and they saw the two of them stop by the bar near the lobby and then turn and walk out the front door. The view switched to a camera on the hotel forecourt, and they saw the blond woman being ushered into a waiting minivan.

"Get me the plate number on that van," said the team leader.

"Okay," said the security guy.

"And go back into the lobby as they leave. The view from behind the desk."

The security guy tapped a few keys and changed the view and scrubbed back in time, and then stopped the vision and they watched the two step across the lobby.

"Freeze it there," said the team leader.

The picture stopped midstride as the two people passed the front desk. The blond woman's face was partially obscured, but it wasn't her face the team leader was looking at. He was focused on the other face.

"Who is that?" said the guy at the back of room again.

The team leader said nothing. But he grinned. He knew the face. He knew who it was, and it explained a few things.

He said, "Show me the guy."

The security guy did his thing and the video picked up in the elevator lobby and followed the man on screen as he did a tour of the hotel—the rooftop bar, the lobby bar, the restaurant. Then he came to a stop in the lobby. He looked at his phone and just stood there, not moving. It looked like the picture was paused. They got a good look at him. And the team leader knew this face too. He knew this face better.

"Fontaine," he said to himself.

"Who?" asked the security guy as the video continued and the man set off running.

"Get me that license number. And find out where that guy goes," said the team leader, walking out of the room. He took out his phone as he walked. "Fontaine's here. Someone got in before us."

"Who?" said the person at the other end of the line.

"I know who. We need to check all calls to the woman's office between the San Francisco meeting and her leaving for DC."

"That will take some time."

"Fast as you can. He's not going to get away this time."

CHAPTER THIRTEEN_

FLYNN FLICKED HIS COLLAR UP AS HE HIT THE STREET, AND shrugged his daypack onto his shoulder. It felt good to be on the move, to be proactive rather than reactive. His Glock was tucked back in his trousers against the small of his back. It was no comfort. It wasn't part of the plan to use a gun in such a populated area. But there was no telling where this particular blanket thread would lead.

The wind had dropped off some, but it was still plenty cold, and putting their collars up was what people did. Hutton wound a scarf around her neck in an intricate knot and adjusted the strap on the courier bag she had wrapped around her. They headed north from Hutton's building. Crossed 17th Street. Walked a half block and stopped outside a restaurant. It was a hamburger joint. The kind of place one could build their own burger like it was a construction project and pay five times the price for the privilege. They looked at the menu in the window, and Hutton glanced back down and across Park Avenue.

"The Yukon has pulled away from the curb," Hutton said.

Flynn said nothing.

"Doesn't mean it's watching us."

"How often is Hedstrom wrong?"

"Not often."

"There you go."

"But not never either. And we need to be one hundred percent sure these are the guys."

"Wait for it."

She waited. She watched the Yukon pull a wide U-turn across traffic. Slow like an ocean liner.

"It's done a U-turn."

Flynn said nothing.

"It's pulled over again. Just this side of the lights."

"Let's go," said Flynn.

They walked north along Park Avenue. Like Manhattan in general, Park Avenue had many faces. Twenty-five blocks north, it was New York glamor. Grand Central Terminal and then Upper East Side money. But downtown it was the gateway to the Lower East Side. The buildings were older and the restaurants had more Formica and the convenience stores stocked the lower end of the liquor spectrum.

Flynn and Hutton stepped into one such store. The lottery was heading for a big jackpot, so there was a long line for tickets. Flynn didn't see the logic. A bigger pot didn't improve your chances of winning. You were more likely to get hit by lightning. Twice. In the same spot. But the human mind held power that it hadn't even yet shared with itself. Dreams were powerful. So people were lined up. Flynn waited his turn.

"How many?" said the guy behind the counter.

"I don't want a ticket."

The guy behind the counter looked at him.

"A fifth of Irish whiskey," Flynn said.

The guy took a moment to process the request of anything other than a lottery ticket and then turned to find the bottle. He didn't ask which brand. The cheapest possible was the biggest seller.

Hutton frowned. "Really?"

Flynn nodded.

The counter guy turned back with the bottle, and Flynn said, "Actually, make it two."

The guy huffed like he'd just painted a house and had been told the owner didn't like the color. He turned and grabbed a second bottle and put it on the counter and offered Flynn a face that asked if he was going to cause the guy any further unwarranted hassle. Flynn just handed him the cash and the guy made change and slipped each bottle into its own paper sack, and Flynn slipped the sacks into his daypack.

Flynn stepped out onto the street and took a moment to position his collar just so. It was a good distraction. It allowed for more body movement than was necessary. Allowed for a good look around without taking a good look around. He saw the Yukon parked down the street. It was as obvious as a billboard on Times Square. It might as well have had neon in the window saying *I'm watching you.*

THE DRIVER FELT EXPOSED. The street was lit like a football stadium. Not a side street or an alley. Park Avenue. Even a dark vehicle stood out. Especially a truck, and especially one that kept stopping on every block. He had to drop back. He had no choice. Even an amateur would notice him, sooner or later. He told his partner what to do, and the twitchy little guy dropped from the vehicle to the sidewalk. He shrugged his shoulders to settle his coat on his light frame and then walked on. The driver waited. He saw the target and the woman walk north, and soon they were lost in the pedestrian traffic. He followed his partner and hoped his twitchy little eyes could keep the target in sight.

They slowly made their way up Park Avenue. He stopped at red lights and watched his partner walk on, hands in pockets. He had a bouncing gait, like a young pony or Travolta in *Saturday Night Fever*. But plenty of people in New York walked with an attitude. So he looked like just another guy, and his speed and direction suggested the target was making no attempt to evade a tail. He clearly didn't know they were behind him.

The driver crawled north, cars behind him sounding their horns at his slow pace. It was a concern to be attracting so much attention. But in Manhattan, the noise of horns blaring angrily was part of the cacophony that was the sounds of the city. He kept his eyes on his partner and saw him turn right toward the river. The twitchy little guy glanced back to make sure the Yukon was following, and the driver sent up a silent prayer that his partner wouldn't get too close to the target and get made.

They headed east. This street was much less busy than Park Avenue. Like most of the east-west streets in this part of town it was one-way, but unlike most, it didn't really go anywhere. It didn't end at an important park or reach a bridge or even bank onto the FDR. There was traffic, but it wasn't busy. Not Manhattan busy. He liked that. Enough cover for him, but less annoyed traffic behind. After a couple of blocks he saw his partner standing on the sidewalk, hands in pockets. He had the stiff posture of someone looking in a restaurant window, deciding whether or not to go in, whether or not the place had exactly what he had a hankering for.

But there was no restaurant. As the driver got closer, he saw that his partner was looking at a vacant lot. Such lots came and went in a city constantly reinventing itself. Buildings were vacated, razed to rubble and then built again. But the driver had heard stories. The planning process was a nightmare. A bureau-cracy fit for only the bravest souls to navigate. He recalled some-thing about air rights. How high a building could be. He found the idea ridiculous in a forest of skyscrapers. But he had heard stories. Planning permissions denied, or investors getting skittish or even running out of money before rebuilding could begin. Sometimes lots sat vacant for decades waiting for a white knight to ride in and save the day. Sometimes the knight never came.

The lots moved location around the island, but they moved slow. And the hobo network moved fast. Homeless people found plenty of vacant land to camp on, even in Manhattan. When the ownership of land was in dispute, there was usually no one to take responsibility for security or fencing. Groups of men would gather around fires in spaces that sprouted green at a surprising rate. Sometimes the NYPD would move them on. More often the NYPD had bigger problems to deal with.

The driver stopped a half block down and pulled out his burner phone. He called the second of two numbers stored in it. Saw his partner pull his hand from his pocket and answer the call.

"Where are they?"

"They had a fight."

"They what?"

"A fight. They were arguing."

"About what?"

"Not sure. I think the guy had some booze, and she wasn't happy about it. Didn't like him drinking."

"So what happened?"

The twitchy little guy turned to look toward the Yukon. "The woman took off. Kept going toward the river."

"Where's the guy?"

The little guy looked back at the vacant lot. "In there."

"What's he doing?"

"I don't know. I can't see him. I guess he's drinking."

"Well, go in and find out."

"I'm not going in there. It's full of bums."

"Who aren't going to care about you. Now go. Try to be cool."

The driver shook his head and ended the call. The twitchy guy looked at his phone and then back at the Yukon. The driver shook his head again. The guy was going to get them busted.

CHAPTER FOURTEEN

THE VACANT LOT WAS MORE LIKE A FIELD. LONG GRASSES waved in the breeze like an early crop of wheat. Pathways had been trodden through the grass, leading deep into the lot and breaking left and right. The right side of the lot was lit by the adjacent building, except for a copse of trees, which made the guy wonder how long the lot had been vacant. The left side butted against the brick wall of another building, red bricks that had been whitewashed and then had some kind of advertising painted on them and then been whitewashed again. Only the very top section of the brick wall was lit. The lower portion of the lot was dark.

The twitchy little guy shrugged his shoulders into his coat and shivered involuntarily. He pushed up a section of chain-link fencing and stepped under it and into the lot. Looked around. Right, left or straight? The right was lit, so he went that way. Most of the lot was undisturbed, as if the homeless men were honoring some code to keep off the grass. He followed a path where the grass had been crushed down to the perimeter of the space. Came upon a man lying on a large piece of cardboard the size of an unfolded refrigerator carton. He was wrapped in newspapers and snoring loudly. His arms were wrapped around a black garbage bag. Perhaps his worldly possessions. He made the little guy think of an abandoned dog. The guy was tempted to give the hobo a kick, just for the hell of it. But he might screech and holler, and the guy didn't want to draw attention to himself, so he wandered on.

The right property line of the lot was marked by another chain-link fence that separated it from a lane that ran beside the next building. Along the fence line, men had made camp. Some in groups of two, most alone. They were spaced out enough to give each some version of privacy. Most of the men were sitting silently. A couple were muttering to themselves. One man sat cross-legged with a small dog in his lap. He fed what looked like bologna sausage to the mutt. The little guy felt colder the further he walked. It wasn't the air as much as the silent stares of the men that chilled him.

They all watched. He was coiled and ready. Ready for what, he didn't know. He expected some begging. Got a quarter? Or was it a dollar now? He didn't know the going rate for panhandlers these days, and he wasn't giving anyway. He kept the fence behind him to make sure none of them got the bravado to attack.

But no one spoke. They didn't ask for anything. They just watched him. As if it were a zoo, and it was he rather than they that was on display. He shivered again. A nervous twitch. He reached the far-right corner of the lot and found no sign of the target. He looked across the lot and considered just trooping across the long grass to the other side. It was only a vacant lot, but it felt like a minefield. He turned and retraced his steps along the worn path.

The left side of the lot was different. There were more groups of men against the wall of the next building. He heard their whispers as he approached. Four men sat around a small fire burning in a pit dug into the earth. They fell silent as he stepped into the light. He was reminded of cowboys around a campfire, way further west and way back when. The men around the fire watched him. One of the men lifted his bearded chin. He was wrapped in a long coat and looked as old as the hills but might have been no more than forty. He held a bottle of Irish whiskey that was mostly full. Perhaps he had just arrived.

"Help you?" he asked.

As if a homeless bum could help him. The little guy looked toward the dark corner of the lot.

"You see a guy come through here? Big guy, ski jacket."

The homeless man looked at him as if considering the question. As if they were sitting on Broadway and he had to go back through a thousand faces that had passed by in the previous ten minutes.

"There was a guy. Headed back there."

The man nodded toward the dark corner of the lot. The little guy sniffed and looked again. And he shivered. Without a word he stepped along the path. There were more men sitting against the wall, dropping their whispers as he passed by. He moved slow, looking at each of the hobos. Lots of big guys but no ski jackets. He carefully moved into the dark reaches of the lot. Let his eyes adjust as best they could. The back end of the wall was exposed red brick and absorbed the light. He felt like he was walking deep into a cave. Someone had made a makeshift shelter out of cardboard boxes. It had collapsed on itself, so it was more a pile of trash. Perhaps they used it to start their fires.

He saw two more guys. They were huddled deep in the lot, as far from the outside world as they could get. They had no fire and their skin was putrid and the only light the little guy could see was reflected in their eyes. They were sharing a bottle of Irish whiskey. Mostly full. He wondered if they had a stock somewhere. He doubted it. He glanced around. There was no guy. No one hiding in the shadows. The big guy had vanished.

FLYNN WAITED. He was good at waiting. He had waited plenty in his previous life. In jungles and deserts and dirty abandoned apartments. Waited and waited and waited and then pounced. A few minutes was nothing. Even crouched low on his haunches. He kept his weight back on his heels and up through his core. It would take an hour for the first twinge of pain from his quadriceps. And he wasn't planning on being there that long. He looked up through the hole in the cardboard and watched. He liked the dark corner. He liked that the two men had no fire going. For more reasons than he wanted to admit. The little guy was looking at the two homeless men in the corner. Then he looked back across the lot. And Flynn launched.

He sprung from his low position like a jack-in-the-box. Pushed hard, out and up and was moving fast by the time he took the two strides necessary to reach the little guy. In a movie he might have been screaming or yelling, expelling the anguish in his guts as he thrust toward one of those responsible for killing Beth. But he wasn't in a movie. He moved silently, the rustle of falling cardboard the only noise.

His right fist hit the side of the little guy's head. Hard but not too hard. It took some concentration because every fiber in his body wanted to drive the punch on through the guy's temple and out the other side. To crush his skull like a car in a compactor. But he needed the guy to keep the gift of his short-term memory and the power of speech. So he held back.

The little guy's head snapped and he was launched side-ways like a wide receiver catching a ball on the sideline, dragging his feet to remain in bounds. He fell like a cut tree and landed hard, his momentum only broken by the thick matting of grass.

Flynn was on him before he could think to move. But the guy wasn't thinking or moving. He was seeing stars, or in Flynn's experience, blue and red swatches of color. Concussed but not completely out of it. Flynn rolled him onto his front and pulled his coat down to the middle of his back so his arms were useless, and then rolled him over. The little guy was blinking hard. He was ugly up close. Hair thinning in patches and pock-marked cheeks. His face had the texture of cauliflower. He took a couple more hard blinks and then his eyes stopped on Flynn's face. The beginnings of a snarl split his lips and Flynn saw defiance in him. Defiance that would make it a lot easier for him to do what he was going to do next.

He punched the guy in the face. Not too hard. More a right jab than a full-on haymaker. No broken bones. It sent a message. *We can do this such that there is no end to it.* It was a cheap shot, a ruthless move. But it always got their attention.

"How many of you are there?"

The guy blinked hard and said nothing.

Flynn punched him again. His head snapped sideways and he spat blood. Flynn grabbed his ear and pulled him back so they were eye to eye.

"How many?"

He could see the answer on the guy's lips, but it didn't come. He wasn't a brave one. He was just stupid. His brain wasn't working some clever plan to get out of his situation. Flynn punched him again. This time it was hard. It hurt. Both of them. Flynn felt the pain stab through his fist. The guy's eyes grew large. He was working some stuff out. Flynn reached into his left pocket and pulled out a chunk of concrete. It was all that remained from when the lot been razed. It was the size of two baseballs, side by side. Jagged and rough. No point breaking his fist on a cheekbone. He held it up so the guy could see it. Pulled back his left arm ready to launch.

"Just us," said the guy.

"Who is us?"

"Me and Cust. That's it."

"Two of you?"

The guy nodded to the extent he could lying on the ground. Flynn lifted the concrete chunk higher and poised it ready to slam into the guy's face.

"I swear, just us. Me and Cust. That's it."

Flynn had more questions, but now was not the time. He had the tactical advantage and he planned to use it. There would be time for questions later. He grabbed the little guy by the shirt and picked him up and flopped him over. Pulled the coat off him like he was skinning a beast. Left him in just a T-shirt. He put his boot into the middle of the guy's back and rifled through the pockets of the coat. Found some gum and a cell phone. The phone was a basic model. He knew them well. Prepaid, and if done right, untraceable. He slipped it in his pocket.

He threw the coat to the two men watching him quietly nearby, sipping the whiskey Flynn had given them. Then he reached into his pocket and pulled out a plastic tie that he had gotten from Hutton. It was thick plastic, hard but flexible. He looped it around the guy's wrists and pulled tight. The tie bound his wrists together and he groaned as it dug into his skin. Flynn lifted him again, like a big bag of rice. Dropped him against the wall of ivy that marked the rear of the lot. The ivy hid another chain-link fence. Flynn got on his knee and saw the markings on the guy's arm. Tattoos. Not designs he knew, exactly. But he knew the type. He pulled the guy's other arm

BURNED BRIDGES / 129

out and saw more ink. Different markings. Much poorer quality. Like the tattooist had been drunk. He knew that type too.

Flynn used another plastic tie to bind the cuff around the guy's wrists to the fence. He could pull and pull and never break the plastic. He'd cut his wrists off first. Flynn stood over the guy and looked at the two homeless men.

"Can you guys watch this one for me? I'll be back shortly for him."

"You got it, mister."

"If he starts making too much noise, feel free to slap him around." Flynn raised his eyebrows at the little guy. The guy didn't move. The inside of his mouth was bleeding, and his already limited cognitive function was further impaired. He wasn't going anywhere. Flynn nodded at the two homeless men.

"Thanks for the drink, mister." The man held up the bottle of Irish whiskey. Flynn nodded. Then he turned and walked away. He ventured off the path into the knee-high grass and made a wide berth around the four men and their open fire. Such was his instinct. He opened his phone as he walked, and called Hutton.

"You okay?" she asked.

"All good. One down. There's only one to go. The guy in the car."

"There are only two?"

"Amateur hour. You find a spot?"

"Yes. One block east, two blocks south."

"Let's do it."

CHAPTER FIFTEEN

THE DRIVER WAS GETTING TWITCHY AND HE UNDERSTOOD the irony of it. But his partner had been gone too long. It was a vacant lot. What was there to see? A few bums standing around a fire. And the guy. Either he was there or he wasn't there. One or the other. It didn't require a high school diploma. Then the driver got really twitchy.

The woman came back. The one who had been with the target. Hutton. He recognized the scarf and the hair. Not manly exactly, but not sexy all the same. She walked like she took no nonsense. Fast and angry. The way women walk when they stride a little too long and flail their arms right through their full rotation, front to back. Power walking. Like she was full of opinions that the driver didn't want to hear. She strode right up to the vacant lot. Stood for a moment with her hands on her hips and then slipped through the fence and out of view.

She was gone no more than a minute. She pushed her way back under the hole in the fence and then stood on the sidewalk. She looked both ways, east first, then west toward the driver. Then she snapped back around and looked east again.

Searching for something. Or someone. She pulled out a cell phone and put it to her ear and then started pacing. Up and down. Five paces one way, five paces the other. She stopped and looked at the screen of her phone as if it were malfunctioning. Then she held it to her ear and paced again.

This time her mouth was moving. The driver was no kind of lip reader, but he knew what pursed lips meant. She was angry. She spoke, and then she seemed to listen. She glanced into the vacant lot and said something more. Then she shoved her phone back into the pocket of her coat. And she turned on her heel and stormed away.

The driver watched her and then looked at the section of the vacant lot he could see. There was no movement. No one came out. Not his twitchy partner, not the target. No one. The woman kept going toward the end of the block. The driver gripped the steering wheel hard. Where was his partner? Where was the target? Where was the woman going?

He watched the woman turn right, down the cross street and out of view. Behind the building that sat next to the vacant lot. Then the driver began to panic—the vacant lot had another way out. He started the Yukon and pulled slowly by the lot. He passed the chain-link fence and the section that had been pulled open and was curled up like a mouth. Beyond the fence was darkness. Nothing to see. No movement. No way to tell if it was bricked in by its neighbors or if there was another fence back there, opened like another mouth, out onto another street.

The driver kept going. He turned right. The street was quiet. Vehicles parked along both sides of the road. Hard to see the woman, but he picked her up nearing the end of the block. He eased off the gas as she waited for the light at the crosswalk. She crossed over the next street that took traffic back to the west side of the island. He struggled to find the burner phone in his pocket. Pulled it out and looked at the small display that told him there were no calls. He couldn't call his partner. If he was still following the target, that might blow his cover.

The woman reached the end of another block and turned east and crossed the street in front of the driver. She didn't look back at the Yukon. Her eyes were firmly on the blacktop in front of her. She strode behind the corner building. The driver tapped the gas to move to the intersection. Reached it and looked east and saw the woman less than half a block away. Fortunately the street she was on was an easterly thoroughfare. He turned a wide left to get a better view. The woman walked by a streetlight. Moving purposefully now but not as fast. As if the anger inside was abating. She moved into a dark section of the sidewalk. No streetlights.

She didn't come out.

The driver instinctively took his foot from the gas pedal and coasted forward. As he reached it he realized that the sidewalk was dark because it crossed a laneway. Not a posted road, not a city responsibility. A private lane. Perhaps for delivery access to the buildings either side. He was wary. Lanes were dark and tight. But he was in a big SUV. A Detroit tank. He flicked his headlights off and checked his mirrors and saw nothing behind, so he pulled across the traffic lanes and into the alley.

It was pitch black. There was no sign of the woman. There was no sign of anything. Perhaps he had been mistaken. Perhaps she had walked on and he had missed her. Then he brushed the thought away. She hadn't walked on. She had gone down the alley. He was certain of it.

He looked in his mirror again and saw the yellow glow of the street behind him. He wondered if the woman had gone into one of the buildings. He couldn't see any doors. He couldn't see anything. He needed to see. He put his hand on the headlight switch. Hesitated a moment and then flicked it on. The alley burst into light. And he saw the woman. She was standing in the middle of the alley.

She was looking straight at him.

CHAPTER SIXTEEN_

THE DRIVER HESITATED. THAT WAS HIS FIRST MISTAKE. HE thought about reversing straight out of the alley. But he found his hand had moved to the console between the bucket seats, where he had dropped the burner phone. He picked it up and glanced at the small screen and clicked on the second of two numbers and let it ring. He jinked his head to the right to hold the phone between his jaw and shoulder, and put his hand up to the gear selector on the steering column. Gave it a hard thunk into reverse.

The phone was cheap and the call answered hollow in his ear. He pressed his jaw harder into his shoulder.

"Hang on," said the voice.

The driver hesitated again. That was his second mistake. He kept his foot firmly on the brake pedal, phone cradled to his ear, the woman standing in the headlights in front. *Hang on* was not the response he had expected.

"What?" he replied.

All he heard was a loud cracking sound.

FLYNN STAYED IN THE SHADOWS. Followed the Yukon following Hutton. Saw the Yukon pull a wide left turn into the alley. That was the spot. That was where Hutton had led him. Now he moved fast. He had reached the corner of the alley when the phone in his pocket rang. Not his phone. The burner. He pulled it out, flipped it open. He knew who was calling.

"Hang on," said Flynn.

Six long paces from the sidewalk, he was in the alley and at the rear bumper of the Yukon. The driver had made many mistakes. He had driven into a dead end with only one way out. Flynn didn't know the alley. In theory it might not have been a dead end. But he did know Hutton, and he knew she would make it so. The Yukon driver had ensured his defeat by charging into the small space and then blazing his headlights. All pretense of tailing his quarry had gone out the window. He was made. And in the process, his headlights had blinded him to the only place an attack could come from.

The rear.

Flynn let go of the little guy's phone as he reached the rear tires of the truck. Let it drop from his hand to the blacktop. It made a hollow plastic thunk. It wasn't likely to have broken. It wasn't a big fall, and in his experience cheaper phones were often hardier than the expensive ones with glass screens and expensive casings.

His only concern was the door. If it was locked, things would get difficult. But he wasn't overly concerned. People didn't lock their cars when they were in them. It was as if they sat in some impenetrable bubble. But carjackings happened every day, in every city of the world. So newer models did the job for the driver. Once the accelerator was engaged, the doors would lock themselves. But not in a truck that had to be fifteen years old. The Yukon was old school, and the driver would have to do it himself. And if the tattoos on the driver's little friend told Flynn anything, they told him these guys thought they were tough guys. Flynn knew a lot of tough guys. A lot of tough guys joined the French Foreign Legion. A lot of tough guys failed to make it through training. And those guys, just like the driver of the Yukon, didn't lock their doors.

Flynn timed his movement like choreography. It was practiced. Not this move specifically, but the idea of it. He had learned how to move, how to box, from his father. He had learned how to fight dirty in the Legion. Then he had learned how it all fit together from an Israeli officer on the West Bank.

His right foot landed just before the door. Not too close and on the ball. He reached forward and grabbed the handle on the door with his left hand. Pressed and pulled at the same time and yanked the door open hard. His right foot pivoted as the door flew open, and his body spun with the centripetal motion so he was looking at the driver over his right shoulder.

He let go of the door and it continued on its arc, falling wide open. Flynn continued on his arc, rotating at his core, letting his left shoulder move away and his left arm cock and his left hand ball into a fist.

The plan always went to hell as soon as the boots hit the ground. That was Colonel Laporte's theory, one that he had acquired from Napoleon, who had probably stolen it from someone predating him. In Flynn's experience it was universally true, and no less so now. Often things got a lot harder than the plan had ever foreseen. Sometimes the opposite. Flynn had assumed that a few punches would be required. He anticipated and planned one, two, three shots to the face, right at the nose. He had left the concrete chunk back in the lot, and he didn't like using the butt of his Glock. It was as hard as a rock, but in close combat a gun could get dropped—or lost. Sometimes the other guy ripped it away. Flynn had never stared down the barrel of his own weapon, and he wasn't planning on trying it.

So it would be his fist. Hard and savage and designed for maximum impact. It would have to be his left hand. His dominant hand. He had learned to shoot right-handed because that's how most guns were designed. Not such an issue with a pistol, but the ejection port on a Remington rifle spat hot spent shells that had burned his arm the first time he had tried to shoot it left-handed. So he'd gone the other way with shooting—but not with a baseball pitch and not with a punch.

Plastering a guy's nose all over his face usually had the desired effects. Shock and disorientation. So he spun and cocked his arm and looked at the driver and saw that the plan had changed completely and the whole thing was going to be a lot easier than he thought.

The driver was leaning right. His head was cocked toward the interior of the truck. Flynn assumed the phone was tucked in there, between the lower mandible and the collarbone. So his reaction to the door opening was to spin around. His head jerked left and the phone fell from his shoulder and he tried to move his focus from the front of the Yukon, where Hutton stood, to the more immediate danger of the opening door.

He didn't quite make it.

Doctors called it rotational force. Flynn had learned about it after a transport he was in was blown up by an IED in Burkina Faso. It was some kind of prehistoric thing, an evolutionary quirk, like having eyes in the front of the head, rather than the sides. More subjects became unconscious from side impacts because the head wasn't designed for them. That was the working assumption, according to the doctor in Burkina Faso. The brain bounced off the side of the head with maximum force. The doctor said the worst was rotational force. When the head was moving one way and the impact was the other way. For example, turning to see who had opened the door of your truck, spinning your head left and getting a massive fist into your chin as you did. Two opposing forces, one winner.

Flynn's punch drove into the driver's chin and continued through, snapping his head both up and away. Circuit overload. The brain bounced and the synapses fired in disarray and the whole thing went into reboot. The driver was unconscious before Flynn had finished his follow-through. He flopped sideways toward the console between the seats, and his right foot slipped off the brake pedal. With reverse gear engaged, the Yukon moved backward. Not fast. There was no great acceleration. But the truck was determined to follow the transmission's command and get out of the alley.

Flynn didn't want that. He didn't want to do what he needed to do sitting perpendicular across a Manhattan street. He gripped the back of the driver's seat with one hand, and the door frame with the other, and pulled both feet off the ground. Slammed his right foot onto the parking brake pedal in the footwell. The Yukon jerked to a halt like it had been shot.

He moved fast. He didn't know if the driver would be out for five seconds or five minutes or forever. Knocking a guy out was an inexact science. It was dangerous. An event that should result in a cumulative effect to the brain could just as easily be catastrophic. A punch might only stun one guy but kill another.

First thing Flynn did was flick the headlights off. Better for night vision, and better not to attract the attention of passing vehicles. Then he pushed the gear stick into neutral and dropped back to the blacktop. He passed Hutton at the front bumper without a word. Ran around the truck and opened the rear door on the passenger side and jumped up and in. He grabbed the driver under his arms and pulled him back onto the rear seat. He wasn't wearing a seat belt, but he was dead weight, so it took some doing. He got the driver's back onto the seat by stepping out of the truck himself. Hutton jumped up into the driver's seat and flopped his legs over the seat back. The guy came to rest half on the rear seat and half on the floor. It wouldn't have been a comfortable position had he been awake to feel it.

Flynn slammed the rear door home and opened the front door and jumped in. Hutton punched the gear into reverse and was moving backward out of the alley before she pulled her door closed. The Yukon hit the street and she pulled away, not too fast but not too slow.

"Is he alive?" she asked as she crossed the lanes and cut to the right.

"Yes."

"Sure?"

"I'm sure."

"Will he be okay?"

"He wasn't okay to begin with."

Hutton drove a big circle. Right, right, right. They came back up Park Avenue. Flynn watched the guy in the back. No movement. Some breathing. They did a loop and stopped by the vacant lot. New Yorkers parked wherever they could. It might not have been Los Angeles freeways, but there were way more cars than spaces. The monthly rent on a single compact car space in a downtown garage would get a four-bedroom ranch house with acreage in Kansas City. But even New Yorkers shied from parking out in front of a vacant lot. As if the lot were vacant because the building had been swallowed whole by the earth, and any nearby vehicle might be next.

Hutton stopped adjacent to the hole in the fence. Flynn jumped out and lifted the wire and stepped through the gaping mouth. He marched toward the back. Found the little guy still tied to the fence at the back of the lot. The two homeless men were still watching him.

"He was yellin'," said the guy with the whiskey bottle. "But he gave up on that pretty soon."

Flynn nodded and stepped to the men. Pulled a roll from his pocket and peeled off a couple of hundreds. He handed one to each of the men.

"Get something to eat."

The men nodded silently and pocketed the money. Maybe they would buy more alcohol. Maybe they would visit the buffet at the Four Seasons. He couldn't say and he couldn't decide for them. He pulled out his Glauca knife and flicked it open, the blade as dark as the shadows. The little guy saw it and he squirmed and gave a whine like gas releasing from a bicycle tire. Flynn dropped to a knee and cut the second plastic tie from the fence. He left the first one as a cuff around the guy's wrists.

Flynn pulled the guy to his feet and pushed him forward to set him marching. The guy stumbled along the track as if having his hands behind him disrupted his equilibrium. They reached the fire where the four men sat. One was the bearded man who had directed the little guy to the back of the lot. Flynn kicked the little guy in the back of the knee and he dropped to the ground. Then Flynn removed four more hundreds and moved around the outside of the group and gave each of the men around the fire a single bill. Flynn felt the warmth of the fire. It should have felt comforting on a cold evening, but it didn't. It made him sweat and he felt his pulse beat harder in his neck.

"Thanks," he said to the bearded man as he handed him the money.

The man looked at him. Or maybe through him. His face was grimy, and sleeping rough had aged him, but it was his eyes that Flynn saw. They were ancient eyes. As if they had seen the Lenape people roam the fields of this nameless island, and then watched as the Dutch had arrived and the place became New Amsterdam and then the English had arrived and changed the name to New York, and then Washington had lost and then won, and the people had come and the buildings had grown and the greatest metropolis on the planet had flourished around him.

The man just nodded. "Be good."

Flynn pulled the little guy up again and marched him out and under the fence and onto the street. His pulse should have been rising now, dragging a man onto a Manhattan street. The opposite was true. The further from the flames he moved, the calmer he got. It wasn't logical, Flynn knew that. There were a few people on the street but Flynn paid them no mind. He opened the tailgate of the Yukon and motioned for the little guy to get in. The guy hesitated, but Flynn's face hardened and the little guy got the message. Getting in with his hands tied was difficult, so he sat on the edge and leaned back and Flynn spun his legs in and slammed the tailgate closed before the legs could spring back out again.

Flynn looked around and saw no one calling for the cops or taking cell phone video. No one was paying any attention at all. He got in the passenger seat and Hutton pulled away.

"What now?" she asked.

"We need somewhere quiet."

"I'm not sure I want these guys in my office."

"No. Somewhere different. I need to talk to Hedstrom."

CHAPTER SEVENTEEN

FLYNN USED HUTTON'S PHONE TO EXPLAIN WHAT HE needed to Hedstrom. Hedstrom spoke in staccato, and Flynn could picture his eyes moving over the environment wherever he was protecting the Russian oil guys.

"I know a place," said Hedstrom.

"No eyes."

"You'll have to use some of your cash."

"You know about that?"

"I know everything that comes into my office."

"Okay. Tell me."

"What are you prepared to do?"

"Everything."

"To protect Laura?"

Flynn glanced at Hutton. She was focused on the road, but she was listening.

"Everything."

"Listen up, then."

FLYNN SAT HALF-ROTATED in his seat. He kept his eye on the two guys in the back as they drove north up FDR, along the west side of the East River, and then followed the curve of the island up the Harlem River. As they passed by, he glanced across at Yankee Stadium, the giant ballpark dark and dormant. He had grown up listening to stories of the house that Babe built, and had watched the World Series on Armed Forces Television. The Yankees had moved one block north to their new stadium before Flynn ever got to see a game live. He still hadn't.

"Your friends are quiet," said Hutton.

"One's out of it. The other wishes he was."

"They don't seem top drawer."

"No."

"Like Iraq."

"No."

"You don't think?"

"No," said Flynn. "Dennison wasn't top drawer, for sure. But someone in Iraq was."

"So this is one but not the other."

Flynn said nothing. He watched the lights across in the Bronx.

Hutton glanced at him as she drove. "You have to consider it."

Nothing.

"Can we be sure Dennison is dead?"

"I shot him."

"Not the same thing."

"Usually is. When I do it."

"Did you see the body?"

"The building exploded. Our driver, Yusuf, pulled me out. I was near the door. He didn't go in looking for Dennison."

"Everyone thought you were dead. They were wrong. Maybe we're wrong about Dennison."

Flynn looked at her and then focused on the backseat.

"They're inked," he said.

"These two?" she replied, nodding toward the rear.

"The driver has military ink."

"How does military ink differ from any other kind? Like a unit designation?"

"Military tattoos are badges of honor. Like permanent medals. They get them all over the world from all kinds of places. But the common link is the precision. They tell of a certain time in a certain place, but they get them done well."

"Like drunk sailors?"

"I'm not talking about the back room of a bar in Saigon. I'm talking about Operation Iraqi Freedom."

Hutton nodded. "So at least one of these guys was there?"

"They were both there. But the little guy has a second set of ink."

"Where?"

"Prison."

"He's not a gangbanger."

"No, he's not. Prison tattoos are a different kind of badge, and it's not about honor. It's about picking a side in order to stay alive. And prison ink isn't high art. It's amateur. Done in less than optimal conditions with less than optimal tools. It's more like branding a bull."

"Where did he do time?"

"His markings don't tell me that. But he will."

THE WAREHOUSE LOOKED ABANDONED. There were no vehicles in the lot, no lights around the building. A ten-foot chain-link gate lay partly open like a lazy sentry. Hutton cut the headlights, edged the gate fully open with the Yukon's grille and drove in. The George Washington Bridge shaded any moon-light, and Hutton seemed to drive by sonar. The building wasn't large by warehouse standards. Not designed for masses of freight or large semitrailers. There were no loading bays. There was a large roller door that looked as if it hadn't been opened since the Reagan era. Hutton pulled the Yukon to the rear, between the warehouse and the river. There were cars here. A dozen of them. All new models, mostly European.

"Interesting," said Flynn.

"They call it a boudoir. I saw some with the Bureau. It might not be a high-end area, but it's a white-collar place. Designed for people with other lives that they really want to keep separate from their secret life." She put her hand on the door to open it.

"Let me do the talking," she said. "At first anyway."

"You got it."

Flynn opened the tailgate and found the little guy curled up in the fetal position. But he was awake.

"Open your mouth and I'll make you swallow every tooth you own," Flynn said.

The little guy shook but said nothing. Flynn took his agreement as implied.

Hutton led them back to the end of the warehouse that was closest to the street. Not the front of the place. Logically the longest side was the front, with the roller doors, even though it was perpendicular to the road. But Hutton found a door on the street side. It was unmarked. No company name or street number. There was a rusted rectangle where a post box might have once been attached to the steel cladding.

Hutton stopped short of the door. "If you don't want to make a lot of noise, we'll need some cash."

Flynn reached into his pack and pulled out a brick of bills. He handed it to Hutton.

"What is it you do for a living?" she asked.

"Tell you later."

Hutton tapped on the door. It was metal and solid. The door opened and a big black guy who was wider than he was tall blocked the space. He didn't speak.

"Party of four," she said.

The big guy looked at her. Didn't look her over. His eyes never moved off hers. Then he jinked his head toward the interior. The three of them stepped inside and they felt the pressure change as the door closed behind them. They were in a dark room. The walls were painted black. Strips of red fabric cascaded from the ceiling, giving the space a sense of movement. Like being underwater. Hutton spoke to a thin woman sitting on a stool behind a small black table.

"Four," she said.

The woman gave her a look of distaste like the finest French maître d', and then ran a long finger down a register book.

"Private?" she said.

"Yes."

She tapped her finger on the book as if she were deciding something. She glanced at the little guy. He was twitching, genetically incapable of standing still. The woman turned her eyes to Hutton.

"Two thousand."

Hutton peeled the cash off Flynn's brick and handed it over. The woman opened a drawer, put the cash inside, and stood. She was built like a reed and moved with a similar rhythm. Hutton dropped in behind the woman, and Flynn kept the twitchy little guy between them. They walked through a large room. Soft lighting made it possible to discern shapes but nothing more. The space was filled with giant beanbags. Some had people in them. The room smelled of sweat and Chanel No. 5. More fabric dropped from the ceiling, making it difficult to discern the true dimensions of the room. There was a bar at the end of the space. The bottles gave the occasional glint in the muted light, but there was no bright display of color one might expect in a nightclub. A man in black stood behind the bar, his silhouette like a hole in the glint of the bottles behind him. Flynn noted the music. The stuff that had been new age in Europe when he was a boy. Flutes and harps and organs mixed with ocean waves and rain splatter. Soft and formless. Like the room.

They reached a hallway, and the woman led them past a series of doors. The walls were still black, but the light was red. She stopped at a door and opened it and then stood aside for them to enter. The space was about the size of a hotel room. There were a couple of the beanbags designed for one and another designed for a party. It was the size of a small bed. There was a table with a landline phone and a bar fridge stocked with Fiji water.

"Do you require anything?" the woman asked.

Hutton looked at Flynn. Flynn looked at the woman.

"Privacy."

The woman waited a moment, as if there was more to come, and then nodded.

"If you require anything, you can reach the concierge with the phone."

She closed the door and left them alone. Flynn dropped the little guy in one of the smaller beanbags. They were useful. There were no surprises, no sudden moves getting out of a beanbag.

"You watch him, I'll get his pal."

Hutton slipped her Glock out of its holster and held it casually. No need to point it at the guy. Flynn opened the door and walked back down the corridor. His eyes were adjusting and his view was better. He made his way through the large room slowly. He didn't want to step on anything, or anyone. And it gave him time to get a fix on the space. It could have been a dance club. He had seen those in Europe, back when his job had necessitated tracking guys down to places like that. Deserters from the Legion often found their way to nightclubs, bars, brothels. Dance clubs were like mainlining humanity. After being locked away from society on Legion barracks, doing nothing but marching and make-work for what seemed like a lifetime, some guys broke. Some broke and were discharged. Some broke and ran. And more often than not, they ran to get a fix of humanity, such as it was. He had found a lot of deserters in places like this one. Just not exactly like this one.

No one was dancing. The music was more white noise than rhythm, and it was better suited to an elevator than a club. It was suited to lying back in a beanbag. He hadn't picked up on it the first time through, but now he heard the subtle moans coming from the floor. Sounds of release. He stepped to the right to avoid a pair of legs stretched out in his way. He followed them up and saw they were joined to a man sprawled in a bean-bag. He was in a business shirt. His tie was loosened like a noose and his collar splayed open. His suit jacket lay discarded beside him. He was white, maybe forty. His left sleeve was rolled up, a rubber tourniquet around his arm. His hand lay open, having dropped a syringe onto the floor. His eyes were closed and he wore a smile.

Flynn kept walking. Out to the entrance lobby, where the thin woman gave him a silent glare, as if she disapproved of the whole thing. The big guy was still at the door. He opened it and Flynn stepped back out into the night air. It was cold and he realized that the inside of the warehouse had been warm. He marched around to the Yukon. It was the oldest vehicle in the lot by a decade. He opened the rear door and slid the driver half out. Flynn dropped to a squat and slid the driver the rest of the way out, over his shoulder and into a fireman's carry. Then he pushed up, closed the door, and walked back to the front of the warehouse. He tapped on the metal, and the door opened. The big doorman stood there silently.

"May I?" asked Flynn.

"No readmission."

"My friend hasn't come in yet."

The big guy looked at the body hanging over Flynn's shoulder. "He can come in. You need to pay again."

"My cash is in the room."

"That's a problem."

"For you."

The doorman puffed out his chest like a rooster. Flynn considered his moves. There were plenty of ways to take him down. Most involved dropping the driver from his shoulder, which he didn't want to do. Picking him up again would be hard. Humans didn't lift like barbells. They weren't so compliant.

"I'll put it on his account," said the woman from her perch behind the table.

The doorman took a good few seconds to move, as if he had a point to prove. Flynn just waited. He'd gotten what he wanted. The doorman would keep. He turned sideways to get around the big guy and marched past the woman without a glance, as if carrying a man like a side of beef was a nightly occurrence. He made his way through the large space with the beanbags and back to the private room. Hutton leaned against the table, sipping on a bottle of water. The little guy lay in his beanbag.

Flynn dropped the driver into the large party-sized beanbag. It boomed like a timpani. Then he took a water from the fridge and gulped some down.

"How does a place like this not get shut down?" he asked.

"Money. You see the parking lot? This is where Wall Street comes to hide its dirty secrets."

Flynn shook his head and sipped his water. He opened his pack and took out a roll of duct tape and placed it on the table. Then he stepped over to the little guy and dropped to a crouch.

"Your buddy's taken the easy way out. Looks like he's out for the duration. So it's just you and me."

The little guy's eyes shot from side to side.

"Who is in charge?" Flynn asked.

The little guy said nothing.

"This could get hard real fast. Who's in charge? Ox Dennison?"

"I don't know who that is."

"Do better. Who and where?"

"I don't know who. I don't know where. Cust got the job. I don't know nothin'."

Flynn glanced at the driver. He was breathing, but he could have been closer to a coma than awake. Impossible to tell. Flynn cursed his luck to knock out the brains of the operation, such as they were. He turned back to the little guy.

"Where's the woman?"

"Gone."

Flynn swallowed the impulse to hit the guy into tomorrow.

"How did you know the woman? How did you know she was the one?"

The little guy said nothing. More than nothing. He pursed his lips as if physically clamming up would prevent the words from leaving him.

"This doesn't end well for you if you don't tell me what I want to know."

The little guy set his jaw firm. Ready for another punch to the face. Not happy about it but prepared to wear it. Which made Flynn think about the reason why. People clammed up for three reasons: ideology, money and fear. Which really amounted to one reason.

Belief.

Flynn pushed off his thighs and stood. He stepped to the table and grabbed the roll of duct tape. His experience was that belief in future events was often overtaken by current events and the human instinct for survival. However bad the future might be, one needed to survive the present. He picked at the tape and then pulled a length of it out. The sound of the tape ripping away from the roll was loud against the white noise of the waves and the harps. He tore the tape with his teeth and let the roll drop to the floor.

"How did you know the woman?"

The little guy's eyes were wide, but not wide enough to talk.

"How did you know the woman was the right one?"

The little guy said nothing.

Flynn leaned over him and plastered the length of tape across the top of the little guy's head from ear to ear.

"How?"

Nothing.

Flynn stood. As he stood he ripped the tape away. Like a giant Band-Aid. Or a wax job. One vicious yank. The tape came away covered in hair. Some of the hair was still attached to skin. A flat patch ran across the guy's head, like a freeway blasted through a hill. Hair at the back and hair at the front. But in the middle, from ear to ear, most of the hair was gone. Blood oozed from the guy's scalp, black in the dark room.

The guy howled like he'd been shot. Flynn dropped and punched him in the guts to knock the sound out of him. His scream turned to a sucking sound. Then wheezing as he tried to breathe. Wheezing and whimpering. Sudden and extreme pain and then no oxygen. Flynn hadn't invented it. He'd seen it in Africa, from a guy who swore waterboarding was superior but problematic when stuck in a parched desert. It had worked then, and he had every reason to believe it would work now.

Flynn searched the floor and found the roll of tape. Turned and picked it up. Stood and found himself face-to-face with Hutton. She was frowning. He didn't expect her to approve of his methods. She was one of the righteous ones. And he was thankful for that. He knew that without the righteous ones like her, the world would belong to the ones who tended to the barbaric. Like him. But the two were like scales, keeping the world in balance. Those like Hutton fought hard to protect the laws by following the laws. And Flynn accepted that bad people never just spilled the beans voluntarily.

He turned back to the little guy. Picked at the tape and pulled it out a couple of inches. The little guy shifted in his beanbag at the sound. Flynn crouched beside him.

"How did you know it was the right woman?"

The little guy shivered. He was crying. Not audible sobs, but there were tears on his cheeks.

"There was a code word. Like a phrase," he wept.

"What phrase?"

"Something she said. I don't know."

Flynn pulled the tape out another inch.

"No, please no. I don't know. It was a kid's thing."

"A kid's thing?"

"Like a saying. Something about the bogeyman."

"The bogeyman?"

"Yes. I'm not making it up, I swear. The bogeyman." Now the guy began sobbing. Flynn sat back on his haunches and stared into the darkness in the corner of the room. He thought of a phrase, a remnant of a past life that had stuck with him. Then he turned back to the little guy.

"Even the bogeyman can't hide forever."

The little guy stopped sobbing and looked at Flynn. "That's it. That's it. The bogeyman."

"Where did you hear that?"

"I don't know. I swear. She said it. She knew it. Said it was Spanish or something. Where she got it, I don't know. I swear."

"Tell me again, who gave you this job?"

"Cust, Cust. He knows them. All I know is, he's scared of them. That's all I know. Cust don't scare easy, but he's scared of them."

"Why is he scared?"

"Because of the last guy. The last guy was burned to death. That's what Cust said. Burned alive."

Flynn looked at Hutton. He could see she was thinking what he was thinking. Burned. Like Iraq. Like Ox Dennison. Burned alive.

Or not.

"Where are they?" Flynn asked.

"I don't know." He started sobbing again. "This really hurts, man."

"Tell me where and I'll take the pain away."

"We meet in White Plains. A parking lot in White Plains. We don't get out of the car."

"How do you set up the meets?"

"I don't. Cust does it. Cust makes the calls. I don't know nothing. Jesus, man. This really hurts." The last line was a swallowed scream. The guy was in serious pain.

Flynn nodded and stood. Opened the door and stepped out into the corridor. Walked back out into the large room. His eyesight had gotten better. The guy was still behind the bar. He was chopping something delicate with a blade. Flynn guessed cocaine. He paid the guy no mind. Just marched back to the smiling guy with the suit. He hadn't moved. The smirk was still plastered to his face. Flynn looked at him for a second.

Wondered what a guy like that was trying to escape. He obviously had a good job, a nice car, an expensive suit. The ring on his finger suggested a wife, maybe a family. Not the worst situation in the world. Not poverty or disease or war. Flynn shook his head. Pulled the tourniquet from the guy's arm and picked up his syringe. It was empty. A second syringe lay on the floor, still wearing a plastic cap over the needle. Safety first. Flynn picked it up. The syringe was full. No burning flames under spoons here. Everything was catered for. One for now, one for later. Flynn stood and turned and headed back toward the room. The barman had stopped chopping. He was watching. Watching Flynn walk across the space, around the beanbags and the prone bodies and down the corridor.

Flynn stepped back in and closed the door. He stood before the little guy and then dropped down on him. The beanbag exhaled more air, and Flynn's knees pressed the guy's arms into his ribs. He pulled the guy's right arm out from under his left knee and ripped the guy's shirtsleeve. Then he wrapped the tourniquet around the guy's arm.

"What are you doing, man?"

Flynn held the syringe up and tapped it. A dribble of liquid squeezed from the tip of the needle.

"What are you doing?" the guy repeated.

"Making the pain go away."

Flynn stabbed the needle into a vein and pressed the plunger. Pushed it in about halfway. It wasn't that he didn't want the guy to overdose. He didn't care about the guy. Not anymore. He had chosen his side and he had chosen poorly. But Flynn only had the one dose. He pulled the needle from the guy's arm and stayed on top of him. The drug coursed through his body quickly, and his head lolled back as the analgesic properties of the heroin took hold and the pain drifted away. The little guy smiled.

"Thanks," he said.

Flynn got up and stepped to the driver. Repeated the dose. The driver didn't offer thanks. Flynn wiped the syringe with his shirt and dropped it on the table. Hutton was still watching him.

"Was that necessary?"

"You want them to leave and warn Ox that we're coming?"

"So you think it's him?"

"That phrase. We used to use it in the unit. And I used it just before I killed Ox Dennison."

"So how does it relate to Beth?"

"I used it the night I met Beth. It became a thing. Something we'd say to each other. She traced money and convertibles for a living, so it appealed to her."

"We need to leave," said Hutton.

"Got that right."

They took their water and their bags. Strode down the corridor. Out into the main room, past the beanbags. The barman was gone from his station. Flynn swept a ribbon of fabric away and stepped into the hall that led to the exit.

The woman was standing behind her table. The barman was talking to the big doorman. The doorman caught Flynn's eye and the barman spun around.

"That's him. He took the other guy's stuff."

The doorman pushed past the bar guy and headed for Flynn. Like they were teenagers in cars, playing chicken. Flynn heard the woman behind the table call him a thief, which he thought was rich, given the environment. But he kept his eye on the big guy. He was the right size for the job of a doorman. His girth alone intimidated the white-collar clientele. Kept them in line. Stopped the odd disagreement with intimidation more than force. But the job had just changed. Flynn wasn't intimidated. So now the guy was all wrong for the job. Because he was too big and too wide and too slow.

"We owe you some money," Flynn said. The doorman didn't stop coming. It was past time for cash payment alone. Bruises needed to be left, lessons learned. But the big guy watched Flynn's right hand reach back toward Hutton behind him. Handing her his water bottle, maybe reaching for some cash. It was natural that the big guy's eye would follow the movement. Instinct.

But the doorman's instincts were off. His size gave him a false sense of strength. Flynn recalled something by Mark Twain. It's not the size of the dog in the fight, but the size of the fight in the dog. Size was never a guarantee of victory. Not by a long shot. The doorman's eyes moved to his left, watching the motion of Flynn's right hand, but they failed the see the motion of his left hand. It moved in a straight line, harder to judge than side-to-side movement. Close to impossible to see in the dark room.

Flynn used the rocking back right to propel himself forward on the left. It was a jab, not the most powerful punch. But the follow-through was tremendous. He put his whole body into it, pivoting at the waist, his core wrenching and creating torque that propelled his fist into the big guy's throat just above the manubrium. There was plenty of flab there, but it all moved en masse, collapsing his trachea, cutting off his air and sending his entire body into emergency life support mode. The doorman grabbed at his numerous chins and gurgled as he dropped to his knees. Flynn's left punch had positioned his right foot in the perfect position for a kick, which he delivered like a penalty goal attempt. Full and straight, plastering the doorman's nose across his face.

The woman had ducked under her table, and as Flynn landed from his kick she came up holding a gun. It looked like a pistol on steroids, but the way she swung it in a two-handed arc told Flynn it was a Heckler and Koch MP5K. It was a snub-nosed version of the MP5 submachine gun. Flynn knew the K stood for *kurz*, German for "short". The fore-end was little more than a stubby handguard at the front, so it could be hidden and handled like a pistol. But the woman had taken it up two-handed. That would give her greater control, but slowed her movement to target.

It slowed her too long. The short gun swung toward Flynn, but before the muzzle reached him he wrapped his hand around the women's front hand grip and drove it back. Her arms folded from the violent action, and Flynn forced the gun back into her chest. She fell down and let go of the gun. Flynn didn't. He kept hold of it by the front handguard and flipped it around and aimed it at the woman. She cowered back against the wall, her hands in the air.

Flynn didn't break stride. He kept moving straight toward the barman, who saw the gun and threw himself at the wall to get out of the way. That was okay with Flynn. It saved any further exertion, and his heart rate had already burst past two hundred. He hit the door at pace, pushed it open and held it for Hutton. The night was bracing. Hutton led him back around to the Yukon. Once more she started it before Flynn had closed his door, and she peeled out of the lot.

CHAPTER EIGHTEEN

FLYNN WANTED TO STOP AND BUNKER DOWN AND REASSESS. Hutton knew just where. She pulled onto Route 9A and took the Henry Hudson Bridge off the island, and then followed the road north until it became Saw Mill River Parkway. East of Yonkers she pulled into a motel that made low rent look polished and new. The place looked closed. There was a lit sign on the corner, a utilitarian announcement of the establishment's name. No more, no less. No mention of amenities, no claims of spa tubs or HBO. The place was surrounded by leafless trees. The rooms were in one long strip, three stories. Twelve rooms on each of two levels, twenty-four total, with parking underneath on the ground level a thoughtful concession to rough winter conditions. Attached to the end of the row was a solid block that housed the office and some kind of breakfast room and probably the manager's billet above.

The only light in the place came from the office. It wasn't lit like Times Square. A soft, dull glow more than the proverbial well-lighted place. There were six vehicles parked under the rooms, all large sedans. Businessmen. The kind of road warriors for whom even the cheap chain business hotels were out of the budget. No light came from any of the rooms. Heavy drapes had been pulled, warding off the cold.

Hutton stopped short of the office, and Flynn wandered inside. The office was as plain as the exterior. Linoleum floors, worn thin and colorless. A wooden rack of dusty tourist brochures. The counter was peeling gray laminate. Behind it stood a young guy in a hoodie. Maybe a college student working the graveyard shift. Plenty of time to study or sleep.

"How much for a room?"

"Fifty," said the kid.

"Okay."

"Credit card and ID."

Flynn pulled a hundred from his roll.

"Fifty for the room, and the rest is my ID."

"We need a credit card for incidentals."

"You offer a minibar?"

The kid shook his head. "The rooms don't have fridges."

"So no incidentals."

He shrugged and pocketed the money and handed Flynn an old-fashioned key on a ring attached to a large wooden tag with the number 24 burned into it like a brand. Flynn offered the kid a nod and walked out to the end of the block. Hutton parked the Yukon under cover and gathered their bags. They used the fire stairs at the end of the building. The stairs were rusted and small flakes of concrete fell from where they were fixed to the wall as Flynn and Hutton took each step.

Room 24 was last in the block on the top level. The original owner was clearly a no-nonsense guy. He had eschewed the convention of including the floor level in the room number. So 212 was plain old 24. The door was a solid item, some kind of old-growth hardwood that would outlast the stairs. The room was as expected. Everything they needed and absolutely nothing they didn't. A queen-sized bed with a bedspread in a pattern designed to mask stains and wear. The carpet was a gold-brown, with a trail worn thin between the door, the bed and the bathroom. There was a wall unit opposite the bed that featured a desk, a TV cabinet and a wardrobe. All one unit, all impossible to steal without a trip to a hardware store. The bathroom had a stall shower in the corner, surrounded by a flower motif plastic curtain, and a small sink. A little soap in paper and a small bottle of shampoo. There was a paper sash draped across the toilet seat, signifying that the bowl had been cleaned.

"One room?" asked Hutton.

"I wasn't planning on staying."

Flynn shrugged out of his jacket and hung it in the wardrobe, and then splashed some water across his face and wiped down with a thin towel. He could hear the main road outside, but only because the bathroom window was fused open an inch. He came out and sat on the bed, and Hutton sat on the old chair under the desk. Seeing Flynn's face, she decided as an afterthought to splash some water herself. She spoke to him from the bathroom.

"Those guys aren't all there is."

"No."

"They're reporting to someone."

"Yes."

"So is it Ox Dennison?" Hutton came out wiping her face.

"Maybe."

"Army grunts, deployed in the same place as Dennison. After the same shipment, and they knew about the phrase. Your bogeyman phrase is not exactly the most common phrase in the world. It's hardly *veni, vidi, vici*."

"No, it's not. But they didn't know the phrase. Whoever was operating them knew the phrase."

"Dennison."

"Maybe. But the thing that doesn't fit is why. Why would he

be after a container of arms, biological or otherwise, after all this time?"

"Maybe the shipment isn't what we thought."

"And how does Dennison link to Beth?" asked Flynn. "She was a lawyer. Big corporate stuff. Not Dennison's circle at all."

Hutton opened her laptop and turned on her phone and connected to the internet.

"Did you get their phones?" she asked.

"I dropped one in the alley. I was more focused on landing a good punch."

"You did that. What about the other?"

Flynn stood and went to the wardrobe and felt the pockets and pulled out a plain black phone. He threw it to Hutton and she caught it in one hand. Turned it on and scrolled through previous calls. Flynn took his spot back on the edge of the bed.

"All the recent calls are to two stored numbers. Both 917 numbers. New York area cell phones. All three were probably bought at the same time."

"Do they have to provide ID to get them?"

Hutton shook her head. "Technically, yes. But did you give ID when you registered for this room?"

"In the form of a dead president. I see your point."

"But—" said Hutton. She turned the phone over and used her nail to flick the cover off the back of the unit. Underneath was a thin battery. She used her nail again to remove the battery. In the cavity of the phone was a small SIM card in a metal brace. She pulled the brace back and it opened on a tiny hinge and she removed the small SIM card. She held it up to Flynn.

"Now we know the cell phone carrier."

"Okay."

"These burner phones can be registered online. To facilitate topping up with credit, that sort of thing." She tapped a few keys on her laptop. "But lots of people don't bother. They just add credit via the phone itself, or in a store. Which means it might not be registered."

"How does that help?"

Hutton wrote down a couple of numbers. One from the SIM, the other from inside the phone. Then she put the device back together and powered it up.

"With the phone, the SIM number and the phone IMEI, we might be able to register the account."

"How does that help us? They aren't going to make any more calls. They don't have the phones."

Hutton didn't answer. Her focus was on the screen. She tapped away, and then the phone beeped. She looked at the phone's screen and tapped some more.

"Voilà."

Flynn stood and looked over Hutton's shoulder. Despite spending the evening on the streets of downtown Manhattan and in a drug den on the north end of the island, she smelled fresh like lavender.

"I just registered the phone to a dummy email account."

"So we can add credit to the phone for them?"

"Yes, smart guy, we could. But we can also see this."

She tapped a key on her laptop, and the screen rolled out a register of the calls made to and from the phone they had. It showed that all the calls were to the same two numbers that were in the phone. But the register showed more. It showed the location where the phone was when it received incoming calls. And it showed where the other phones were when it made outgoing calls. Manhattan was repeated over and over. Outgoing and incoming calls made and received in Manhattan. That was not news to them. But in between all the calls to and from Manhattan there was one other location. Outgoing calls made. To Katonah, New York.

"Do you know this place?" asked Flynn.

"Yes. It's not that far from here. About thirty miles north and east, straight up the Saw Mill. It's a stop on the Metro North rail line. A commuter town for Manhattan. But not for janitors. It's money."

Flynn stepped back and sat down on the bed. "That's where they are."

"Whoever they are."

"No, you sold me. It's Dennison. It fits. Think about it. In Baghdad, what was his MO? He liked to hide in the suburbs, such as they were. The place I met him, the first time."

"That place looked like a war zone. Katonah is where Manhattanites go to breed."

"It's all relative. Baghdad was a war zone. The coalition bombed the hell out it—twice. Our driver, Yusuf, told us as much. He said it had been where rich people lived. People who could afford to flee. But it was as close to a nice suburb as you got outside the green zone. And Dennison wasn't going to do business in the GZ, or anywhere near Camp Victory. That suburb was as safe and settled as it got. Close but not too close. Where regular people came and went. Sometime in the past, it was a nice suburb. Maybe a commuter suburb for downtown Baghdad."

"Like Katonah."

Flynn nodded.

"Okay, that narrows it some. But Katonah is still a decent-sized place. And the surrounding areas probably count, as far as reaching a cell tower is concerned. We've found the right field, but not the right haystack."

"Think about the MO," said Flynn. "What did Dennison do in Iraq? He didn't rent. He didn't take over a warehouse."

"It was a residential property. Someone's home."

"Right, but an empty one."

"So he's in an empty residence in Katonah?"

"Not just any empty residence. There was something else important about the place in Baghdad. It was abandoned. The owners weren't coming back."

"A house for sale?"

Flynn shrugged. "Close, but it still doesn't feel right. Properties on the market can be visited, right? By prospective buyers."

"And lookie-loos."

"Lookie-loos?"

"People who look at real estate with no intention of buying it."

"Why would you do that?"

"Sometimes just to see the inside of someone else's house," said Hutton. "To compare a neighboring house to yours. You haven't done that?"

"I've never owned a house. I've never needed to buy one."

"What about in San Francisco?"

"It was Beth's place. She had it when we met."

"Oh. Well, that's something normal people do."

"Okay. But that's additional traffic. Not an ideal place to hide."

"Right. So we're looking for a residential property, vacant but not on the open market. Not likely to be visited."

"Abandoned would be best," said Flynn.

"I don't think there's too many abandoned houses in Katonah. It's not that kind of place."

"Okay."

Hutton put her finger in the air like she'd just had an epiphany. "Abandoned, but not completely. For a fixed period of time."

"What does that mean?"

"REO properties."

Flynn shook his head.

Hutton smiled. "You really didn't pick up a lot of the civilian world in the past few years, did you?"

"I got a smartphone."

"Do you have a car?"

"No. I like to walk."

"In Manhattan, I get that. But Marin County?"

"We lived in downtown San Rafael. Walking distance to everything. Even the bus depot."

"Did Beth have a car?"

"Of course. You want to explain the REO thing?"

"Real estate owned. It means owned by the lender who has the lien on the property. In layman's terms—the bank. If the homeowner doesn't pay their mortgage, eventually they default on the loan. The lender calls in the loan and takes possession of the property. Sometimes the owners get evicted, sometimes they leave. But often the houses sit vacant while the bank processes everything. There's a whole legal process they have to go through, with the city or the county. And it doesn't always move fast. It can take months."

"But is the property on the market?"

"No. Not until the legal process is finished. Then the place is often put up for auction. Often sold sight unseen. No visit. Sometimes by developers or flippers."

"Flippers?"

"People buy the houses cheap at auction and fix them, paint or whatever. Sometimes the old owner is angry when they get kicked out and they do damage to the place. Flippers fix it and sell for a profit. But the point is, the date the legal process is finalized is a known date. No one will visit until then. Maybe a drive-by, but nothing more, and maybe not even that. And then the auction date is set, and that's a known date too."

"So how would Dennison know which properties are REO and what those dates are?"

"Easy. He'd ask a real estate agent."

"Okay. I'm assuming those guys aren't at their desks at midnight."

"No. Strictly regular people hours."

"Can we find that stuff on the internet?"

"Not really. Limited information, maybe. They like to keep that stuff close to their chest. We should visit an office, first thing."

"In that case, we should sleep. Then get a good breakfast."

Hutton closed her laptop and spun her chair around and looked at the bed. "So we're staying after all?"

"I'll take the floor," said Flynn.

"Don't be silly. I think we can be grown up enough to share a bed."

Hutton kicked off her shoes and padded to the bathroom. Flynn heard the shower running. He stepped out of the room and onto the landing that ran the length of the building. He could hear distant traffic noise. An artery to the city that never sleeps. The air was cold and he was in his shirtsleeves, but he liked the feeling. Brisk, his mother would have called it, on a morning in Brussels, decades ago. He watched the bare trees sway just so, in time with the silent rhythms of nature.

When he came back inside, Hutton was in bed, in a T-shirt. Her hair was still damp.

"Mind if I have this side?"

"Not at all." He used the bathroom and then turned the room light off and slipped out of his trousers and shirt and laid them out on the floor. The sheets felt cold and crisp. The bed was just large enough to lie side by side. Hutton had her hands up behind her head. Flynn did the same. They touched at the elbows.

"You okay?" she asked.

"Sure. Why not. We're making progress."

"I didn't mean that."

"You mean Beth? Yes, I'm okay. We're making progress."

"You're an emotional fountain."

"Falling apart won't bring her back."

"Neither will vengeance. You know that, right?"

"I know."

"And it probably won't make you feel any better."

"We'll have to agree to disagree on that point."

"Does it usually make you feel better? Catching the bad guys?"

"Yes, it does."

"Really?" She shifted her weight, turned to face him in the dark.

"Yes, but not how you think. It's not about vengeance. It's much more simple than that. My dad always said that he served because he could. Because there were many good folks who couldn't, and it was his responsibility to keep those people from harm."

"That's noble."

"He was. He believed all that Semper Fi stuff."

"What happened?"

"When?"

"To your dad. You don't have to tell me if you don't want."

Flynn shifted his weight but not his position. "I don't know. Not exactly. Dad was doing a stint in Iraq and I'd just finished my senior year of high school in Brussels. We were in the United Arab Emirates. On vacation at a resort, just outside of Abu Dhabi. There was an explosion. A terrorist attack."

They lay listening to the sound of distant traffic for a time. Then Hutton spoke.

"Is that why you wanted to track down terrorists?"

"I was assigned that job."

"Ordered?"

"Asked more than ordered. My CO was tasked with putting together a unit to track down enemies of the state. I had been assigned for the previous couple of years to a unit that tracked down deserters from the Legion, and he thought I was good at it."

"Was that a big problem, deserters?"

"It's a problem in any army. A PR problem."

"How so?"

"Guys go AWOL for a lot of reasons, but it pretty much boils down to the fact that they don't want to be there. In a conscription army, that's a manpower problem. But in a volunteer force, you really don't want those guys there. No one wants to go into battle with a guy who has deserted before. There's no trust, and trust is everything."

"So why bother finding them?"

"That's why it's a PR problem. In the Legion you sign a contract for five years. And then they do their best to kick you out. The training is brutal. It's like special forces training. It's the methodology. How do you take a bunch of guys from different countries, speaking different languages, with different motivations for being there, and turn them into a cohesive force? You break them. You strip away their individuality and then build them back up as a team. It's complete mental and physical disintegration. Most guys fail. Most guys who make it say they would never have joined if they really knew how hard it would be. Every military force does a version of it. But in the Legion it's harder to do, so the training is harder. The breaking is harder. The rebuild is more important. And once it's done, if you're in, you're in. They put a lot of time and money into you. And that's the PR problem. If guys know they don't have to honor their contract, if they believe they can walk away whenever they choose, you don't have an army anymore. You can't plan around that. So they have to make a point of hunting down the guys that desert."

"Did you find many?"

"More than we should have. Because it's a PR problem, not a real problem, so they don't resource it. If you want to get away, you can. If you use your brains a little. A lot of guys didn't though. They followed certain patterns. Armies love patterns, they love procedure. They can teach procedure to anyone. So guys who've been in the army, especially the low-level grunts, aren't taught to think. They're taught to follow procedure. So when they go AWOL, they often follow procedure subconsciously."

"So you were like a military cop?"

"More like a bounty hunter."

"Did you like it?"

"I didn't dislike it."

"Not quite the same thing."

"Ultimately it was pointless. Deserters didn't want to be there and the Legion didn't want them back."

"So you were asked to find terrorists instead."

"More or less."

"Did you find them or eliminate them?"

"Sometimes one, sometimes both."

"You don't like rule of law?"

"You know I do. It's important. But life isn't so black and white. Real life is shades of gray."

"But you could have caught them. Put them on trial."

"Sometimes we did. But sometimes that's not practical. Sometimes bringing a bad guy in only serves to give his buddies a recruitment tool, something to get angry about."

"They don't get angry when a guy ends up dead?"

"Sure. But it's not as effective for them. There's no evidence, no video to show around. A guy's just gone."

"Was the rumor about bin Laden true? Was that really you?"

"No. That was SEAL Team Six."

"So you weren't there."

"I didn't say I wasn't there."

"You found him?"

Flynn shrugged.

"So why didn't you take him out?"

"Politics. The way I figured it, there was still bad blood between France and the US after the second Iraq war. The French didn't think it was justified. And the US knew that Europe's position made the US look bad. They asked questions the administration didn't want asked. But later, when the rebuild started happening, it was just like after World War Two. It was US companies that were invited in, it was the US that put the government back together. The French had done a lot of business in Iraq historically—with Saddam and before—and they were losing a lot of that business."

"So they made a deal?"

"The particulars were above my pay grade, but I don't think it was an exact quid pro quo—this for that. It was more like they were establishing the relationship again, opening doors for French interests to at least get a look in."

"So you passed bin Laden to the SEALs?"

"The CIA came first. We watched the CIA watching bin Laden's compound for a long time. I think they were keen to glean any intel they could before they took him out, because there were not going to be any long conversations later."

"You don't think they ever planned to capture him?"

"No."

"Do you agree with that?"

"*Cent pour cent.* One hundred percent."

Hutton released a long slow breath. "What would your dad have thought?"

"My dad was a Marine. He worked at NATO. Diplomacy was his business. But he was a believer in the big stick method. He would have said that when you have the chance to cut off the snake's head, you don't mess around with the tail."

"So after Abu Dhabi, why did you join the French Foreign Legion? Why not follow your dad into the Marines?"

"It's complicated."

"You don't have to tell me."

"It's not that. I've just never verbalized it."

"You didn't tell Beth?"

Silence, then: "No. Jacques Fontaine was dead. I figured it was better that way."

"You don't have to verbalize it now. It's okay."

"I joined the Legion because the Legion was there when I needed it, and the Marines weren't."

"What does that mean?"

Flynn let out a breath. "I was a teenager, remember. I guess I wanted to carve my own path or something like that. I applied to West Point and got in."

"The army? That wouldn't have been popular with a Marine."

"It wasn't. My dad didn't see my side at all. And I probably didn't explain it very well. We argued over it."

"I'm sorry," Hutton said. "So why didn't you join the army?"

"On the day it happened, we argued about West Point. After the argument I stormed off. Went for a walk. While I was gone, a suicide bomber drove a sedan full of Semtex into the resort."

"You got lucky."

"Luckier than some. Eighteen people were killed, including

my parents and my brother, who were eating lunch without me."

"I'm so sorry."

"Nothing you can do about it. But in the mess that followed, I kind of slipped through the cracks. I got interviewed by some guys from the State Department. I was in shock and they didn't have the greatest bedside manner, so I gave them a false name. They asked a bunch of questions that I realized were about my dad. They were suggesting he was involved in the bombing."

"You're kidding?"

"No. Then a guy from my dad's unit arrived. He was my dad's CO, more or less. He found me and told me the government was trying to position my dad as the brains behind the bombing."

"That doesn't make any sense. You don't blow yourself up as part of the plot."

"Making sense didn't seem very high on their list of priorities. Placing blame seemed to be very important though. And if they couldn't get him, they were happy to get me. So my dad's CO helped me get out. He managed to get my passport from the resort, and he gave me some money and arranged passage through Saudi Arabia to Egypt. I got a fishing boat to Marseilles. He had a villa there, a vacation place. He told me I'd be safe, until the smoke cleared."

"What happened?"

"I got cabin fever. So I went to a bar. I met a guy there, started talking. I met him again and again, over the course of a week. It turned out he was an officer in the Legion. I didn't tell him exactly what happened, but I told him I had been interested in the military, but maybe it wasn't an option anymore. He said if I was interested, and if I didn't have any criminal record on file with Interpol, I could try out for the Legion."

"And you did."

"I did."

"And what happened?"

"I got broken down to my constituent parts and then rebuilt. Exactly what I needed."

Hutton said nothing. She rolled over, put her hand on Flynn's chest, and fell asleep.

THE TEAM LEADER was dozing when his phone buzzed. The call logs for the lawyer's office had been obtained from the telephone company, and the extension for the woman had been isolated and all the calls to her between the time of the San Francisco meeting and her leaving for DC. had been isolated. The numbers were checked and cross-checked. They came from corporations and lobbyists and banks in Washington and Los Angeles and New York. One number stood out. It was from an unregistered pay-as-you-go phone, bought from a cell shack in Manhattan, New York. The team leader took the number of the PAYG phone and hung up. He punched in the numbers and waited. It was early. There was traffic outside, but the sun was barely there. The call rang on, that familiar electronic pattern.

"Hello?" The voice was alert, as if it belonged to someone who rose early rather than someone who had stayed up late.

"Do you recognize my voice?" asked the team leader.

There was a pause. "I do."

"You've been at the Watergate."

"How do you know that?"

"Let me guess. You got a call from Baghdad?"

There was no answer.

"He's coming for you," said the team leader.

"Who?"

"Fontaine."

"My guys have him covered."

"Are you sure?"

There was no answer.

"When was the last time you heard from your guys?"

"I thought you was them."

"Time to choose a side."

"There are things I want."

"I know. Just tell me what I need to know."

"You're in Washington?"

"Yes."

There was a pause. "You're in the wrong city."

CHAPTER NINETEEN_

THEY WOKE BEFORE DAWN. FLYNN RETURNED THE KEY TO the office. No one was there. Perhaps the young guy was sneaking in a snooze. Perhaps he was using the bathroom. Flynn dropped the key next to the ancient computer that had served no purpose during his check-in the previous night.

Hutton pulled into the first diner she saw that wasn't a chain. She said she preferred the mom-and-pop places to the chains. Something about better distribution of wealth. Flynn didn't care either way. He always expected diner food to be plentiful if lacking in imagination, the service to be brisk but professional as a minimum, and the coffee to be dishwater. He was wrong on two of those counts.

The waitress was in her midthirties with long hair tied back, and offered a smile that belied the early hour and warmed the frosty morning. She called Flynn sweetheart and told him the cook did poached eggs like a French chef, and he took up that challenge, with bacon and sourdough. Hutton had an omelet, Denver style.

The waitress told no lies. The eggs were done to perfection, with just the right amount of yolk running onto his toast. The cook sprinkled the top with cuttings of chives and a few shards of parmesan, which was unexpected but totally worked. The bacon was thick and artery-clogging perfection. His countrymen might have needed a few tips when it came to coffee, but no one came close to American bacon. Thick-cut and smoked to within an inch of existence. The check came in under twenty dollars, so Flynn left a fifty on the table. He figured people who rose that early and were that cheerful about it deserved all the encouragement he could offer.

Hutton looked up a couple of possible options over her omelet, and they were standing across the street from a local real estate office in Katonah when it opened. Unfortunately the person opening the office was the office manager. She didn't know much about foreclosures or real estate owned, other than it was a terrible shame when good people got kicked out of their homes. She wasn't keen on suggesting an alternative office, which Flynn figured was a good quality in an office manager, but under gentle interrogation gave up the name of another office at the other end of the street.

They walked the length of what appeared to be the main street. One side was occupied by colonial buildings housing general stores and restaurants and real estate agents and little places selling a pointless array of what were referred to as home goods. Hutton called them *tchotchkes*. The opposite side of the street featured a similar design aesthetic—a wine shop, hardware store and framing place, all backed by the rail line that ran south to Manhattan and terminated at Grand Central Station. They walked from one end of the downtown to the other, having passed three more real estate brokers before they found the office recommended to them.

Hutton went in alone. She looked more professional, like she might even be one of those flipper type people. She also reasoned that a couple would offer more hope to the agent of a family home sale, and thus provoke more questions. Flynn happily waited on the sidewalk. The clouds had come in overnight and a gentle misty rain began to fall as he stood watching the parade of expensive European cars drive up and down the street.

It took twenty minutes. Hutton offered her apologies—the agent had insisted she have an espresso from their new machine. Flynn shrugged. They marched back to the Yukon. A film of water had settled on the windshield. Hutton pulled out a computer printout of all the current REO listings. The agent had also provided a separate list, with a nudge and a wink, that she got from a banker friend, of REOs not yet formally listed. All told, there was a total of sixteen properties.

They decided to do drive-bys. The Yukon had no GPS, so Hutton used her phone to input each location and Flynn navigated. They started with the closest to town and worked their way out. The first couple of houses were two and three blocks back from the town's main street, and both bore small and tasteful For Sale signs on their lawns. Flynn scrubbed both off the list.

"If they're being marketed, they can be visited. Can you tell if that's the case?"

"Not from this list."

"In that case, *on y va.*"

They broke north and then east of the town, and then worked in quadrants back to the south. Nothing fit Dennison's MO. The houses were on busy roads or they were still for sale or the neighbors were too close. One home backed onto the local firehouse. Hutton drove slow and took her time, and Flynn watched hard and studied the approaches and surroundings and the buildings themselves. He got out and walked three possibles, but wrote them off on closer inspection.

Hutton studied her list and said the next best region was to the north, and they would have to backtrack through town. They stopped for lunch in the quaint downtown. Hutton dropped into a store and bought a small umbrella, and they moved next door to a cafe for sandwiches and iced tea. Neither spoke of the notion that they were on the wrong path, that they were wasting time. They pulled out into building rain and set off up Saw Mill River Parkway. The REO properties to the north were further out of town.

Property fourteen of sixteen ticked all Flynn's boxes. Hutton steered into a cul-de-sac surrounded by woods. There were only three homes on the street. One on the right, with a driveway about a hundred yards in from the cross road. The second on the left, a further fifty yards in. The third was at the end of the cul-de-sac.

It was a colonial that wasn't really. Part of it maybe, originally. But it had been expanded back and to the side, and had risen like a loaf of bread. The listing said there were 3,500 square feet, which came out at a touch over 325 square meters. In France there were palaces that weren't that large. Hutton suggested that wouldn't include the garage, which had two roller doors, one the width of two vehicles, the other the width of one. A three-car garage. The property backed onto thick woods, lots of trunks but few leaves. Hutton drove slowly to the end of the street. There was no rounded turning area. More a dead end, so she stopped short of the property like an interested investor might do.

"It's secluded," she said. "Neighbors, but they aren't close. No line of sight, even with the winter trees."

"The woods are a good second exit, if they've been scouted out. But the lawn looks mowed."

"The lender is probably required by the city to maintain it. So it doesn't affect everyone else's property prices. But yard guys wouldn't go inside."

"It looks empty," said Flynn.

"It is empty."

"No, I mean it *looks* empty. As in abandoned. There are leaves in the gutters. Yard guys might not do that if the bank is paying the bare minimum to do the bare minimum. And it looks cold. No lights, no heat."

"No power. Con Edison has probably cut it off."

"Even better. And there's no lockbox. No real estate agent."

"But no vehicle."

"A vehicle would look wrong. The place is supposed to be abandoned. Either they jimmied the garage door and it's inside there, or they have a path scoped out through the woods to another location. Maybe another street or a lot or something."

"I'm going to take a look," said Hutton, unbuckling her seat belt.

"Risky."

"Like an investor. Taking a quick peek."

She grabbed a folio from her messenger bag and opened the door. Then she popped the umbrella open and slipped down from the truck. Flynn watched her walk away through the rain. She looked like one of those people. An investor, or a banker. She still wore her black trousers and was in her expensive-looking greatcoat, scarf wrapped around and knotted stylishly. The umbrella was in one hand, the folio in the other. He watched her walk up the driveway. She stopped at the garage and tried to pull up the door. It didn't budge. Not jimmied. She walked up to the porch and dropped the umbrella down. Then she walked the width of the house, stopping several times to peer in through the windows. She got to the end and turned and walked back, looking at her folio, appearing to take notes. Like an investor. She stopped at the front door and tried the knob. It must have been locked, because she collected her umbrella and disappeared down the side of the property. She was gone a tick

over two minutes. She returned down to the end of the driveway, where the concrete met the blacktop, and she took another
look at the property. Then she turned and strode back to the
Yukon.

"No one's home," she said as she landed back in the driver's
seat and tossed the umbrella in the rear. "Not for a while. The
blinds are mostly closed, but I could see in a few places. The
kitchen looks a mess."

"Dishes?"

"Demolition. I'd say the previous owner was pretty
unhappy about getting evicted. Probably had a high-paying job
and got laid off and was trying to hide their financial worries
from their golfing buddies. Happens a lot. Big house, nice cars,
but still paycheck to paycheck. Anyway, they seem to have
taken most of the kitchen cabinets, and the appliances. They
left the sink. On the floor."

"Any signs of life?"

"Nothing visible. But there's something else."

"What?"

"The trees kind of hide it, but the land at the back rises up
some. The back section of the house is higher."

"So?"

"So there's a basement under it. I couldn't see into it, but I'd
guess it joins up with the garage."

"A basement," Flynn said to himself. "This feels right."

"What do you want to do?"

"We need to go in. See if they're in there."

Hutton frowned. "Now?"

Flynn looked around. The clouds were heavy and damp
and the afternoon light was failing.

"No. Let's wait. As soon as it's dark."

THEY RETURNED to the downtown in unrelenting rain and bought plastic rain ponchos. Most of the options were bright colors—oranges, pinks, yellows. Hutton went with a forest green, and Flynn chose a clear version. Hutton got two espressos in the cafe and they drank them in the Yukon. The night came on like lost consciousness. Gray was overlaid by black. The rain found its rhythm, not hard but not giving up. Workers from the city started returning, spilling from the train station into expensive cars. They waited until the cascade of commuters became a trickle, and Hutton drove back toward the house.

Flynn told her go about three-fifths of a mile further up the cross street.

"Three-fifths?" she asked. "Not a half, not three-quarters?"

"I like three-fifths."

"You're very strange."

"It's close to a kilometer. I like kilometers."

"The metric system, hey? You didn't learn American measures?"

"Of course I did. Twelve inches to a foot. Three feet to a yard. Seventeen hundred and sixty yards to a mile. Tell me how that makes any sense."

"Don't start. Tell me how metric makes sense?"

"Ten millimeters to a centimeter, ten centimeters to a decimeter, ten decimeters to a meter. Simple."

"You really are strange."

"Let's go."

They hiked back along the road under their ponchos. Hutton left her scarf behind but kept her coat underneath. She had repacked her courier bag and wore it strapped across her so the bag sat just above her butt, under the poncho. Flynn discarded his snow jacket. The poncho provided no respite from the cold, but he preferred the freedom of movement. He could live with the cold.

They walked back along the road to the mouth of the street. The first house in the cul-de-sac burned with warm light behind closed drapes. The second house offered only patches of lamp light. The kind of lights that were probably on timers, as if the owners were yet to get home or had gone out for the evening.

The REO property at the end of the cul-de-sac was dark.

There were no night lights, no path lights leading up the driveway, nothing on a timer. The white garage door and the trim around the windows glowed through the rain and gave the house a sense of structure. Flynn followed Hutton up the side of the house where she had gone earlier in the day. They followed the property up as Hutton had described. The rear was ten feet higher than the front. The yard went back for an indeterminable distance, possibly fifty yards, before meeting the tree line. The rear of the house was a bank of sliding glass doors that opened onto a deck made of some kind of slip-resistant wood substitute. Perhaps it was easier to maintain. Hutton led Flynn to the sliding doors and stopped under the eaves. Her poncho was shedding water everywhere.

"This looks like the vulnerable point," she said.

Flynn nodded. He had to agree. Glass always was. He noticed that the sliding doors had been covered with large sheets of paper. Perhaps a nod to security. Maybe the kitchen had been damaged by someone other than the owner. He pushed the hood of his poncho back and walked under the eaves along the glass doors. Windows were easy, but noisy. He wasn't so worried about rousing the neighbors, but he didn't want to tip off anyone who might be inside before he needed to. He stopped before a conventional door at the end of the windows. It was white painted wood with six panes of glass slotted into it. Flynn could see that the door led into the kitchen. He crouched to look at the deadlock. It was new. Probably installed by a contractor working for the lender. And like the yard guys, probably getting paid the bare minimum and therefore installing the bare minimum. He looked up at Hutton.

"You have a force tool?"

"What about the glass?"

"I prefer to leave no footprints. If possible."

Hutton nodded and reached in under her poncho. She pulled out a small purse, like someone might keep pocket change in. She unzipped it and handed the tool to Flynn. It was like a rudimentary screwdriver, long and thin at one end, a broad basic square-edged handle at the other. Flynn pushed the thin end into the keyhole. Then he pulled out his Glock and ejected the magazine and the round in the chamber and handed them to Hutton. It was a safe weapon with three passive safeties. But there was a fourth safety, the most important of them. His brain. He didn't want the gun loaded for what he was about to do.

He slotted the end of the force tool in through the trigger guard of the Glock and then turned the gun until it was tight on the corners of the tool. Then he pushed the barrel of the gun like a wrench. He needed to create torque in order to turn the force tool in the lock. There was potential to damage a good handgun, but he was reckoning on the gun being of better manufacture than the lock.

It was. The barrel moved and the gun turned and the force tool rotated in the lock as if it were a key. Flynn slid the gun off and Hutton handed him the magazine, where she had pushed the previously chambered round back into place. Flynn slipped the magazine back in and pulled the slide and chambered the round again. He handed the force tool to Hutton as he stood and then looked at her. Her hair was damp despite the poncho. She nodded.

Flynn pushed the door open and stepped inside, Glock held up and ready. The kitchen was large and long, with an island that ran up the middle. He crossed the space to the other wall, where a space in the cabinets had previously housed a wall oven. He took a couple of steps to just short of where the wall stopped and the kitchen opened up into what he assumed would be the living space. Open concept, they called it. Hutton closed the door and dropped low. She moved along the wall of windows, until she reached the end of the island. Flynn saw her stop, but he couldn't hear her above the rain landing on the deck outside.

He edged to the end of the kitchen wall and then spun around so his weapon swept across the open space. It was dark but there were few hiding spaces. There was no furniture. No lounges or sofas or china cabinets. Just a pale Scandinavian-style wood floor that almost glowed in the darkness. He moved around into the room, and Hutton followed on the other side. They worked together to sweep the lower floor and found noth-ing. No sign of anyone having been there in some time. Then they moved upstairs. Slowly, up the stairs, crossing over each other as the steps banked around on themselves, and then a little faster as they entered each room. Every one was empty. Four bedrooms. All vacant.

Flynn led the way down. Got to the bottom and listened hard. Heard nothing but the distant patter of rain through double-glazed windows. The house gave no other sounds. No shifting or easing of the structure. Not the hum of electronics running through the walls. No bursts from a heat pump pulsing on and off. Nothing. Flynn stepped back toward the kitchen side of the living space. Off to the side was another door.

The basement. Flynn turned the knob and opened the door slowly. Looked around as much as he could without sticking his head through the doorway. The kitchen where he stood was dark. The basement was another order of darkness altogether. Like a black hole in space. It smelled like a cave, damp and musty, with overtones of latex paint and two-stroke motor oil. He stood at the head of the steps, listening. He heard nothing. No shifting, no bursts, no hums. It felt like the house. Empty. Ox Dennison wasn't here, if he ever had been. If he had ever gotten up from that small room in Iraq, where Flynn had shot him before the building exploded. Flynn realized that Dennison was a dream he was chasing. Events were real, but the explanation behind them had to be something he hadn't thought of yet.

Then he heard the grunt.

It was soft and involuntary and barely audible over the white noise of the rain outside. A uniquely human sound. Not a cat or a dog or a rodent. The sound of someone trying to be quiet but trying so hard that they betrayed themselves. Perhaps discomfort or just from trying to hold their breath too long.

Flynn backed away from the door. He couldn't see into the basement, so any kind of attack was madness, despite holding the high ground. Hutton was waiting behind him.

"Pitch black," he whispered.

Hutton held out her hands. They were balled into fists. Flynn held out his hand and she dropped military grade glow sticks into his palm. He nodded. She had thought of everything. Glow sticks worked via chemical reaction, which determined how long they lasted. The brightness was a function of the temperature. Warm weather meant a brighter glow. In the tropics one stick would do. Hutton had given him three. And she had warmed them up some.

Flynn cracked the sticks and tossed them into the basement. At the three corners he could hit from the top of the steps. He didn't wait. He spun through the door and angled his Glock across the space. It was lit a familiar eerie green. One side was rock work. The outside wall of the basement. The rest had been finished in drywall. He moved down the steps. Saw a dormant hot water system in the far corner. Then a door that he guessed led to the garage. He dropped the last few steps onto the concrete floor and spun back toward the other end of the room. One corner of the room was an empty green. The glow stick gave off enough light to almost reach the ceiling. And enough to almost reach the space beneath the steps. Enough to show an irregular shape protruding from the shadow under the steps. Irregular for a basement. Not irregular for the human eye. Flynn knew what it was immediately.

A human shoulder.

"Freeze," he said, extending his Glock at the space just to the right of the shoulder. The middle of the torso that he couldn't see. The person grunted again, this time louder, like they knew they couldn't hide now. Hutton picked up the glow stick from the corner behind Flynn and tossed it toward the person. It skidded across the floor and came to rest under the steps, illuminating the person from below, like a horror movie. They were chained to the wall, hands tied behind, feet wrapped in the same kind of tape Flynn had used in the drug den the night before.

Flynn lowered his gun. Hutton did not.

"It's a woman," she said.

"Not just a woman," said Flynn. "It's Beth."

CHAPTER TWENTY_

FLYNN RAN FORWARD.

"Beth," he said.

In the green glow, he saw fear stretched across her face. She recoiled from him. He stopped moving. Considered it from her point of view. He was a wet formless mass, his poncho waving about, the only solid part of him the Glock in his hand. He dropped to his knees and grabbed the glow stick Hutton had tossed under the steps, and he held it to his own face.

"Beth, it's me. It's John."

He watched her face tell the tale as her brain worked it through. Fear became confusion, confusion became hope. Hope burst through. He saw the tears form in her eyes. He edged forward. She had tape over her mouth.

"Try to lick your lips."

Beth frowned but did as he suggested and licked the tape away from her mouth.

"This might hurt a little."

Flynn pulled the tape from her face. He didn't see the logic of extending pain by doing it slow. Beth gave a yelp.

"John," she said. "I didn't think I'd ever see you again."

"I'm here. Let me get you out."

He pulled out his Glauca knife and cut the tape around her feet, and then used the cuff cutters on the knife to remove the plastic cuffs around her wrists. He yanked on the chains. The kidnapper had placed a standard handcuff on her left wrist, then attached the other end of the handcuff to a chain. Flynn used the glow stick to follow the chain to the wall.

"It's attached to a pipe," Beth said. "I couldn't break it."

Hutton stepped out of the shadows. Beth recoiled again and Flynn put his hand on her shoulder.

"This is Laura. She's a friend."

Beth gave Hutton a look of distrust.

"We can get those off," said Hutton softly. She pulled out her little coin purse and removed a key. She unlocked the cuff on Beth's wrist and Beth threw her arms around Flynn.

"I can't believe you're here." She hugged him tight and then suddenly pulled away. "What if she comes back?"

Flynn frowned. "Who?"

"The kidnapper."

Flynn shook his head. "I thought you said *she*."

"I did. My God, I can't believe you're here."

"The kidnapper was a woman?"

"Yes."

Flynn looked at Hutton and she shook her head.

Hutton said, "Whatever, let's get out of here. We can talk later."

"Can you walk?" Flynn asked.

Beth nodded.

Flynn helped her to her feet. He took the lead, Beth's hand in one of his, his Glock in the other. Hutton brought up the rear with her Glock held down but ready. Flynn led them up the steps and paused at the door. It was habit more than anything. Never just waltz through an open door. But there was something in his dinosaur brain, a prehistoric notion, a gut feel. Something was different, as if the atmospheric pressure had shifted. He stopped for a moment. There was no sound other than the rain, which didn't seem to have dissipated. He picked up the tiny vibrations that people give off, their breathing and movement and component molecules putting microscopic waves into the air. But that was all expected. Beth was hanging just short of a panic. She was giving vibrations off like crazy.

Flynn glanced right toward the front of the house as he stepped into the wide living area, and then moved to the left. Toward the rear of the house. They would exfiltrate the same way they had come in. Always less footprints that way.

The shot hit him in the leg.

Right on the hamstring, which contracted immediately and pulled him to the floor. He dropped Beth's hand as his entire body was wracked with pain. It pierced through him as if he'd been hit by lightning. He convulsed massively, writhing and flopping on the hardwood floor. He'd never had a heart attack, but he wondered if he was having one now. He thought it would be more localized to the chest. But this was unrelenting and all-engulfing. He felt it to his fingertips. And it wasn't just his body. He was sure that his brain was frying, like a potato in a microwave oven.

Hutton heard the shot. It was all wrong, but there was no time to think about it. She grabbed Beth by the back of her suit jacket and pulled her back into the basement. Hefted her around on the landing and pushed her down a couple of steps. Then she turned back, two hands on her weapon, back hard against the wall, which she reconsidered. It was nothing more than two sections of drywall. A bullet wouldn't lose but a fraction of its momentum going through it and into her, so she crouched low on the step and edged up to the landing.

Flynn heard the footsteps about the same time as the agony

began to abate. His brain was the first thing to kick in, although it was doing a full reboot and was a long way short of full capacity. Life support systems only. He realized that he wasn't having a heart attack. He knew he had been shot. But he'd been shot before and it hadn't felt like this. With a gunshot the shock reached right across the body, but the pain was focused on the entry point or the exit point, or both. In his case it had been both. He had been shot during an attempted coup in Central Africa. From a distance, a rifle shot. Still enough velocity to puncture his chest and collapse a lung and continue into the wooden wall of a building behind him. It had hurt and it had damaged him. Sections of his chest and lung and rib bones remained in the wall. In the Legion there was a concept known as *Français par le sang versé*—French by spilled blood. Legionnaires injured during service were offered French citizenship. It was an offer Flynn had never taken up. But he recalled the pain. And this was not that.

This time he had been shot in his leg. He felt for the location as he saw a black-clad figure approach above him. The figure was dressed in an urban tactical assault uniform. Black from top to toe, with black body armor, on which were numerous pockets and webbings and sheaths. The figure looked down at Flynn through a single eye that Flynn realized was the business end of night-vision googles. The figure held a shotgun across his chest. A Mossberg. It was the only thing on the figure that wasn't all black. The stock and the fore-end both glowed in the darkness as if they were bright yellow. It didn't make sense. And then Flynn's hand arrived at his hamstring.

A shotgun wasn't like a rifle. It didn't fire a bullet—in and out. It was closer to an incendiary explosive. It spewed pellets across a wide arc, indiscriminate and unfocused. A Mossberg from close range could take a man's leg right off. At best, Flynn's hamstring should be a bloody mess. But it wasn't. There was no blood, no mess. But there was a shell. It was stuck into his leg like a genetically modified super bee.

"Confirm, X target is down," said the black-clad figure, pointing the shotgun at Flynn.

Then the figure's shoulder exploded.

He was thrust across the room from the impact, and blood rained down over Flynn, splattering across his poncho. He watched the man hit the floor and then turned to the basement door and saw Hutton crouched there, her Glock hot in her hand. Then it all fell into place. For reasons he couldn't begin to fathom in his current state, the assault team had fired nonlethal rounds. He'd seen them before but never used them. Never had cause to. If it got to the point that he had to fire his weapon, he generally didn't care if the other guy ever got up again. But the assault team did. He'd been hit by an electronic round, like a Taser XREP, but more powerful. It was a shell that could be fired from a standard shotgun, but instead of opening up and spraying lead pellets everywhere, it fired a capsule topped by electrodes that lodged in its victim and shot an electric charge through them. It was designed to immobilize, not kill.

From somewhere toward the front of the house, Flynn heard someone call out.

"Y target has live rounds."

Flynn shouted to Hutton, "Nonlethal rounds."

He couldn't see her face, but he guessed she wouldn't take it well. The guy she'd shot had a weapon. The shooting was right-eous. She couldn't see the yellow stock denoting a shotgun whose firing pin had been reconfigured such that it could only fire nonlethal rounds, not a regular shotgun shell. No way for her to know that. But that wouldn't make her feel any better. The special agent in her took those things seriously.

Hutton edged forward.

"You're okay?"

He could hear the amazement in her voice. She had expected major damage.

"Severely annoyed."

"Did you say nonlethal rounds?"

Flynn tried to speak, but the sound of the doorjamb erupting into a thousand splinters above Hutton's head rendered him mute. She fell back on the landing. Flynn realized he had heard the tap-tap-tap of a triple burst. An automatic weapon. Not a nonlethal round. Not this time. But he was lying on the floor, open and vulnerable. He looked up and saw nothing but darkness. Clearly the assault team, whoever they were, all wore night-vision equipment. Probably heat-based. In a cold house on a cold night he would be lit up like a deer in the spotlight.

But they didn't shoot him. He lay there begging his eyes to work harder, to no effect. But they didn't fire. He leaned toward the basement.

"I can't see."

Hutton got the point. She always did. That was one of the things he liked about her. She cracked two night sticks and threw them around the corner, into the living area of the house.

Another figure stood there. It was the same look all over again. Tactical assault gear, night-vision headwear. The figured held a weapon. Impossible to say exactly what it was. Maybe an M17, or perhaps an HK416. But it was possible to tell what it wasn't. It wasn't a Mossberg. It wasn't a shotgun. That was for damned sure. And its stock and fore-end were as black as the rest of the room. Not yellow. Not in the slightest.

Flynn sat straight up, bending from the core. As he did he brought his right hand around to the front. In it was his Glock 17. The electronic burst that had shocked his body had caused him to clench his fist, right around his firearm. Now he fired one-handed. Not his preferred method, not in the dark with a recently fried brain. But the target was close and he was a decent shot. Not sniper material, but as good as anyone in close quarters. He fired three times. Fire burst from the muzzle. He saw the figure begin to move, brain kicking into gear. But there was nowhere to go. An open room. No furniture.

Flynn kept his shots low. The body armor the figure was wearing would stop a 9mm Parabellum. But there was no armor on the legs. The fire burst blinded him but he heard the dull thud of a round splattering into flesh. The figure cried out in pain, hit and down but clearly not dead. Flynn checked the room for any other figures but found none.

"Let's go," he said to Hutton.

"They'll be coming from the rear too," she said.

"Yes. So keep low. Behind the island."

Hutton grabbed Beth's hand and yanked her up the steps and out of the basement. Flynn stayed in his sitting position, Glock outstretched, watching for more gunmen. Hutton dragged Beth past him toward the rear of the house. He waited two seconds and saw no further movement. The figure in the living room had fallen on his rifle. He gripped his leg. He wasn't firing again anytime soon.

Flynn spun to his feet and took four long strides and found Hutton crouched by the corner leading into the kitchen.

"Someone's there," she said.

"Light 'em up."

She held up a flashlight, for Flynn to see. She was out of night sticks.

"Strobe," she said.

Flynn took a breath. "Go."

Hutton went up and Flynn down. She held the flashlight around the corner of the wall and trained it on the kitchen and flicked it on. It was a powerful unit. The light would have been seen miles away in an open field. But they weren't in an open field. They were in a suburban kitchen. The space exploded in cold light. It was blinding to everyone. But it was worse to the guys in the assault gear. They were facing it, and they were wearing night-vision equipment. Their world burst into a disorienting whiteout. And then not. The flashlight was in strobe mode. Alternating bursts of light and dark, like flash bangs without the bang. Blindness and confusion. For a second or two.

Flynn charged across the end of the kitchen island toward the bank of sliding doors. Focused his vision on the middle of the kitchen. On no one thing in particular. The flashlight pulsed on and he saw the first guy. He was on the rear side, by the windows. The side Hutton had come along when they had first entered the house. Then absolute darkness. Flynn kept moving. A second burst of light. The first guy held a weapon. Maybe a shotgun, maybe not. No time to tell. Not in a split second of light, not using peripheral vision. But Flynn saw the yellow stock. Then darkness again. He was halfway across the opening to the kitchen. A third burst of light. A second guy. Farther back, against the hole in the wall where the oven had been. More darkness. More light. The second guy had a rifle. All black.

That meant the second guy would be first, and the first guy would be second. Flynn dropped below the end of the kitchen island and skidded on the polished wood floor. He was two seconds into it and getting up to fire over the top of the counter, when the second guy opened fire. The guy couldn't see, that was for sure. He was shooting blind. But he'd recovered from the initial disorientation and knew the source of the strobe light, so he swung his rifle in the general direction and opened fire. It was loud in the empty room, and the sound of rounds discharging added the bang to Hutton's flash. Drywall and wood splattered everywhere and Hutton dropped the light.

The guy kept firing. He should have stopped. He should

have retreated down behind the opposite end of the long kitchen island. But he stayed standing, firing his weapon in Hutton's direction. Her flashlight hit the floor aimed square and true at the gunman. He was lit up, and then not. And then lit again. He only stayed firing for a couple of seconds. But it was a couple of seconds too long. Flynn swung his arms up over the top of the island. His Glock swept by the first guy in light toward the second guy in darkness. The next burst of light saw him aiming at the second guy, who had finished firing at Hutton.

Flynn started low. The first shot might have just missed the countertop itself and hit low on the wall. He let the recoil lift his hands as he fired again a little higher. And again, higher still. In the strobe it looked like slow motion, like an old movie box where the viewer turned the handle to make the movie run past a lamp. The guy was launched backward, firing into the ceiling as he went. Flynn knew he had a hit, but he didn't spend time thinking about where or how bad. Instead he turned back toward the first guy, who had become the second guy because of his shotgun.

When a tactical team made an assault, they made sure they were fully equipped. And if they intended nonlethal force, like a civilian SWAT team might do, they made damned sure the guys carrying the nonlethal weapons had secondary weapons with what Hutton would call *stopping power*. Flynn rotated and saw the guy. He had changed his mind. To hell with nonlethal force. He had dropped the Mossberg and was reaching down for his sidearm. In full light he wrapped his hand around the butt. In darkness he began pulling it out of its holster.

And in full light again his head exploded.

There was no angle to aim low, so Flynn aimed for the torso. He got it wrong. The shot went high and up through the guy's chin and out through the back of his head and deposited a crucial part of him into the crown molding at the top of the wall. Flynn dropped so his armpits were hard against the corner of the countertop, and surveyed the room. It was like watching a series of snapshots, each one the same. No one appeared, no one fired. He didn't wait around for anyone to start.

"Follow me," he said to Hutton. Hutton pushed Beth forward so she was behind Flynn. Despite the situation, Beth wasn't panicking or screaming. Hutton picked up her flashlight and flicked it off.

Flynn pulled the door open and scoped the rear lawn. The rain made hearing enemies impossible. But there was a little more ambient light outside, and he swung his Glock from one side to the other and then back. The space was empty. But it was surround by trees. And it was fifty yards to the tree line. A lot of open ground. If they went across the backyard.

So they didn't. Flynn pulled Beth up and along the bank of glass doors, across the deck to the other side of the house. He peered around the corner. It was completely dark. He couldn't see five feet. But there were trees overhead with branches hanging low toward the roof. Most houses had two sides along the property line, two ways to move from front to rear. But in most houses one side was more easily passed than the other. Perhaps one had a path, the other didn't. One housed the miscellaneous junk that regular people collected. Discarded garden furniture, a wood pile. The other had a gate and a way through. He guessed this side was the path less traveled.

He tightened his grip on Beth's hand and dragged her across the space to the trees at the side of the property. Maybe ten feet of clear land, and no need for a privacy fence. He plunged into the darkness of the woods and kept going straight for another ten feet. Then he turned hard left and marched toward the back of the property. He took fifty long paces until he felt they were level with the back edge of the yard. Made sure Hutton was tight behind Beth and then turned right and marched on through the woods.

It was dark. It was wet. There was nothing to see and nothing to hear. Flynn moved fast but not too fast. Footing was inconsistent. There were depressions in the ground. There were fallen branches. Beth tripped several times but made no complaint. They made no noise other than the sound of crunching leaves, which was barely audible over the rain. Flynn used the compass in his head to keep true. He wasn't worried about the natural tendency to bank down the hill. That suited his purpose. He just kept marching and counting. Marching and counting.

He didn't stop until he had hit a thousand in his head. His stride length over rough ground was approximately a meter. He had tested it, time and time again. In mountains and in jungles and on sand. It was as much a part of him as his nose and his eyes and the lines on the backs of his hands. And a thousand steps meant a thousand meters. And a thousand meters meant a kilometer. Approximately three-fifths of a mile.

He made sure Hutton was still with him and then he turned hard right and marched on. The house had been at the end of a cul-de-sac and they had made part of their initial approach to the house on blacktop, so returning that same distance in the woods took longer. Then suddenly one step he was in the woods, the next step he was not. He burst from the trees and stopped. Beth bumped into him, and Hutton into her. Flynn felt the ground drop away into a depression. A runoff channel beside a road. He picked Beth up and threw her over his shoulder, and then edged slowly down. It was only about five feet down, but felt like more. The grass was long and deep and although there was no running flow, the channel was waterlogged. His boots felt like they were being pulled from his feet. He hit the other side and used a hand to pull himself and Beth up and out of the channel and onto the road. He set Beth down and turned to help Hutton across, but she was already climbing out of the depression. She stood next to him. They looked left along the road. Saw nothing but road disappearing into the ether. They turned right.

The Yukon sat twenty feet back, wet and waiting.

Hutton got in and started the truck, and Flynn helped Beth into the back and followed her in.

"Go straight," he said to Hutton in the front.

"Way ahead of you."

She pulled away from the curb and headed up the hill away from the main road, away from the house.

Away from the guys with guns.

CHAPTER TWENTY-ONE

Hutton returned to the same motel. There were approximately the same number of cars parked underneath, but they were all different vehicles. It was a one-night-per-stay kind of place. Flynn found the same kid in the lobby, wearing the same hoodie. He was watching something on his phone. He glanced up and saw Flynn and gave a look of surprise at seeing the same face two nights in a row.

"Two rooms," Flynn said.

The kid kicked his chair and slid across the floor to where the keys were kept. He unhooked two and slid back.

"Two rooms. Unlucky or lucky?"

"Lucky not to have to work the graveyard shift in a motel."

"But not lucky enough to not have to stay here."

Flynn shrugged and put down a hundred and a fifty. The kid eyed the money and looked like he was considering asking for an even two hundred, but thought the better of it and slipped the money away and dropped the two keys onto the desk. Flynn picked them up, nodded and walked out.

He had keys for the same room at the end, plus the one next

to it. Rooms 23 and 24. Flynn opened the door to room 23 and let Beth in, and then motioned Hutton to join her.

"You guys need a minute?" she asked.

Flynn shook his head. "We need to figure this thing out."

Hutton stepped into the room, and Flynn handed her the key for room 24.

Room 23 was a mirror image of room 24. The same layout, the same bedding, the same traffic path worn in the carpet. Everything was just in the reverse position. Beth stood in the middle of the room. The rain was soaked so deep into her clothes it had stopped running off her. Hutton helped her to the bathroom to dry off. The motel wasn't a robe-and-slippers kind of place, so Hutton gave Beth a T-shirt and track pants of her own.

Dried except for her damp hair, Beth crawled up on the bed and put her back against the wall and hugged a pillow. Flynn figured that shock was starting to set in, now that things had quietened down. Hutton took the chair from under the desk. Flynn stayed standing. He touched Beth on the shoulder. She looked up at him as if he had just appeared out of thin air, or she had. She studied his face and then dropped her gaze to the bed and stared into middle distance.

Flynn got a glass of water from the bathroom and placed it on the bedside table by Beth. Then he moved away and leaned against the door and turned his attention to Hutton. He wanted to sit with Beth and talk it through, but he knew that he was too close. Hutton would know how to ask the questions that needed asking.

"Beth, my name is Laura, remember? I was formerly with the FBI. I handled this kind of thing. Can I ask you some questions?"

"FBI?"

Hutton nodded.

"FBI? Okay."

"I need to ask you about the hotel."

Beth glanced up and around the small room, and then she frowned.

"What about it?"

"Not this hotel. The Watergate. About what happened at the Watergate."

She dropped the frown and looked at Flynn.

"We need to call the firm."

"The firm?" he asked.

"My firm. It's protocol. Workplace safety."

"Okay, we'll get to that."

Beth shook her head as if something had just that second occurred to her.

"And the police, John. We should call the police." Beth looked at Hutton. "But you're FBI?"

Hutton ignored the question. "Tell me what happened at the Watergate. You mentioned a woman. You said you were taken by a woman. Was that correct?"

"Yes. A woman."

"Not a man?"

Beth shook her head. "No. No, the prospective client turned out to be a woman."

"Tell me about her."

The frown stayed, but her focus seemed to return now that she was thinking things through. "She was strange. No, not strange. Out of place. She was dressed up like a business-woman." Beth bit at a fingernail and pressed her hand against her lips to stop it from shaking.

"Why was that strange?"

"Because she was dressed up."

"Weren't you dressed in business attire?"

"No, you don't understand. She wasn't dressed like a businesswoman dresses. She was dressed up like a businesswoman. Like a costume. Like she was going to a Halloween party as a businessperson. She had the right clothes, but they were wrong."

"How were they wrong?"

"Nothing fit. Not quite right. People who meet at the Watergate don't have ill-fitting clothes. And they didn't match. The trousers with the jacket. All wrong. And the shoes. As soon as we got into the van, she peeled off her shoes. Like they hurt. Like she didn't normally wear heels."

"Okay, that's good. Tell me about the meeting. Where did you meet?"

"In the hotel. Like we were supposed to. We went up to the rooftop bar, but it was too cold. So we tried another bar. One near the lobby. It was very busy. She said she knew a place, nearby, that wouldn't be so busy. She said she had a car."

"So you headed out?"

"Yes. She sort of took my arm—you know the way an old lady wraps her arm through yours to keep her balance when she walks? Like that. It felt too familiar, but I let it pass. Some people are like that."

"How did you leave?"

"There was a car waiting for us."

"What sort of car?"

"The wrong sort, I suppose. I didn't think. I should have thought." Beth looked at Flynn. "You always say keep your eyes open."

"No reason for you to suspect anything," he said. "Tell us about the car."

"It was a van, really. Like a family wagon. A soccer mom's car."

"A minivan?" asked Hutton.

"Yes, a minivan. Dark. Blue or black. I wish I could remember. That's important, isn't it?"

"Not really. They'll have dumped that vehicle."

"But there might be prints. The police could find them."

Hutton pressed on. "Tell me about *them*."

"There were two men. One in the back row, another driving. I got in the van and the woman was right behind, a bit pushy I suppose. The door slid closed before I really saw the man in the back." She looked at the bed again as if replaying events through her mind.

"He had a gun. He told me to sit tight. Then the woman told me we were going for a little drive. Nothing to worry about, if . . ."

"If what?"

Beth turned her gaze on Flynn.

"If you did what you were told."

Flynn nodded.

"Why would *you* do what you were told? What does my client have to do with you?"

"That's what we're trying to figure out," said Flynn.

Hutton said, "The meeting at the Watergate was clearly a setup. It links back somehow to your original client. Can you tell me about them?"

"Some of that is privileged."

"I understand. I don't want to know anything that isn't public record. Okay?"

Beth nodded. "I guess that's okay."

"Who were they?"

"Just an investment company. Clients hand over their portfolio and these guys invest it and take it abroad and distribute funds where the IRS can't touch them."

"Is that legal?"

"Of course. I don't write the tax laws, Laura. I just follow them."

"Okay. So how did they bring up the meeting at the Watergate?"

Beth pushed herself back up against the bedhead, straightening her posture. She noticed the water on the bedside table and took a sip.

"They didn't organize it. Not exactly. I met with the client the first time in our offices in San Fran. Then we arranged to have a follow-up meeting to sign papers in DC. In their office downtown." Beth's face dropped. "That was supposed to be this morning. I missed the meeting."

"Beth, I think that's okay. Let's focus on who abducted you."

"You're right. Of course, you're right."

"So how did the Watergate meeting happen?"

"They called me. Not the same people I had met in our office. She said she had heard from the client that I was going to be in DC., and asked if we could meet."

"Who suggested the Watergate?"

"I think I did. We were staying there. John and I." Beth glanced up at Flynn. He was leaning against the door again.

"No, that's not right. John wasn't staying there. You weren't coming then."

Flynn said, "You asked me to come. You said there might be some business in it."

"Yes. That's right. The woman said she couldn't go into great detail on the phone, but she had some money that needed to be traced. And a person. She said she needed to find a person."

"What did you take that to mean?" Hutton asked.

"We don't just move money, we find money. Kind of forensic accounting. If a company is embezzled, for example, we might track down the money for them."

"Doesn't the Bureau do that?" asked Hutton.

"Of course, if there are grounds. If there's an investigation. Sometimes there's not. Sometimes there isn't enough proof." Beth shrugged. "Sometimes the client doesn't want law enforcement involved. For PR reasons."

"Okay. Is that what you thought this woman wanted?"

"Yes."

"And finding the person?"

"I took that to mean they had sustained some kind of loss, and they wanted to find both the money and the person who took it."

"And how does that relate to John?"

Beth frowned and then dropped it. "It's what he does. He finds people. Right?" She looked up at Flynn. He nodded.

"So I thought he might get some work from it. We would trace the money, and he could trace the person."

Hutton nodded. "All right. Let's go back to the Watergate. How did you know the woman was the right person? You hadn't met."

"She approached me in the rooftop bar. I assumed she had looked me up on our website."

"And what did she say?"

Beth stopped. Stopped talking, stopped breathing. She froze in place, the words trapped in her throat, unable to escape. Then she turned her head, toward the door. Toward Flynn. Then her mouth moved and the words came softly.

"She said, *even the bogeyman can't hide forever.*"

Flynn glanced at Hutton and then back at Beth. Beth was frowning at him.

"That's your phrase, John. Isn't it? You say that."

"I do. I did. Did you?"

"What do you mean?"

"Did you ever use it? Other than with me, I mean."

Beth stared into middle distance as she tried to recall. After the night's events, Flynn was surprised that her memory was functioning at all.

"I'm not sure. I may have said it in the initial client meeting. In San Fran. I think I did. I think I said it like you do."

"Like I do?"

"In French. Yes, I seem to recall the client asked how traceable their money would be, I assume from the IRS. I said your phrase more to myself than anyone. I recall the client asked what it meant. I translated it."

"What did he say?"

"Nothing. I think he smiled, like it was a little joke. Just like it was with us."

Hutton said, "But that client never spoke of it again. It was the woman who said it."

"Yes."

"Okay. So you were taken down to the minivan and drove to New York?"

Beth nodded. "Yes. How did you find me?" Her eyes darted between Hutton and Flynn.

"I tracked your cell phone using the lost phone app on your tablet."

"Huh. I wouldn't have thought of that."

"Did you go straight to New York City?" asked Hutton. "Stop anywhere?"

"No."

"For gas, anything?"

"No. We drove straight to Manhattan." Beth paused for a moment, and then continued. "Then we stopped."

"What happened then?"

Beth took a moment to answer. "They tied me up. I was pulled out of the minivan and dumped in something else. A van. Not a minivan—like a delivery van. There were no seats."

"And then?"

"We drove for a while. Much shorter."

"Who's we?"

"I don't know. The woman I guess. We stopped and she pulled me out. We were at the house. She dragged me into the basement and locked me up there." Beth looked at the pulled drapes and back at Hutton. "Where are we?"

"The house was in Katonah, just outside of New York City. Now we're near Yonkers."

"But the house? Those men were shooting at us."

"Yes, they were."

"We need to call the police. You said you are FBI or *were* FBI?"

"Was."

"We need to call the police," she said again, this time at Flynn.

"We will," said Flynn. "Just help Laura understand what happened first."

Hutton said, "What happened after the woman left you in the basement? Did she stay, did she leave?"

"She left."

"Did she come back?"

"No."

Hutton looked at Flynn. "So there were two meetings arranged," she said. "The client meeting arranged in San Francisco, and then later a meeting arranged at the Watergate."

"But the second meeting was scheduled to happen first."

"Yes."

"And two teams," said Flynn. "The kidnappers—the woman and the two guys in New York were the first. And I think we can agree that whoever that was back there at the house, it wasn't the kidnappers."

"Agreed," said Hutton.

"Everything up until then had been amateur. Done on the fly. The initial abduction, allowing me to track them. The guys following us. None of it was top-shelf. But the team at the house . . ."

"They were very tooled up."

"And despite us getting away, they were well drilled."

"You think? They made mistakes."

"They made plenty," said Flynn. "But lucky for us they were all the result of one big error."

"Which was?"

"Nonlethal force. They shot me with an electronic round."

"A Taser?"

"More or less."

Hutton's face dropped. "So I shot an unarmed man?"

"No, you shot a man before he had a chance to use his sidearm on you."

"I noticed the rounds fired at me seemed lethal enough."

"They were, and we should remember that."

"They need you alive."

Flynn nodded. "And that was the beginning of their errors. They were well drilled. A four-man team. Fast, mobile. The Navy SEALs prefer that formation."

"You think they were SEALs?"

"Not specifically. But military, yes. Or ex-military. And that was their problem. They weren't used to less than full commitment. They were used to shooting to kill. Nonlethal force was foreign to them, and it made them slip up. It gave you the chance to get your shot in. Thanks for that, by the way."

"Anytime."

"So it's Iraq all over again."

"How is it Iraq all over again?" asked Beth. She was still hugging the pillow, but she was watching and listening.

Flynn didn't move from the door, but he focused on Beth.

"Best we can tell, this all has something to do with an operation we did in Iraq."

"Who's we?" Beth's eyes were on Hutton.

"Laura and I met in Iraq. We worked on an investigation together."

"So what does this have to do with me?"

Flynn wanted to sit down and tell her everything. He had never lied to her about his past life. But there were lots of gaps, plenty of chapters left unspoken. She had said she understood. He had been in the military. His was a black-ops unit. There were things he did and places he went and people he dealt with that he could never speak of. She hadn't asked. He knew she had filled in the missing pieces herself, the way people do. He knew she had filled them in wrong. But she had said she wasn't interested in his past, she was only interested in his future.

And he had told her that his future was hers.

Now the past and the future had collided. So he explained to her about the container. About Staff Sergeant Dennison and their standoff in an abandoned building in the desert of Iraq. About it all going to hell.

"So you disappeared?" Beth asked.

"Yes."

"In San Francisco?"

"I went to Colorado. San Francisco just kind of happened. You kind of happened."

A smile almost made it onto her face, but it faded before it began.

"Is your name really John Flynn?"

"Yes. I was born John Weatherston. When I came back to the US after Iraq, I adopted my mother's maiden name, Flynn."

Flynn glanced at Hutton. She was watching Beth.

Beth said, "So that's you. Who are they?"

"That's what we're trying to figure out."

"And you think there are two groups of people after me?"

"After me," said Flynn. "It looks that way. And it did in Iraq."

"Why? What happened in Iraq?"

Flynn glanced at Hutton. Hutton nodded.

"We felt like there were two teams there as well. The actions didn't fit one person, or even one coordinated group. It was like there were two sets of actors and they had the same endgame, but they either didn't know about each other or someone didn't care if they went against each other."

"How so?"

Hutton said, "Sergeant Dennison was a grifter. He was a guy who could get things for other soldiers. It happens in places like war zones or prisons. Places cut off from normal society. Certain things become commodities. In prison it might be cigarettes. In a war zone it might be unofficial guns or drugs."

"I get it," said Beth.

"So Sergeant Dennison was a quartermaster. He could get things in and out. He did a lot of that sort of trade. And then he did more. He essentially became a drug dealer."

"In the army?"

"Sure. The military is a big organization. It contains a broad cross section of people, similar to regular society. So it has the same problems. Only add in the fact that these people's lives are in real danger on an ongoing basis. There's a lot of stress, PTSD, you name it."

"He was a drug dealer? Doesn't the army stamp that kind of thing out?"

"Of course," said Hutton. "They might turn a blind eye to a bit of weed during downtime, or a few sleeping pills here and there, but they don't condone drug abuse. The MPs root it out where they find it."

Flynn said, "The point is, Dennison moved on. He started

dealing in weapons. The US was pulling out of Iraq and he was disappearing munitions and selling them on the local market."

"To terrorists?"

"To anyone. But his operation was low-level. He was the equivalent of a cashier stealing a twenty from the cash register. The way he ran things—and when he got wind that he was being investigated, the way he handled things—it was amateurish."

"So?"

"So there were things that happened that were very professional. And it wasn't him doing them."

"I don't understand," said Beth.

"He tried to have us killed," said Hutton.

"Really?"

"Yes. And he kidnapped someone to do it. Sound familiar?"

Beth said nothing.

Hutton looked to Flynn and he urged her to continue.

"Have you heard of the Green Zone in Baghdad?"

"Sure," said Beth. "It was like a safe area."

"More or less. John and I were there. We were on foot and a truck came out of nowhere at us. There was a man inside with an explosive strapped to his body."

"A suicide bomber?"

"Yes," said Hutton. "Only this one wasn't what you think of when you think that. This wasn't about religion. It was a sloppy attempt to silence us, to stop our investigation."

"How did you survive?"

"We got lucky," said Flynn. "A guy I once served with, a Scotsman by the name of McConnell, had become a private security contractor and happened to be on patrol with his unit. He took the bomber out."

"Took him out?"

"Sniper shot."

Beth said nothing.

"We realized that bombers didn't just come and go from the GZ, so someone had to help them get the explosives in. We figured Dennison for it."

"He had a hideout," said Hutton, "away from the military base, in the suburbs. Kind of like the Baghdad equivalent of Katonah. We deduced that the bombers had to be motivated by more than money. That's when we came up with the idea that Dennison had taken the bombers' families hostage."

"Kidnapped them," said Beth.

"Right," said Hutton.

"But we figured it all out too late," said Flynn. "We went to his hideout and found the bodies of the bombers' families. Women, children. All executed."

"Oh my goodness," said Beth. "And this Dennison did it?"

"No. It was professional. Double taps to the head. Dennison could hardly hold a gun."

"There was a French operative though," said Hutton. "Right?" She looked at Flynn.

Flynn nodded.

Hutton said, "He was pretending to be the driver for a general, but when the general left the country the operative stayed. We think he may have taken out a member of John's team, and possibly been the professional behind the deaths of the women and children."

Beth fell silent.

Hutton continued. "Then we discovered a container shipment Dennison was moving, and the investigation went south. People way above Dennison's pay grade got involved—high-level officers, NATO MPs and more. So we came to the realization that there were two groups—Dennison, the amateur, and another group, more professional. We never got the chance to figure out how the two were connected. But now there are two again. An amateur side—this woman and the two men—and the professional side. The amateur side is just like Staff Sergeant Dennison, except we thought he was dead, and the professional side feels like it might be this French operative."

"Except we know he's dead," said Flynn.

"We do?" asked Hutton.

Flynn nodded. "Guaranteed."

Beth rubbed her hands across her face. She looked pale and tired. Flynn didn't know how much sleep she had gotten in the basement, but he figured on somewhere between not much and none. He pushed off the door with his hips, stepped to the bed and put his hand on Beth's shoulder. She put her hand across his and looked up at him.

"You've had one heck of an ordeal," he said. "You should get some rest."

"I don't think I can sleep," said Beth.

"I have something to help that, if you like," said Hutton.

She took a pill from a plastic bottle in her satchel and placed it in Beth's palm.

"Vicodin," Hutton said.

Beth took the pill with a swallow of water and then settled down into the bed.

"You get some rest," Flynn said to her, but she was staring into middle distance and she didn't respond. He stepped to the door with Hutton.

"You should get some rest too," said Hutton, opening the door.

"Too many questions," he replied.

Hutton glanced along the walkway toward her room. "Work it through?"

Flynn looked back at Beth, eyes closed.

"Yeah, let's work it through."

CHAPTER TWENTY-TWO

Room 24 felt colder. Hutton flicked the lights on and Flynn followed her in. They stood for a moment in silence before he spoke.

"Will you be okay?"

Hutton nodded. "I wish I had my whiteboard. I think better with my whiteboard."

"Use me. I'll be your whiteboard."

"Okay." Hutton shrugged off her jacket and Flynn turned up the heat.

Hutton said, "Let's start with what we know. Two men, one woman. None of them is Dennison. They arrange a meeting at the last minute. A meeting arranged on the back of a wealthy client of Beth's. The woman meets Beth, gets her in the minivan. The men are there. They drive her to Katonah."

"No, they drive her to Manhattan. That's where Beth's phone signal stopped, and that's where it stayed. They made the transfer in Manhattan. The two guys stayed in Manhattan and the woman came to Katonah with Beth."

"Why?"

"The guys didn't know the Katonah location. Not exactly. A moat between them and the woman."

"And they kept Beth's phone. Why?"

"By that time, they'd worked out that I was tracking them on it. They could see my blue dot just like I could see theirs. So they knew I was headed for Manhattan. The two guys stayed partly because of the moat, and partly because it was their home turf. They had the advantage. Or so they thought."

"Okay, so the woman has Beth. She leaves the house. Why? And permanently or temporarily?"

"Permanently. Because of the other team. The professionals. They were sending a hit squad."

"To get Beth?"

"Maybe, initially."

"That doesn't work," said Hutton. "The assault team had nonlethal weapons. Especially for you."

"Maybe for Beth?"

"No, they had her hostage already. No need for it. Besides, you said it yourself. It was like the Iraq thing. The suicide bomber's family. Dennison held them hostage, but the other team killed them. Why did they do that?"

"They didn't need them alive," said Flynn. "Prisoners are a liability."

"Right. I think that's what happened here. The amateurs abducted Beth. They kept her prisoner. The professionals figured they didn't need her. They were okay to kill her. They shot at me, remember? I could have been Beth. They didn't care. Everyone except you was to be eliminated. Just like in Iraq. No prisoners."

"All right. I buy that. But who is this woman?"

"I don't know."

"Whiteboard it. What do we know about her?"

"She's linked to Beth's client."

"But she isn't Beth's client. She's on the amateur side of the ledger. There's some kind of link between the two, but it's tenuous. Because the amateurs keep doing their own thing and the professionals keep cleaning it up."

"Right," said Hutton. "And she didn't fit in at the Watergate. The costume. It wasn't her kind of place. She's not a mover or a shaker. She not Washington. She's Katonah."

"No, she's not," said Flynn, pacing the room. "Think about Katonah. Think about the stores and the cars and houses. You said it yourself. It's money. It's a commuter suburb for Manhattan. But not for the janitors. For people who would fit in at the Watergate. But this woman didn't fit in."

"So why was she in Katonah? Your rationale was sound. Dennison's MO. A familiar location, a quiet street, an abandoned property. So why Katonah?"

Flynn spun around and looked through the window. The drapes were open in room 24, but all he could see was his own reflection.

"There's a link with Dennison. Got to be. Maybe he told someone. Maybe the woman was in Iraq with him."

"Lot of maybes."

"There's always a lot of maybes. You just keep checking off the maybes until all that's left is definite. So she's following Dennison's MO and she's on the amateur side of the ledger. Just like he was."

"Maybe."

"No, more than maybe. The link is there. Somewhere. What do we know about Dennison? Associates in Iraq?"

"You know what I know," said Hutton.

"None, to speak of. What don't we know? What about his jacket? Do you have it?"

"It doesn't say a lot." Hutton opened her courier bag and

found the file she had on Dennison. It wasn't very thick. She pulled out some sheets that were stapled together.

"This is all I have. It's all I got. The DoD didn't like to share, especially with the Department of Justice."

"Don't take it personally. I'm sure they don't like to share with anybody. Let's look at what you have."

"Same as what we went through in my office. The basics. Family history, deployment locations, date of MIA."

"Whiteboard it."

"Family. Father and mother, Enoch and Mary. From some small town in Pennsylvania. Both deceased. Two kids, Cameron and Oxnard. Like we said before, typical story. Nothing to do, no future. The boys find trouble. The older brother gets into some trouble, does jail time. The younger brother does what younger brothers do when they don't want to follow their sibling down that path. They join the army."

"The brother did time. The two guys in New York did time. Maybe they met."

"Doesn't explain the woman."

"Not yet. Follow the links."

"Okay. You think Dennison talked to his brother and he's behind this?"

Flynn said, "Maybe Dennison was the Iraq end and his brother was the US end."

"Of what? There was no evidence anything was coming or going to or from the United States. No need. Easier to make stuff go missing in the field in Iraq or Afghanistan than it is in a warehouse at Fort Lee."

"All right, I buy that. But the woman chose Katonah for a reason. Maybe the brother was the reason."

"A jailbird from Pennsylvania isn't really Katonah material either."

"You're assuming he did time in Pennsylvania. Does Dennison's jacket say anything about that?"

"His jacket doesn't say anything about his brother. Just a name and a DOB. Department of Justice info says he did time. The stuff I have doesn't say where."

"You're sure?"

"Positive. I spent a long time looking at this file, after Iraq. It's got its own entire section in my brain."

"So we don't know where. But suppose it was in this area. It's not uncommon for inmates to stick around a general vicinity of the location of their incarceration. They're like military guys. A lot of guys who get discharged hang around the towns near their last posting. It's a thing. When I used to search for deserters, one of the first places we looked was the town, but one from their last posting."

"And that worked?"

"About thirty percent of the time. So what prisons are around here?"

"It's New York. There are plenty. City and county lockups, state prisons, federal penitentiaries."

"Not lockups. Not long enough inside. And there needs to be a reason to stay. Think the kind of prison that would run a community program to help inmates get back into society."

"Sing Sing isn't far. It's in Ossining. Over on the Hudson."

"Possible. But I'm thinking closer. An inmate from Sing Sing is more likely to end up here in Yonkers, or back in New York."

Hutton pulled her laptop and tapped some keys.

"I'm searching for prisons around Katonah. The closest is in Bedford."

"Is that close?"

"Katonah isn't actually an incorporated town. It's a hamlet, within the city of Bedford."

"That'll do."

Hutton kept tapping and reading. "Huh."

"What?"

"The jail in Bedford. Its full name is Bedford Hills Correctional Facility . . ."

"So?"

". . . for Women."

"That's a wrinkle. Maybe it's the woman who did time. It's possible she had a parole officer in Bedford. Maybe she met Ox's brother there."

"Still a lot of maybes."

"What would keep an inmate in the local area? Apart from a parole office?"

"A work release program?"

"Right. Maybe the woman worked in Katonah."

"Doesn't narrow it that much."

"Hutton, it narrows it plenty. That town is practically one street deep. We could canvas the whole town in a morning."

"Okay. Maybe we should. But what about Beth? Can we leave her alone for a few hours?"

"It won't take a few hours. It'll take a few minutes."

"The town's not that small."

"No, but the suspect pool is. Think about it. The woman does work release, which keeps her in the area. But it's the kind of work that allows her to scope out vacant properties. And not just any vacant properties. REO properties. Properties that haven't even gotten onto the public record yet."

"You think she worked for a real estate agent?"

"There's one way to find out, and not too many places to ask."

"Okay. That's a plan. First thing. I'll start with the place I got the list from this morning and work from there. You can stay with Beth here."

"No. We'll all come. We need to go out for breakfast anyway."

Hutton closed her laptop with a shrug. She slipped it into her courier bag and put the bag on the desk. She looked at Flynn.

"We should get some sleep."

Flynn nodded but didn't move.

"You should go and look after Beth," she said.

He looked at Hutton looking at him. For a second, and then two.

Then he walked out.

CHAPTER TWENTY-THREE_

They ate breakfast at the same place as the previous morning. The same waitress served them. She remembered them. Waitresses remember big tips. She offered them the same early-morning smile. Flynn ordered the same thing, poached eggs with bacon and sourdough. Hutton repeated the Denver omelet. Beth went with coffee and oatmeal.

Flynn arched his back to stretch out. He had slept in the chair in room 23, watching Beth sleep. He had spent time trying to reconcile his two worlds colliding. Iraq was gone. Not forgotten, but brushed under the carpet. Now the carpet had been removed and the stains spilled all over his new life.

He had given Beth an overview of their thinking and their plan. She hadn't commented on it. She hadn't mentioned the police or the woman. She pushed her food around her plate. Flynn wanted to tell her to eat, that she needed to get food in while she could. That you never knew when your next meal might come. But that wasn't her world. Her next meal would come when she was hungry. That was how her world worked. Flynn ate his breakfast and wiped the runny yolk from his plate with the last of his sourdough toast.

They drove into Katonah and waited for the town to open. The real estate agent who had given Hutton the list of REO properties was their first stop. The rain had stopped and the sky was a patchwork of gray clouds and pale blue sky. Flynn sat in the front of the Yukon and watched Hutton walk away, and then he turned to Beth in the rear. Her clothes were still damp, so she was wearing Hutton's T-shirt and track pants. Her hair was a mess. She didn't seem concerned by it.

"You okay?" he asked.

She didn't look at him. She stared out the window at the dark wood of damp trees. "Who is she?"

"Who? The woman who took you?"

"No. Laura."

"Hutton? She is what she told you last night. Former FBI."

"I wasn't at my most attentive last night. How do you know her?"

"We met during service."

"She was in the army, too?"

"No, she was FBI then. The US government sent law enforcement to train local police in places like Iraq and Afghanistan."

Beth nodded. "What does she want?"

"Hutton?"

Beth shook her head. "The woman who took me."

"I don't know."

"I remembered something. Did we talk about it last night? The meeting I had with the client in San Francisco?"

"A little. What do you remember?"

"The bogeyman. That was your phrase. You said it the night we met. Remember?"

"I do."

"And I said it. In the meeting with the client. I remember when they asked if we had the ability to track down people, as well as money. I said we did, and I was thinking of you. They said this person might be very hard to find. And I said, *Même le croque-mitaine ne peut pas cacher éternellement.* In French, just like you do. And they asked me what it meant, and I told them. *Even the bogeyman can't hide forever.* I didn't think anything of it at the time. But there were two men, the clients. They just smiled like it was cute, like it meant nothing."

"Maybe it meant nothing to them."

"But then the woman called, after the meeting. And she knew the phrase. How did she know?"

"I used the phrase. To the guy who we investigated in Iraq."

"When you met Laura."

"Yes."

"Tell me what you were doing. Back then."

"There's a lot I can't tell you."

"Tell me what you can."

Flynn looked across the street, where storefronts were opening and starting the trading day. He turned back to Beth in the rear of the Yukon. He told her about his military service. About how it had been with the French Foreign Legion, not the United States Army. She listened without interrupting him. Flynn felt the weight lift from him as he spoke. He had never meant for it to be a secret between them, but he found it a relief to speak of it regardless. He told her about his parents and his brother, about fleeing Abu Dhabi and ending up alone in France.

When he was done, Beth spoke.

"I wouldn't have guessed," she said. "I always figured you for a patriot."

"I think I am a patriot. I fought for everything that our country stands for."

Beth sat back in her seat. "What did you do for them?"

"I did more or less what I told you. I found people. In the

beginning it was deserters. I had a talent for it. Then in 2007, terrorists exploded two car bombs in Algiers. A group calling themselves Al Qaeda in the Islamic Maghreb took responsibility. They claimed the attacks were aimed at 'the Crusaders and their agents, the slaves of America and the sons of France.' As a result of the attack, the officer who recruited me was tasked with creating a special team. A team designed to hunt terrorists."

"You hunted terrorists?"

"Yes."

"Like bin Laden."

"Yes."

"Only we found him, didn't we? Navy SEALs."

Flynn let out a breath. "Yes."

"So which terrorists did you find?"

"I can't tell you that."

"Can't or won't?"

"It won't help you to know. It might hurt you."

"You mean someone might kidnap me?"

She offered him an expression that he had never seen before. Not anger, not even distrust. It was a face of disappointment.

"I'm sorry, Beth. I made a mistake. I thought I could leave it behind. I didn't think it would come after me. I thought it was done. I would never put you in this position if I thought for a second they would come after you."

"Who are they?"

"I don't know. Not exactly. My last mission was in Iraq. That's where I met Hutton. I was working with her and with some people from the United States Army. There was an arms shipment. The US was pulling out, coming home. The bad guys were gearing up. Preparing to fill the void. I found a shipment and I made it disappear. So they couldn't use it after we were all gone."

"And they want you to find it."

"Yes."

"And they used me as collateral."

"Yes."

"So where is it?"

"I don't know. Like I said. It's lost."

"But they're not buying that."

"I'm not sure they know that."

She turned back to the window and looked away for a time. Took a deep breath.

"What did you do with these terrorists that you found? Did they stand trial? Did they end up in Guantanamo?"

"No, they didn't end up in Guantanamo."

"So what happened to them?"

"Mostly they were disposed of."

She took another breath and turned back to look at him.

"You killed them."

He looked over her face. It was stressed and taut. A face unfamiliar yet at the same time completely known to him. He had run his fingers across every inch of it, kissed every curve and every line. He had watched her sleep and seen the way it looked when it was at complete repose, like a contented baby. It was a face he loved. It was a face he thought he could grow old beside. But that face was gone. Like visiting a college town thirty years after graduation. Familiar but foreign.

"Yes," he said. "I killed them."

The door opened and Hutton dropped in from the cold.

"No dice," she said. She looked at Flynn and then glanced back at Beth and then back at Flynn.

"We okay?"

Flynn nodded.

Hutton started the Yukon. "My new friend said she would never hire such a person. That was her phrase. *Such a person.*

But she thought there was someone who might. Another agent. Her place is on the next street back. Apparently this agent's husband owns an auto store that works with parolees. Worth a shot."

"Yes. Worth a shot," said Flynn.

HUTTON WAS happy to try the next office. The dynamic in the truck had gotten weird. She figured it was reasonable that it would, but it wasn't a place she wanted to spend too much time. The second agent's office was on the second street back, which was far less busy than the main street. There was a library and a park and a church. Not as much walk-by traffic.

The agent's office was in what looked like a Victorian-era house. Hutton opened the door and a little bell rang. There was a table in the entranceway that appeared to be the reception desk, but there was no one behind it. Hutton was about to call out, when a small-framed woman appeared from a hallway. She was jiggling a tea bag in a mug.

"Sorry, just making some tea. Can I help you?"

"Yes, my name is Laura Hutton. I have my own firm, and I was given your name."

"Great. How can I help?"

"It's a delicate matter."

"Come into my office."

They walked down the hallway, past a kitchen and into a room that might have been a bedroom or a study, once upon a time. It was now the woman's office. There was a desk and a computer and a printer. There were neat shelves with thick folders detailing real estate codes of conduct. There was a photo on the wall of a leafy fall scene, all orange and gold and red. The woman sat behind her desk and pointed Hutton to a visitor's chair. She was wearing a heavy sweater with a turtleneck. Her hair was blond, but that came at considerable expense and via the expertise of a hairdresser, probably on the main street. She was well maintained but easily sixty years old.

"I'm Cheryl Barclay. How can help?" she asked for the third time.

"Well, you see, I have a business. I'm part of my community."

"Are you a broker?"

"No, nothing like that. But I'm thinking about hiring some help. I was at a function, and I was told about some women. These were women who may have taken the wrong path, you might say. And they may need a helping hand. To get back on their feet. Back into society, you might say."

"I see."

"I was told that you might know about such a program. Perhaps have some experience with something like that."

Cheryl dropped the string on her tea bag and sat back in her chair. She didn't slouch. Her entire body slid back until her back was against the rear of the chair.

"You're referring to a community re-entry program. For former inmates?"

"That's right."

"I am familiar with it, but it's really my husband who has the involvement."

"Oh, I see."

"He has helped a number of men and women. He owns a chain of automotive supply stores, you see. He occasionally hires people who are in the program. Mainly to drive his pickups. They make deliveries to workshops, that sort of thing."

"I see."

"I can give you his number, if you like."

"That would be most helpful, I'm sure. But I wondered.

From your point of view. I'm sure you understand, as a woman. I'm a little nervous about the whole thing. Have you had someone working for you recently? In your office?"

"I understand your concern. These people are looking for a second chance. I did have a girl doing a little for me. But it was really through my husband. She was driving for him. So she did a little extra work for me. Driving around to properties, taking photographs, installing signage."

"So not here in the office?"

"Rarely. Not that I wouldn't have a girl here, but I'm not a big broker. I specialize. Not every client fits, you see. So I don't have a lot of need for office help."

"How did the woman driving for you and your husband work out?"

Cheryl shifted in her seat. It was subtle and involuntary but all too obvious to Hutton.

"It went well. As far as these things do."

"Is she still with you?"

"Well, no. Look, I don't want you to get the wrong idea. Most of these women are a little unsettled, in their home life. Sometimes their families live far away."

"So she's moved on?"

"Yes, that's right. Moved on."

"Was there a problem? Don't worry, I understand that these women will not be perfect."

"No, perfect they are not. But she was a good worker. They usually are. As good as regular people." Cheryl shifted again. "I mean, we had an issue with the truck, but that was a misunderstanding."

"An issue?"

"Nothing, I assure you. They don't have the same understanding of things as you and I. She just made a couple of trips in my husband's truck. The one she used for deliveries. She took it a couple of times."

"Took it where?"

"Pennsylvania."

"Pennsylvania? Really? How do you know?"

"Oh, my husband has tracking on all his vehicles. Not to track his staff, of course. It's a fuel management thing. But it was sorted out. It was odd though. She collected used tires from some of the garages she delivered to. Took the tires to Pennsylvania." She shook her head.

"So why did she leave?"

"In this case, one day she was here, the next day she was not. That is all. Nothing major. Nothing sinister. A few weeks ago she just stopped coming into work. Often their parole will end and they will go home, if they live interstate. I'm not sure if that was the case. As I say, she only did a little work for me."

"Well, it sounds like a worthwhile program."

"It is, it is. And we all must do our part, mustn't we? For the community."

"Yes, absolutely." Hutton stood. "Thank you for your time."

"Of course, anytime. It was Laura, wasn't it?"

"Yes. Do you have your husband's number, in case I have some questions?"

"Yes, let me get you a card. From reception."

Cheryl led Hutton back to the entranceway and took a card from a holder on the desk. It was for an auto supplies company, and Francis Barclay was the CEO. Hutton shook Cheryl's soft hand and stepped to the door. Then she stopped.

"By the way, what was the name of the woman who worked for you?"

"Cameron. Her name was Cameron."

CHAPTER TWENTY-FOUR

HUTTON OPENED THE TAILGATE OF THE YUKON AND ruffled through her bag. She pulled out her file on Ox Dennison. Looked at it and groaned. She paced around the vehicle and dropped into the driver's seat.

"I made an error."

"Why, what happened?" Flynn asked. "Did she not talk to you?"

"Not now. Earlier. Much earlier. Maybe years ago."

"What error?"

Hutton handed Flynn the document in her hand. "Family."

Flynn scanned it, but he knew what was written there. "Mother, father, both deceased. Two children. Ox and his brother."

"No."

"No?"

"Where does it say brother?"

Flynn looked at the document again. "It doesn't. It says children."

"The real estate broker I just spoke with. She had a woman working for her, part-time. The woman's name was Cameron."

Flynn looked up at Hutton. "Ox's sibling is a sister."

"I should have seen it."

"You're right, we should have. But it's not just your error. I didn't see it either."

"But I'm a woman. I shouldn't make assumptions based on gender like that."

"No one should make gender assumptions like that," said Beth from the rear seat. "But don't beat yourself up about it. It's a result of upbringing and education, not gender."

"Does she still work there?" Flynn asked.

"No. She just vanished. A couple of weeks ago. But there's more. The real estate agent was a privileged old thing. See this street? There's no business on it. Not like the main street. It's a poor place to put a realty office. If you want business, that is."

"She didn't want business?"

"I don't think that was the point, no. I got the impression that her husband does well and this was a little project to get her out of the house. But her husband is the one who hires the ex-cons. They drive trucks for him, delivering auto parts. Cameron worked for him, and then did a little extra work on the side for the wife. Putting up For Sale signs, that sort of thing."

"Checking out all the local properties."

"Exactly."

"That tells us how she found the house, but that's old news."

"There's more. There was an issue. She took a couple of trips in the guy's truck. But he has tracking on all his vehicles."

"Trips? Where?"

"Get this. Pennsylvania."

"What's in Pennsylvania?" Beth asked.

"The family farm," said Flynn. "But the jacket says the parents are long dead. Did they leave the farm to her?"

"Possible. But there's something else. The trips she made, before they called her out and asked her not to use company vehicles for private use. The broker said Cameron was using the truck to take loads of tires to Pennsylvania. Old tires."

"Why would anyone want old tires?" asked Beth. "They can't be recycled, can they?"

"Actually, they can," said Flynn. "Primarily as tires. I've seen it before. They're called retreads. Some old tires can have a new layer of rubber laid on them and they're more or less new. As long as the structure of the tire wall isn't compromised."

"How do you know stuff like that?" asked Beth.

Flynn shrugged. "I read."

"So what do we do?" Hutton asked.

"It's Ox all over again. If things go bad, retreat to home base."

"You think she's gone back to the family farm?"

"I do."

"So we're going to Pennsylvania?"

"Excuse me," said Beth, "but shouldn't we be calling the police at this point? Or more specifically, shouldn't we have called them last night?"

"The police can't help with this," said Flynn.

"What are you talking about? That's their job."

"No, their job is to protect taxpayers from local crime. This is bigger. This is beyond their remit."

"John, I don't exactly understand what you did before, but this isn't that. This is now. You are not that guy anymore."

Flynn shifted in his seat to look at Beth. "That's what I thought too. That's what I hoped. But I was wrong. I am that guy. I was always that guy. But more importantly, I know these guys. They are bad people. And we need to stop them."

"No, John. The police need to stop them. I need to go home."

Flynn turned back in his seat. Took a breath and glanced at Hutton.

"Let's go back to the house."

THE HOUSE LOOKED quiet and peaceful. The road was still damp and the trees were waterlogged despite not holding many leaves. Hutton drove past the house on the right and past the house on the left and parked in the driveway of the house at the end of the cul-de-sac.

"This is crazy, John," stuttered Beth. "They might still be there. They probably expect us to come back."

"They're long gone, and they think we're even longer gone. I'll check it out first, okay?"

Flynn got out and wandered around the back, and after about thirty seconds, the front door opened and he walked out and back to the Yukon.

"Nobody's home."

"I don't want to go back in there."

"I know you don't. And I don't want you to have to. But you need to understand. You need to see this."

"See what?" Beth's face contorted with fear.

"Nothing. Come on. You can stay right behind me."

He opened the door and half helped, half dragged Beth out of the vehicle. Hutton got out and followed them up to the front door. From the outside there was no trace of the previous evening's events. The porch was clear and damp, the door unharmed.

The inside wasn't much different. Flynn walked into the open living area and stepped aside. The pale floorboards shone as if they had been freshly cleaned. There were no bodies. There was no blood. The floor and the walls were pristine. Except for the sections that had been removed. Square sections of drywall had been cut out of the walls, leaving holes that looked like they might become built-in shelves for sculptures. Flynn had seen such alcoves in museums.

Beth wandered slack-jawed into the dining space at the end of the kitchen. There was more missing drywall, and a large section of crown molding along the rear of the house had been removed. The floorboards were all intact, but she saw a darker patch in the wood where it looked like the lacquer had been removed. A large section was dull wood against the shine of the rest of the floor.

She turned and looked at Flynn. He stood looking at a similar dull patch opposite the door that led to the basement where she had been held.

"What happened?"

"Quick thinking," said Flynn. "But quick and dirty. They removed all traces of being here. Found all the spent rounds, in the walls, in the molding, and cut them out."

"The floors?"

"My guess is a hydrogen sulfide solution. Sulfuric acid. They cleaned up the blood and then washed the areas in acid. Messes up DNA processing, if that was ever going to happen."

"They are professional," said Hutton. "This is a good job."

"Yes and no. They are pros, no doubt. With four guys down, most people would just flee. But they didn't. They cleaned up. But no, it's not a good job. This is not the work of a cleanup crew."

"Who did it, then?"

"They did."

"At least three had GSWs and the other was most definitely DOA," said Hutton. "You think they bandaged up their wounds and got the bleach out?"

"No. It was the fifth guy."

Hutton frowned. "What fifth guy?"

"In a team of four, there's always a fifth guy. The point guy.

The guy back at the vehicle, directing things. The head guy. The unit leader."

"So this fifth guy comes in with a mop?"

"More or less. They got lucky, and they know it. They know this property is REO. They know it's not on the market. It will go to auction unseen, and probably be snapped up by one of your flippers. An investor. For cash—that's what you said. And an investor is going to open the front door and find this damage and blame the last owner. Maybe cuss a little bit. Then they're going to add a thousand bucks to the budget and they are going to patch the drywall and fix the molding, and they are going to sand and restain the floors. The investor will do the final cleanup for them."

Hutton looked around. The floors were damaged, but not badly. Drywall could be replaced in a day. She turned around 360 degrees and looked at it all.

"That was smart."

"That was lucky. It tells us something. They're a skeleton crew. If they had backup, they would have done a better job. There wouldn't be any damage. We're only an hour from Manhattan. But there is no cleanup crew. So they did it themselves. And you're right—four down, at least one permanently. So they did what they could. Good work in the circumstances. Professional. But I like the math."

"What about the math?"

"Four down. The fifth guy had to do the cleanup. So the fifth guy is the last guy operational. There's only one guy left."

"Unless they get reinforcements. These guys are connected, remember."

Flynn shook his head. "Reinforcements aren't coming. Think about it. It's New York. I'm not saying they didn't have a cleanup crew available. If they have one anywhere, they have one in New York City. Stands to reason. But they weren't called. The assault team didn't call for backup."

"Why?"

"That's the question." Flynn turned to Beth. She was watching him and Hutton talk. She was slack-shouldered, as if being back in the place of her imprisonment had drained the life from her.

"You see now?" Flynn asked her. "The police need evidence. They don't move without it. They can't move without it. And there is none. It's gone. So they'll call it vandals."

"I wasn't abducted by vandals."

"You were at a hotel. Had you been drinking? You're a lawyer. Lot of pressure, right? Do you take recreational drugs? Maybe something harder, or something to make you sleep."

"You know I don't."

"I know. They don't. And they will look for the most obvious answer. They get more crackpot calls than you can imagine. And there's no proof. No kidnapper. And why would the kidnapper let you go? There was no ransom paid."

"Because you rescued me."

"Then three of us end up in interview rooms for days, maybe longer. Maybe they find a terrorism angle. It's a handy law. Can be bent a lot of ways. And they could easily bend it to say I was behind it. That Hutton helped me. It wastes time we don't have. And in the end, there's no evidence of a crime being committed. No autopsy, no foul. You're a lawyer, think about it from the DA's point of view."

Beth stayed still, but her eyes flickered around the room. Thinking, processing. Then deciding.

"What's to stop them from trying to get me again?"

"Me. I'm going to get them first."

Beth blinked hard and ran her hand through her hair.

"So we're going to Pennsylvania," she said.

THE FIFTH MAN WAS ANGRY.

Angry with himself, angry with his team. But mostly angry with his superiors. They had given the orders. They had put him in this position. They'd had him chasing ghosts for years. It could have been worse. He knew that. He was on the good end of the deal. But they had been adamant. No harm must come to Fontaine. Or Flynn. Or whatever he wanted to call himself. The team leader told them he could take him out with a leg shot, a sniper round from a thousand yards. They had said no. Might hit an artery. He might bleed out. And they needed him alive. No doubts about it.

So his team had gone in with mixed rounds and lost. He knew Flynn was good. But Flynn had the advantage. He was prepared—no, allowed—to use deadly force. The woman, Hutton, had killed one of his team. Unlucky. Off the shoulder bone and into the ear canal. And Flynn had ended one other. The other two would be no good for some weeks. So now it was up to him. That was okay. That was just fine. It was a one-man job, really. He didn't want backup and he didn't need backup and he certainly didn't need them doubting him again. He knew that for sure. They had made that clear. Further doubt would be the end of it. There was no coming back from it. And he couldn't hide from them. Not forever. So it was up to him.

He drove the freeway, sitting only five miles an hour above the limit. He wanted to go faster, but caution was a valuable asset. And he was ahead now. Out in front. The scales were tipping his way. He knew what Flynn knew, and he knew what he would do. He was confident of that. So he kept his speed short of everyone else and stayed invisible and drove on.

CHAPTER TWENTY-FIVE

FIRST STOP WAS AN OUTLET MALL IN NEW JERSEY. BETH wanted out of the track pants. Hutton took the opportunity to buy new clothes. Flynn got an espresso and waited by the truck. He took the wheel from there while Hutton made a couple of calls and tapped away on her laptop. They were passing Easton when her cell phone rang and she took a one-sided call. Then she hung up and turned so she could see both Flynn and Beth.

"My office. Background on Cameron Dennison. She did indeed do time in Bedford Hills for aggravated assault."

"Assault. Nice," said Flynn.

"We also have something on the driver in New York. Daniel Cust, according to his driver's license. He did time for GTA."

"A car thief?"

"There's more. His little buddy. Davie Rankin. Did time for armed robbery."

"I'm betting he wasn't the brains behind the operation," said Flynn.

"He got caught in the act, so maybe he was."

"Point taken."

"Anyway, Cust and Rankin's time away overlapped. Same facility."

"So they knew each other. How does that connect with Cameron?"

"She and Cust shared a parole officer."

"Bingo."

"I haven't gotten to the good part yet."

"Please do."

"Cameron Dennison did time as a juvenile."

"Jail?"

"Juvenile hall, but for a kid it's the same thing."

"What for?" asked Beth.

"She burned down her parents' barn."

"Not nice."

"With them inside."

Beth almost leaped into the front seat. "She killed her parents?"

"Apparently. They couldn't prosecute as an adult, and they couldn't show that it was premeditated. But she did it."

"And got out."

"Eventually. So your theory wasn't far off," Hutton said to Flynn. "The older sibling did time and the younger one joined the army."

"So who owns the farm now?" asked Beth.

"My assistant is looking into that."

Flynn asked, "Do we have an address for the farm?"

"Bent Pines, PA. That's as specific as it gets."

"Where is that?"

"Appalachian Mountains."

Flynn just nodded and drove. Southwest on Interstate 287 and then east on I-78. He watched the topography change, minute by minute, mile by mile. The interstate system was a modern engineering and political marvel, the likes of which couldn't be achieved anymore. It moved millions of vehicles from point A to point B with ease and speed. It wasn't designed for sightseeing, for taking in the countryside. It wasn't designed to prop up the businesses of the towns it bypassed or the communities left to flounder on what were once the main thoroughfares but were now local back roads. It was a boring drive. The landscape felt flat and wide but artificially dense. As they moved across New Jersey and into Pennsylvania, the roadside changed from population centers punctuated by open space into open space punctuated by population centers. They drove by Bethlehem and Lebanon. Both places Flynn had been, just not in the United States.

Flynn stopped for gas outside of Harrisburg. They all used the restroom, and Hutton bought a round of gas station coffees. Flynn pumped the gas, leaning against the Yukon, and Beth wandered back from the restroom.

"You okay?" he asked.

Beth nodded.

"You don't have to be here for this."

"Where would I go?"

He nodded. It was a fair point, one he'd run through his head for miles. She couldn't go home. Not until this thing was done. He couldn't be sure someone wasn't watching their home in California. And he preferred to keep her near. He could protect her if she stayed near. She stood beside the pump and wrapped her arms around herself. Hutton returned and passed around the coffee. Beth watched Flynn take a sip.

"Gas station coffee," she said. "You drink that after all? Is that something else I don't know?"

He shook his head. "It's dishwater. But it's caffeine."

Hutton offered to drive. Flynn accepted. It wasn't his favorite task. He was as good at it as the next guy, maybe better than some. He paid attention for a start. But it occupied more of his brain than he liked, and he wanted to be thinking through options and scenarios and plans. For what, he had no idea.

"I'm wondering if we should dump the Yukon," said Hutton.

"You want to steal some poor civilian's car?"

"We could rent something," said Beth.

Hutton nodded at that.

Flynn said, "We should leave as little a trail as possible."

Hutton shrugged. "They might know the Yukon. Might recognize it."

"I doubt it. This is not a crew that takes inventory of their vehicles. Besides, in this part of the world, a dirty old truck is close to invisible. A shiny new rental sedan will stick out."

Hutton nodded and said nothing. She took the keys and got in the truck. Beth slipped in the back as Flynn topped off the tank, and then they pulled back out onto the Pennsylvania Turnpike and headed west. It took a little over an hour more. The geography changed again, even on the turnpike. Hundreds of millions of years showed their work. The elevation happened gradually. There was a subtle shift in the genus of the trees. Flynn was no flora expert, but they certainly grew thicker with evergreens.

The Appalachian range was a nebulous term, sometimes referring to the mountain country in Virginia, sometimes in Tennessee or Georgia. Backwoods country. But the range itself was the East Coast equivalent of the Rockies, a dividing range that ran from Canada all the way to Georgia. It was famous for the eponymously named trail, over two thousand miles of hiking down the eastern spine of the country. Flynn mused that he might like to do that, after all this was done. He liked walking. He had walked more than most during his lifetime. It was the single most important factor in his making it in the Legion. The training was physical and mental exhaustion. But what got most guys was the marching. The Legion liked marching. A lot. Some guys couldn't handle it. Day after day. The soreness and the fatigue. But mostly the monotony. It wasn't like a walk in the park, enjoying the scenery. It was a hard slog with twenty or thirty kilograms on your back. Luckily for Flynn, he found that he loved walking. Enjoyed marching. The pace and the rhythm. He found a trancelike state, ready to break into action in an instant, but happy to remain in a transcendent place in the meantime.

The turnpike passed through a tunnel in the mountains, and not long after, Hutton followed the GPS on her phone off the interstate. The road got tighter and winding. It didn't take long for her phone to provide a message that it was no longer in range of a tower. But the map stayed on the screen and she could see the town ahead on the one road leading in the one direction.

Bent Pines was barely a town. Katonah was Manhattan in comparison. There wasn't really a main street as such. The road passed the town by. There were no signals and no off-ramps. Just a service road branching off that allowed access to a strip of buildings. Most of the structures were constructed out of wood. Flynn guessed pine. There was a garage that had no gas and looked long closed up. A small church that bore a crucifix but no hint at its denomination. There was a feed store that had another dirty Yukon parked in front. And there was a diner.

Hutton pulled into the lot by the diner. There were two other vehicles, both trucks. The cook and the waitress, Flynn guessed. Not a waiter, not out here. Not in a diner. They sat in the vehicle for a long moment. Hutton looked at Flynn. Beth looked at Flynn.

"I'm hungry," he said.

They got out. The sky was wispy white cloud and the air

was cold and clean. Like breathing oxygen from a tank. Each of them stretched in their own way. Looked at each other. Then Flynn led them inside.

The outside of the diner looked like a log cabin. The inside matched it. The walls were exposed logs, long and thick from a time when trees got old. There was a laminated counter at the back, six red-topped stools overlooking the pass-through into the kitchen. There were five empty tables, all set for four diners. No booths. The chairs were wooden, the tables were wooden. The floor was unpolished, like the sections of the floor in Katonah where the acid had been applied.

A woman of about forty was behind the counter. She was wiping down the countertop the way waitresses are always doing. Their version of make-work. She had long brown hair and her face was lined at the eyes and forehead. She wore the look of a person who had spent time at the bottom of a bottle. She watched them come in and offered a tight smile and a nod.

"Wherever you like." Her voice was raspy, like a country singer.

They took a table against the wall. Flynn sat down facing the door. Hutton and Beth sat side by side opposite him. The waitress wandered over and handed them each a laminated sheet. The menu. Not overly complex. Not the menus Flynn found in the city, as thick as the King James Bible. He liked simplicity. Choice was highly overrated.

"Can I get ya a drink to start?"

Beth and Hutton both ordered coffee. Flynn took water. The waitress nodded and walked away.

Hutton tapped the table. "So, is there a plan in there somewhere?"

"Find the farm, find the bad guys. Finish it."

"Good plan."

Beth leaned in. "I think we should call the police."

"You weren't convinced by the cleanup at the house?"

"I don't know. But what we are doing? Two wrongs don't make a right."

"That depends on your definition of right and wrong."

"Hurting people is wrong."

"What about stopping people from hurting other people?"

Beth wrapped her arms around herself again. "If you sink to their level, you're just as bad as they are."

"Really? You believe that?"

"Of course I do. I'm a lawyer. I believe in the law."

Flynn said, "The law allows your clients to hide millions of dollars abroad so they don't pay tax. But a single mother in Oakland pays a fifth of all she earns for roads and schools. I believe in the rule of law too. But the law is a construct of mankind, and nothing mankind does is perfect. Sometimes the bad guys get away with it. And I don't like that."

"And you're the judge, jury and executioner."

"Not today."

The waitress dropped off their drinks and wandered away again, and Flynn waited before he continued.

"Today you're the judge and jury. You decide. You saw the assault, you saw the cleanup. You were the one abducted. You spent time with this woman. So you tell me. Do you think the police will be able to prove anything? Against an assault team we don't know? And do you feel okay with that, knowing guys who wanted to kill you are out there, above the law, with you still a loose end?"

"That's not fair. That's exactly why we don't allow victims to be jurors."

"Let me put it this way. Is the woman who took you a bad person?"

"Yes."

"Are the guys who turned up with the automatic machine guns bad guys?"

"Of course."

"But you're okay with them out and about, free as birds? To do bad all over again?"

"You don't know that."

"No?" Flynn turned to Hutton. "What does Cameron Dennison's rap sheet look like?"

"Long, and ugly."

"And the guys with the guns. What did they do in Iraq?"

"We suspect they murdered two families, women and children, to cover their tracks."

"Suspect," said Beth.

"I'll give them a chance to defend that one," said Flynn. "But they'll keep doing it. Unless someone stops them. Sometimes the law isn't enough. Our own government acknowledges that."

"I don't think they do."

"Did the president admit to killing Osama bin Laden?"

"He was a terrorist."

"Yes, he was. But he never faced a court of law."

Beth sank silently into her seat. The waitress returned and asked what they would like to drink.

Each of them looked at their drinks and then at the waitress.

"We're good for drinks," Flynn said. The waitress patted down the hair on the side of her head. A reflex action.

"Good," she said. "So what'll you eat?"

Beth said she wasn't hungry, but this time Flynn told her to eat while she could. She ordered soup, Hutton a burger. Flynn asked the waitress what she ate. She was a fan of the country stew. The secret was in the chuck beef and the parsnips. Flynn said that was for him.

When she walked away, Flynn leaned across the table to Beth.

"I know this is way out of your comfort zone. We'll find the farm, take a look. If it doesn't look good to you, we'll go find the cops."

Beth kept her arms folded but looked at him. "You'll do that?"

He nodded. She nodded. Flynn glanced at Hutton, who said nothing.

The waitress returned with food and refills. Flynn told her the stew was pure gold, and he wasn't lying. He thought the real secret was in the bacon pieces, but he kept that to himself. She smiled and poured more water.

"We're looking for a place around here," he said.

The waitress said, "Uh-huh."

"The Dennison place. You know it?"

The woman stopped pouring. A frown crept onto her face. "Yeah, I know it."

"Is it nearby?"

"You friends of theirs?"

"Not yet."

"Looking to get some tires?"

Flynn looked puzzled.

The waitress touched the side of her head again, like it was suddenly itchy, and pulled away from the table.

"Turn right past the town. Stay on the road. It's not marked. But you'll know it when you see."

They finished their meal. No one ate dessert. Flynn paid the check at the counter and gave the waitress a nice big tip. Business wasn't exactly booming in Bent Pines, Pennsylvania. She thanked him but didn't look at him.

They stepped out into the late afternoon. The sun had dropped below the crest of a mountain and threw golden light and deep fingers of shadow across the hills to the east. Bent Pines was getting dark.

Flynn said, "Let's see what we can see, while we still can."

He got in the passenger side and let Hutton drive. He might have been as good at it as the next guy, but Hutton was better. She backed away from the diner and turned right, onto a small road that wound into the mountains.

CHAPTER TWENTY-SIX_

THEY DROVE ON SURROUNDED BY A MIX OF PINES AND naked oaks, the road like a tunnel. Then without notice, the pines fell away and the landscape opened up into fields. Wide expanses of green grass. No cattle, no crops. As if the space had been cleared for no other reason than something to do. The Appalachian version of make-work. But Flynn expected the diner and the church and the feed store had been built out of the trees that had been cleared. Perhaps that was reason enough.

There were mountains either side of them. Not mountains in the Himalayan sense, or even the French Alps. Flynn figured them for somewhere between hills and mountains. He didn't know if there was a technical measure that defined one from the other. But their size was not the point. Their aspect was the point. They ran more or less north-south, with a slight leaning to the northeast-southwest. They were a real physical barrier to east-west travel. And the sunlight that came from the west. All the crests were lit like bonfires, all the valleys were dark.

Which made it difficult to discern what they saw as they approached. From a distance it looked like a fort. High turrets and wide walls. But it was ill-defined, edgeless. Like a painting Flynn had once seen, where the artist was illustrating the permanence of a castle against the illusion of permanence itself. He painted a stronghold that morphed into the surrounding countryside, no defined sides, just gradual change. That's what they saw. A big structure, broad and bold, but bleeding into the shadows. Hutton slowed as they approached.

"It's a black castle," she said.

"It looks like an evil witch's lair," Beth said from the rear, craning between the front seats.

It did look evil. And black. Firelight burned around the perimeter. Flynn was reminded of Dante's circles. He would have thought this the gates of hell, the entrance to limbo. And the fires at the gates of hell were the last thing Flynn wanted to think about. He took a long slow breath that he tried to keep quiet, and he closed his eyes hard. Pressed Dante into another compartment to be dealt with later. Then he opened his eyes again. They got closer to the castle.

"It's not a castle," said Flynn. "They're tires."

The two women strained hard to see. He was right. What they were looking at was tires. Some stacked neatly one on top of another, high into the air like turrets. Between the turrets the tires were more of a pile, thrown in a huge mound as if discarded. Hutton slowed again, but kept moving. They motored past the property.

It looked like a farm. There was a long driveway leading to an old farmhouse on the right. Weather-beaten and in need of a paint. Further back on the left was a huge barn. It was newer than the house but not particularly new. The paintwork was windblown red. It was too large to be a milking shed, but the land behind it seemed too undulating for large farm machinery to be practical. In between the two buildings was an open space. Hard-packed dirt and gravel. The tire fort stood behind the open space, and to the right, so part of it was behind the house when they drove by the driveway.

Hutton kept driving. She left the farm behind and continued on up the mountain. A long, slow climb. She drove for ten minutes. Then she stopped. She didn't pull over. She just hit the brake in the middle of the road and left the headlights on.

"Thoughts?"

"I don't like it," said Beth.

"We need a closer look," Flynn said.

Hutton said, "What's with all those tires? There must be thousands."

"It's a lot of retreads."

"I don't like it," Beth repeated.

Flynn looked at Beth and then back at Hutton. "You should go. Both of you. Drop me off and drive away."

"Not happening," said Hutton.

"You said it was my call," said Beth. "I'm saying we call the police."

"What police? There are no police out here. County sheriff is probably hours away. And what do we say? You were abducted in Washington, DC, and taken to New York and now we think the perp is in a tire fort in your county? No, we haven't seen anybody, but can you come look?"

"I don't like it."

Flynn said nothing. He looked at Hutton.

Hutton said, "We can't see anything. We don't know who, we don't know how many. We don't have a lay of the land and we have no idea what we're walking into. I agree with Beth. I don't like it."

Flynn nodded. "Then let's retreat and regroup. Come back tomorrow. See what we can see."

Hutton did a slow, careful U-turn and headed back toward

Bent Pines. There had been no sign of a hotel in an hour, but perhaps the waitress at the diner could point them in the right direction.

THE TEAM LEADER watched the headlights pass. He was too far away and it was too dark to know if it was the same vehicle that had driven by twenty minutes before. But the spacing of the lights and throaty beat of the engine told him it was another big vehicle. An SUV or a pickup. A mountain country vehicle. The headlights didn't stop or even slow, but he watched the glow on the trees as the vehicle went below his position, and he kept his eye on it until the lights disappeared from view. There had been no other traffic all afternoon. There was really nowhere to go. The darkness had become absolute under the canopy of trees. Out above the farmhouse the stars burned in the sky and the fires burned on the ground. He took his MRE and ripped it open. He would eat while he could. Then he would sleep. He had the feeling the dawn would bring movement, and he wanted to be ready.

THE WAITRESS WATCHED them walk back into the diner. She offered a frown rather than a smile.

"Dessert," said Flynn.

"We're about to close."

He stepped to the counter and put a twenty on the laminate. "We won't stay long."

The waitress nodded. Business was slow in Bent Pines. You took the work when it came. She couldn't say no to a twenty.

"The cook's gone home."

"What can you do?"

"Coffee and pie."

"Three. Thanks."

Flynn sat at the counter. Hutton and Beth stepped forward from the door and joined him. The waitress made the coffee fresh. Not a big carafe, but enough. While it brewed she wandered into the kitchen and came back out with three plates. Apple pie and ice cream. Vanilla. Then she poured the coffee.

"Good pie," said Flynn. "What's the secret?"

"Mix Granny Smiths with Jonagolds," she said, leaning against the counter.

Flynn nodded. "I'll remember that." He took another bite. "You know of a motel around here anywhere?"

"Nothing like that around here."

"Not a B and B, or a guesthouse?"

The waitress shook her head. "No one stops around here. No one passes through. Except you."

"What's happening at the Dennison place?"

"I thought you was friends of theirs."

"No, ma'am. Never met them."

"You find it?"

"The farm? Yeah, we did. Lot of tires."

"Uh-huh."

"What do they do with them all?"

"You delivering?"

"No, ma'am." Flynn ate some more pie.

"What's your business there?"

"Don't have any yet."

"You mind if I make a suggestion?"

Flynn nodded.

"Go home. Don't come back."

"Is that the county's tourist motto?"

"Do what you want. But they're bad people."

Flynn watched her. It wasn't a line. She believed it. She touched her hair again, a nervous tic, perhaps. But her eyes were filled with fear.

"I know they are," Flynn said.

"Then you'll be finishing your pie and leaving."

"Perhaps some more coffee." He hadn't taken a sip of it, so he did.

The waitress turned away and grabbed a filter paper from a stack and opened up the machine. Then she saw the glass carafe underneath, still half-full. She grabbed it and warmed their coffees.

"You lived here long?" asked Flynn. It was a diner kind of question, on a slow night in an otherwise empty place.

"All my life."

"You know the Dennisons, then."

"Yeah, I know 'em."

"The parents died, I understand."

"You could say."

"Suspicious circumstances."

"Nothing suspicious about it." The waitress shifted her look along the counter. From Flynn, to Hutton, to Beth. She settled on Beth. Her pie and coffee remained untouched. Her arms folded, her face ashen.

"What happened?" the waitress asked. She kept her eyes on Beth.

Beth looked up, surprised to be spoken to. "Pardon?"

"I said what happened?"

"To whom?"

"To you."

The two women looked at each other. Unspoken communication. Not ESP, not exactly. But no transfer of actual words. Just the acknowledgment of common ground. Beth breathed in deeply.

"She abducted me."

The waitress offered no surprise. She just nodded, as if she had been told that a bad driver had just been in another car accident.

"You okay?" she said.

Beth nodded.

The waitress turned her eyes to Flynn. "Why would you bring her here?"

Flynn wiped his mouth with a napkin and placed his fork on the pie plate. He looked at the waitress. She wasn't old, but she was beaten down.

"To finish it."

CHAPTER TWENTY-SEVEN_

THE WAITRESS CLOSED UP SHOP. SHE THREW OUT THE dregs of coffee and wiped the counter one more time and turned out the lights. She locked the door and stepped down from the wooden patio onto the dirt parking lot.

"Follow me," she said.

Hutton drove up onto the main road. Not to the right. Straight away to the west, winding through the darkness for twenty minutes. Until the taillights turned off the road. Hutton followed, her headlights showing them a small cottage painted yellow. Empty flower boxes in the windows, a rocking chair on the porch.

The waitress unlocked the door and lit a lamp on a table and they followed her in. It was a small place, a living room with a large puffy sofa and a TV and a fireplace. A door to a kitchen, and another door to a bedroom and a third door to the outside rear. A cat sauntered in and jumped up onto the armrest of the sofa, looking to be petted or fed or both.

"Sorry it's not much, but it beats sleeping in a car."

"It's nice," said Hutton. "Very homey."

The waitress went into the bedroom and came out with a pile of sheets and blankets. She dropped them onto the sofa.

"The sofa sleeps two." She looked at Flynn. "And we can put some cushions on the floor."

"Thanks, you're very kind."

"Would you like something? Coffee, water. I think there's a beer in there somewhere."

"We're good, thank you," said Hutton.

"Well, I don't want to be rude, but it's been a long day."

"Not at all," said Hutton. "And thanks again."

The woman turned to the bedroom.

Beth said, "Excuse me, but why are you helping us?"

The waitress stopped. Her head bowed, and then she turned. She looked at Flynn.

"Because you seem capable. And I've got nothing to lose."

They stood in silence. The waitress looking at Flynn, everyone else looking at her.

Beth spoke softly. "What happened to you?"

The waitress let out a long breath, like she was exhaling a cigarette. Then she stepped toward Beth. She stopped and turned and put her hand to the side of her head. The nervous tic. Then she lifted her hair away and flopped it over the top, showing the side of her scalp.

A long jagged scar ran the length of her head. From the temple to past the ear, and around toward the back. They all looked at her without words. She held her hair up for a moment. Then she let it drop. She looked at Beth.

"She did that?" asked Beth.

The waitress nodded. "No reason. Just angry about something that nobody remembers. I was in a coma for a week."

"When did this happen?"

"Long time ago. High school. I was going to college, you know that? Penn State. My papa was as proud as punch."

"You didn't go?"

She shook her head slowly. "After it happened, I don't remember things so good. I forget stuff. I couldn't remember the classes, even if I wanted to."

"What about the police?"

"I met with a lawyer. Some prosecutor guy. He said because I didn't remember too good, the defense would say that I couldn't be sure who did it."

"She got away with it?"

The waitress shrugged. "They took her away. After she burned down her mama and papa's farm. I didn't get to leave, but at least she wasn't coming back. Until now."

The waitress looked at the carpet and ran her hand along the cat's back. "Well, g'night." She turned, walked to her room and closed the door. The three of them stood in silence for a moment, and then Hutton took the sheets and laid them over the sofa. Flynn kicked off his boots and took a cushion from a lounge chair and dropped it on the floor by the dormant fireplace. The women lay on the sofa with their heads at opposite ends, their feet woven around each other.

They lay in the darkness, listening to the sounds of each other's breathing, and the purring of the cat.

THE MORNING CAME ON AS SLOWLY as the evening had. There was light above in the sky long before the sun hit the north-south valley, lighting the hills to the west. Flynn woke first. He put on his boots and walked around the property. It was small and neat. Well-tended gardens and lawn. He came back inside to find the waitress in the kitchen, drinking water from the faucet.

"I need to get to work," she said. Another long day about to begin.

"We'll get out of your way."

"No rush. But . . ."

Flynn shook his head. "Not a word to anyone."

The waitress nodded. She put the glass in the sink and grabbed her keys and walked to the door.

"Will I see you again?" she asked.

"You got any pie left?"

She nodded again.

"Then definitely."

THEY WERE GONE within ten minutes. Flynn woke Hutton and Beth and they splashed water on their faces and got in the Yukon. Flynn drove. He headed back toward the diner. The lights were on and there were three vehicles in the lot. The waitress, the cook, and a customer. He turned left and headed up the mountain.

The tires looked less like a fort in the daylight. They looked like a graveyard for tires. He drove by again. The house looked older and the barn looked newer than they had in the twilight. There was more debris around the grounds. Oil drums, discarded farm implements, an old car up on cinderblocks.

Flynn drove on, watching the road and the mileage counter. He lost view of the farm in his mirrors and then looked for a spot. Slowed and turned off the road along the fence line of a property above the road. Noted the mileage. Close enough to a mile and a quarter. Two kilometers, give or take. He drove up across open ground. The wheels rose and fell on the rough terrain, and it jostled them about. Flynn kept on into a line of trees. The fence stopped but the trees seemed to mark some kind of property line. They were in an unnaturally straight line, as if planted by a land owner generations ago. He pictured the triangle in his head. The farm at one corner, at right angles to the road and to a point up the hill. He estimated the angle between the fence line and the road and drove the hypotenuse of the triangle.

Eventually he stopped the truck and stepped out. Walked to the trees and looked out across the valley below, and then came back and got in the truck and continued for another minute. Stopped again and looked through the trees and saw the farm below. Smoke was coming from the barn and the chimney in the house. Someone was home and they were having breakfast.

Flynn set up camp. He crept down the hill a short way and looked back up. Between the shadows and the pines and the foliage, the Yukon was invisible. He made his way back up and took Hedstrom's Leupold scope out of his daypack. He scanned the hill above. Trees and bushes. No roads, no homes. Beth and Hutton stood by the Yukon.

"I'm just going to take a quick look up the hill," Flynn said. He took off between the trees. The two women watched him disappear into the foliage. Beth had her arms wrapped tight around herself. Hutton could see her breath in the air.

"I'm getting back in the truck, it's cold out here," Hutton said.

Beth nodded and followed. They both quietly closed the doors. Hutton didn't start the engine, but it was still warmer in the vehicle. She turned in her seat to look back at Beth.

"So you live in San Francisco?" she asked.

"Marin County, actually. I work in San Francisco."

"How did you meet John?"

"In Lake Tahoe. I was up there skiing with friends. John was marching through."

"Marching through?"

"He likes to walk. A lot."

"I noticed. But in the mountains, in winter?"

"He was actually marching from Colorado to San Francisco. He said he wanted to see the Golden Gate."

"There are flights. Busses, even."

"I know. But he likes walking."

"And he stopped in Tahoe."

Beth nodded. "At Northstar. He was sitting by one of those little fire pits they have around the village. Only the one he was sitting at wasn't working. There was no fire in the pit. A girlfriend of mine liked the look of him, so we sat at the same pit. It was freezing, but my friend kept trying to include him in the conversation. She started talking about drinks she liked and didn't like, and she asked John what he thought, and he said he only drank at weddings and funerals. My friend asked what he drank at weddings and he said champagne. Then she asked about funerals, and John and I answered at the same time."

"What did you say?"

"Bourbon."

Hutton nodded. She had seen the bourbon, but not at a funeral.

"And you're sure he only drinks that at funerals?"

"I don't know. I've never seen him drink alcohol at all," said Beth.

"I saw him with bourbon once, in Iraq. And again in New York."

"Drinking?"

"He seemed to prefer doing it in private."

Beth nodded. "Oh, that. He locked himself away, right?"

"In Iraq. In New York he didn't get the chance to do anything with it."

"He doesn't drink it," said Beth. "He opens it and lets the smell fill the room and then he sort of meditates on it."

"Meditates? John?"

"Yes, I know. But his father drank bourbon, he told me. I think it reminds him of his dad."

"He's a complicated guy."

"Yeah. Complicated is the word."

***

FLYNN RETURNED HAVING VENTURED partway up the hill. There were signs of tracks made through the trees over the years, but nothing that he noted as recent. He preferred to take a position higher on the hill, but the rocky terrain up higher obstructed the view of the farm. He clambered down to their original position, got comfortable against a tree, and put the scope to his eye in the direction of the farm. Everything was the same. The house, the barn, the tires. The open turnaround area. Black smoke billowed from the barn's chimney. Gray smoke from the house. All else was still. The grass in the field beyond glistened with dew.

He settled in to wait. Hutton came and sat next to him. They took turns looking through the scope. It flattened the view but gave the colors greater depth than the wan sun. Without a monopod attached, the scope was harder to keep still and there were tiny vibrations in the image, like the whole farm was on some kind of agitator.

"Someone should go in," Hutton said.

"Someone will."

"I mean for a closer look. Get the lay of the land."

"Too risky. When I go in, I'll go in hard."

"What's in the barn?"

"No idea."

"It's a good size barn. Could be anything."

"Damn right."

"So I should go down and take a look."

Flynn dropped the scope from his eye and looked at Hutton. The shadows of the pines were softening her face, blending the angles the way a good portrait photographer would.

"You need to stay here," she said. "For Beth, and for me. To keep an eye on me." She smiled.

"How will you do it?"

"Down the hill, further to the south. Cross the road out of view of the farm and come in behind the barn."

"The barn is what we need to know. Remember, it's not a voyage to make a more complete map of the world."

"Got it."

"In, out."

"Got it."

Flynn looked back down at the farm. "I wish we had comms."

"Radios would have been a good idea. I'm used to New York. Too dependent on cell coverage."

Flynn nodded, unsure.

Hutton touched his shoulder. "It'll be fine. And we don't want to go down there later and discover an arsenal the hard way."

Hutton left her courier bag. She took her cell phone for pictures. She took her flashlight for the shadows and in case a late exfiltration was required. And she took her Glock for everything else.

She stayed behind the high side of the tree line and walked away south. Flynn kept the scope scanning from the southern end of the road to the barn. Looking for her in the foliage, looking for her on the farm. He didn't see her. He took that as a good sign. She wasn't military trained and her patch was an urban environment, but she knew her stuff.

He watched the farm for any movement. Saw nothing in the

first hour. He figured two hours to be enough to get down, take a look and get back. He saw no movement in the second hour. Beth came and sat by him. He saw no movement in the third hour.

It was the fourth hour that he saw something. A person walked out of the farmhouse. A woman. Large-framed and big-boned. Carrying more weight than a doctor would recommend, for sure, but it was more than that. She was just built large. Like an outhouse, was the phrase that came to mind. She had short hair the color of dust and wore a checked flannel shirt. Flynn handed the scope to Beth. Told her to focus in on the house. She did.

She dropped the scope.

Flynn picked it out of the pine needles. "Did you see?"

He didn't need to ask. The color had drained from her face. She nodded, very slowly.

"That's her. The woman who took you?"

Another nod, laborious, like she had whiplash.

Flynn trained the scope back on the porch of the house. Cameron Dennison stepped down onto the dirt driveway and walked across the open area toward the barn. There was a traditional-style large door for farm machinery to get in and out. Within the large door was a smaller door. A human-sized door. Cameron stopped before it, pulled it open and then stepped inside. Flynn kept his scope on the barn. He didn't see anyone come out. He saw no more movement in the fifth hour. The woman didn't come out of the barn. No one came out of the house.

Hutton didn't return.

CHAPTER TWENTY-EIGHT_

THERE WERE ALWAYS PROS AND CONS. ON THE PRO SIDE, the sun was well through its arc, and the shadows in the valley were long. He would be close to impossible to spot. He figured he could be there and back in thirty minutes if he pushed it. An hour if he didn't. The rural environment was his domain. He had trained in it, long and hard. He also had weapons. His Glock, plus the MP5K he had acquired at the drug den. He had a good lay of the land and had spent hours studying the farm.

On the con side was Beth. He wished she wasn't there. He wished she was safe at home in San Rafael, doing lawyer things and going to wine tastings and the farmer's market. He wished, in a roundabout way, that he'd never gone to Tahoe. That he'd never decided to march to the Bay Area. That he hadn't stopped off for a look at the snow. That he hadn't been by the dormant fire pit or offered a smile and been enchanted by her smarts and her wit. He couldn't quite take it all the way and wish he'd never met her. But that was just selfishness and ego. Right now there was no doubt she would have been better off. She wouldn't have been abducted. She wouldn't be sitting in the

Appalachian Mountains watching a farm. And he wouldn't have to leave her alone.

"I need to go down and take a look," he said. He was ready for the *let's call the police* retort. It would be a reasonable response. It was how reasonable people thought.

"I know," she said. "She should be back."

"The keys are in the truck. If I am not back in an hour, get in it and go. Don't stop until you get to a city. Then and only then, tell someone."

She nodded and put her hand on his cheek.

"Come back."

"I intend to."

He left her with the scope. He took both guns. Handing a firearm to an untrained civilian might work in the movies, but more often than not ended in disaster in the real world. He moved south along the trees as Hutton had. Counted five hundred steps and then cut right and down the hill. There was plenty of tree cover, but he took it steady. The long shadows served to mask his movement. The only sound was the underbrush beneath his feet, but pine needles were as close to silent as he could get. He made it to the road in twenty minutes. Five behind his mental schedule. Waited, listening. Then he broke cover and marched across.

The trees around the farm were similar but different. Pines, but a variety distinct from those on the hillside. There were broad oaks near the barn. He reached the edge of the cleared section around the farm. The house was at twelve o'clock to him, the barn at nine. The tire fort was in between. The whole place smelled of rubber. Like a rancid potpourri. Fresh rubber and old rubber. And burning rubber.

Between him and the house was an old vehicle. It was rusted and still intact, but it wasn't going anywhere. It sat mounted on cinderblocks, its tires removed as if sucked off by the gravity of the nearby tire fort. He looked around and listened hard. Nothing but breeze rustling through trees. He moved into the open.

First stop was the old vehicle. It was a sedan of some kind. The badging was long gone, but the boxy shape suggested a 1980s vintage. He slipped to the rear of the vehicle, keeping the car between himself and the house. He slipped the MP5K underneath and pushed it against the cinderblock. Two guns was one too many for a search of the barn. He liked to keep one hand free. And although he didn't expect a full firefight, it was good to have a fallback position. Plans go to hell as soon as boots hit the ground.

He moved along the car and then stayed crouched as he stepped briskly across the yard to the barn. He slipped around the far side of it, the side he hadn't seen from his position up the hill. There was nothing to see. There were no windows, no doors. He moved back to the front end of the structure. The walls were solid, but not solid enough to stop a rifle round from within.

The latch mechanism on the door was a basic bolt-action thing. Pull out to open, push in to close. Easy to attach a padlock. There was no padlock. Flynn dropped to his knees and worked the latch open, inch by inch. He took it slow and kept the pressure on the door as the slide came free. The natural tendency of the door was to fall open. He kept his hand against it and slid down until he was lying on the ground, hand on the bottom of the door. The door didn't go all the way to the ground. It was framed inside the larger barn door, such that there was six inches of the larger door between the ground and the access door. Flynn got as low as he could and readied his weapon. Then he eased his hand off the access door.

It fell open just a crack. Not enough to see in. So he used his shoulder to ease the door open wider. Four inches, then six.

Enough space to stick his head in. Which was always the dangerous part. Cameron Dennison could be sitting in a lawn chair in the barn, waiting to pop him right between the eyes. But his eyes weren't where eyes were supposed to be. It was natural to focus on an area about four feet from the ground. Most people looked for the head, but most people looked low. Which nine times out of ten was okay, because looking low meant they were focused on the largest possible target. The torso. But Flynn's torso was in the dirt. He stuck his head in at floor level.

And recoiled at the smell.

The barn smelled like recently burned rubber. The stench clung to the settled air in the barn. The space was vast. A concrete foundation. Enough room for two or three large tractors, the kind that harvest wheat. Flynn wasn't sure of the terminology. Reapers? Combines? But there were no tractors. There was just a large expanse of dirty concrete floor up the center of the barn. There were fluorescent tubes strung from the rafters lighting the space. Along the right side of the barn were machines. Heavy solid things. On the left side was a small forklift truck, and pallets of black stuff wrapped in plastic. He kept his Glock trained in the barn and pressed himself up, took a deep breath of outside air and stepped inside.

He moved right, against the row of machines, his weapon trained as he swept the space. The machines he passed were both familiar and unfamiliar at the same time. It looked like the motor pool on an army barracks. He had seen similar things, and could guess at others. He had never owned a personal vehicle. His parents had owned cars, and the Legion had had vehicles of all types and sizes. But he had never owned a car himself. He had never maintained one. Never had to tune an engine or rotate the tires. But he had seen such things happen. The machines seemed designed to hold tires upright and spin them. One machine had an abrasive buffer on it. Another was attached to a computer that he had seen a *soldat* in the French army operate. It was meant to balance tires, whatever that meant.

He crossed the floor to the other side. The pallets were stacked high with thin strips of rubber about four inches wide. He followed the pallets to the far end of the barn and then crossed back to the other side. There he found two machines that looked like they were designed to make giant donuts. One was much larger than the other. They were curved like a donut, and when he looked inside, he saw there were bumps on the inside of the shell. The machines were molds. For affixing new treads to old tires. There was a whole process to it. Taking the old rubber off, abrading it so the new rubber would stick, and then heating the rubber and molding it. That was where the smell was coming from. There wasn't sufficient air flow to take it away.

He'd had his fill of the smell. He glanced around the barn, a full three-sixty. Lots of machines, lots of rubber. No Hutton. But there was another door.

It was another access door at the opposite end from the one Flynn had entered through. He checked it over. Unlike the first door, this one wasn't built into a larger barn door. This one was built into the wall. But it wasn't obvious. There was no trim, no jamb. It was as if a rectangular section of the wall had been cut out and then fixed back in place by cheap hinges and some wire. As if someone wanted to hide the door but hadn't done a very good job of it.

There was a wire attached to the door that was clipped to a loop fixed to the wall. Flynn lifted the wire out of the loop with his finger. Held his Glock ready and pulled the door open a foot. Then, leading with his weapon, he stepped out.

He found himself back outside, on the far side of a barn. Unseen from where he had watched with the scope, where

Beth sat waiting for him. That thought gave him a new sense of urgency. Thirty-five minutes down. He let the door fall closed behind him. Large pines and oaks towered over him to his left. To the right was the back end of the tire fort. He could smell the rubber from fifty feet. He moved to the corner of the barn and looked around the open gravel area and saw nothing new. Just the same stuff from the other side. The tires, the farmhouse, the driveway, the car on cinderblocks. He pressed his back against the rear wall of the barn and looked out across the field behind the farm. It was a grassy field, maybe a half mile deep. It stopped at the base of the far side of the valley, where the pines took over and reached up the mountain. Flynn glanced left, past the door he had just come through.

There was another door. This one was a trapdoor, built into a concrete collar in the ground. It was the kind of thing that led to a basement if it was in Kansas. A tornado shelter. Double doors that opened out, so they couldn't be blown in. Flynn wasn't aware of any tornados in the Pennsylvania Appalachians. The door appeared to lead under the barn, but the barn was built on a concrete slab. There was no basement down there.

Flynn knew what it was. The barn wasn't original. The original had burned to the ground. He recalled that from Cameron Dennison's prison record. She had burned it down with her parents inside. But the new one had been built in its place. Much more recently. The storm shelter doors were heavy steel items. They wouldn't have burned. They were original too. From when the barn hid a still. The hatch was an escape route, from back in the bootlegging days. Flynn had read all the stories. There were lots of them, about distilled liquor cooked up in the mountains. Most of the tales related the stories of the southern Appalachians. In Georgia and Tennessee. But there was plenty of anti-Prohibition activity in Pennsylvania as well. He pulled at the door. It was heavy. It required two hands, and even then it didn't budge.

Flynn left the trapdoor and returned to the corner of the barn. Still no movement. He decided to chance a look in the farmhouse. He ran across to the tire fort. At the front of the pile stood two towers of semitruck tires. Big and wide and heavy items. Stacked ten high. One tower was on his corner, on the barn side, the other near the house. He moved around the back. The pile of tires was high, about the same height as the farmhouse. The lower tires seemed to be bigger, and the higher ones were smaller, like regular car tires.

He clambered around the mound and saw the far side of the house. There was a wide porch that ran the full length of the building. An old rocking chair sat in the shade, overlooking the open fields of grass. A bucolic view. Flynn left the shelter of the tires and stepped past some fifty-five-gallon oil drums against the house. He made it to the side of the house and turned back toward the rear porch. There were no stairs, no access to the field. It was a porch designed for sitting back and relaxing after a hard day's work. He climbed up over the railing of gray weathered wood and onto the porch.

It wasn't in great shape. The boards were warped and splintered. They creaked with every step. Better than a Doberman for guard duty. And less upkeep. He moved as quietly as he could, sticking close to the wall of the house, where the boards were less likely to creak. He took long, slow strides, keeping the number of steps on the creaking boards to a minimum.

There was one door leading from the porch into the house. Flynn tried the lever and found it open. He slipped inside. The daylight was fading fast and the house was dark. He was in a living space. There was a ratty sofa covered in a burgundy blanket. A fireplace with cold ash in it. Behind the sofa was a round pine table with four matching chairs. There were three interior doors off the room. He moved to the first and spun through it, Glock held high. It was a small kitchen. An old oven, an ancient fridge. The cabinets and countertop were more pine.

He left the kitchen and tried the next room. It was a bedroom. Two small beds, like prison cots, and a tallboy dresser. The beds were made up with blankets only. He touched the end of the first bed and saw a puff of dust rise in the air. Then he moved out.

The third room was another bedroom. This one looked lived in. A double bed with a wrought-iron headboard. A side table, pine. And an armoire. It was a massive unit, polished rosewood. It bore ornate woodwork inlaid into the doors. It was an impressive piece from a time long gone. Flynn suspected he might have survived a nuclear blast inside it. There was a small iron key hanging in the lock of the one of the double doors. He opened the door and found drawers. Plain women's underwear. Some T-shirts. He closed the door and opened the other side. There was hanging space. Some dresses that didn't match the underwear. Fancy items, in a black-and-white movie kind of way. Frills and lace. And way too small for whoever wore the underwear. There was an old canvas greatcoat and a man's suit. Black with a layer of dust across the shoulders.

Flynn closed the door and felt up on top of the wardrobe. People often put certain things on top of such pieces in their bedrooms. He found nothing. Then he had a thought and he opened the second door of the armoire again. He pushed apart the greatcoat and the suit and reached for the back of the armoire. Thoughts of lions and witches as he did. He fumbled around, running his hand across the back of the cabinet.

His hand stopped around the twin barrels of a shotgun. He pulled it out through the hanging clothes. It was a fine weapon. A Winchester Model 21 with side-by-side barrels. The wood was old and pockmarked but shiny. Flynn cracked the weapon open. It was a breech-loading design, one 12-gauge shell in each of the barrels. The barrels were oiled and clean, but not loaded. It was a working gun, a farm gun. It had outlasted its original owner and was in fine condition. He put the shotgun on the bed and rifled through the drawers in the other side of the armoire. Underneath cotton bras and underpants made from some kind of stretching material, he found the box of shells. Opened it and took four for his pockets and then slipped two into the gun. Then he returned the box to the drawer and replaced the underwear.

Flynn left the house via the rear patio and jumped down onto the hard dirt. He moved along the side of the house to where one of the large turrets stood sentry over the house. Beside the turret sat some oil drums. One was capped, and a tap of his knuckle revealed it to be full. Another two had their tops removed and were charred black on the inside. He crouched behind the capped drum and laid the shotgun down in the long grass that grew at the base of the house. Then he walked back behind the pile of tires. The sun dropped below the nearby peaks, and although the sky above was a light gray the valley descended into darkness. Flynn skirted around the tires and looked back down the driveway. Still nothing. He hadn't found Hutton, and he didn't feel great about that, but he wanted to get back to Beth before his hour was up and she drove away.

He skipped across the open space to the rear of the barn, and then around the far side of the barn, and disappeared into the pines. He had decided that Beth should leave. That was certain. But he didn't want her getting panicked and stopping at the first police station she hit, before he had time to do what needed doing. So he counted five hundred paces through the pines and then turned left back to the road. It was close on full dark down at road level, and he jogged across and clambered up the hillside. He hit the mark for the tree line and turned back toward their position. The light was slightly better high on the hill, but only by degrees. The sunlight was drifting up the mountain leaving a blanket of night behind it.

Flynn saw the Yukon from a hundred yards out. He quickened his pace and tucked the Glock into the back of his trousers. The lights were off, so the cab was dark. He was twenty yards from the truck before he was sure that no one was sitting in the front. He stopped by the driver's-side window to confirm. Then he yanked the rear door open. No one in the backseat, no one in the cargo area. Flynn spun around in place. It was too dark to see very far, and too dark to bother checking footprints. And Hutton had the flashlight.

"Beth," he whispered to the night.

He waited for a reply but heard nothing but breeze in the pines and the chirping of insects.

"Beth," he said again.

But there was no reply.

CHAPTER TWENTY-NINE_

BETH WAS GONE. NOT TO PHILADELPHIA OR WASHINGTON or New York. Not to the local cops. The keys were in the Yukon, and Hutton's courier bag was in the back. Flynn's daypack was right beside it. Hedstrom's scope was gone. Flynn stood still and let his breathing settle so he could hear the sounds of the night. Most night noise outside of cities is made by insects. There are a million varieties and their combination of sounds make each location unique. Flynn suspected there was probably an entomologist at a university somewhere that could tell him where in the world he was just by listening to a recording of the bug noise.

But bug noise was most of what Flynn heard. There was some rustling in the trees—a combination of breeze and squirrels—and rustling on the ground—rodents and cottontails. But there was no human noise. No voices, no crunching of underbrush by human tread. He couldn't even hear his own breath.

What caught his attention was the light. He saw the first flicker in the corner of his eye, and moved to the tree line to observe. The source of the light was the farm. Someone was lighting fires in the empty fifty-five-gallon oil drums that were scattered around the property. First one, then two, then three. Like a moat of flame around the perimeter of the tire fort. Without the scope, he couldn't see any people, but it was not the work of a timer, like in a suburban house. Someone was lighting the fires. Someone was drawing attention to the farm.

His attention.

Then he noticed the spread of the flames. They were contained within the drums, each like an individual spotlight, but the drums being lit were spread from a central point. Starting at the front of the tire fort, close to the center of the driveway, then moving to drums left and right. Simultaneously. That meant at least two people were lighting fires. He figured neither Beth nor Hutton would be helping. At least not without a gun to their heads. And that meant at least two enemies.

Flynn pulled back and dropped to the ground, his back against a tree. He felt the cold sweat on the back of his neck, and his breathing became shallow and rapid. It was, various psychologists had told him, a panic attack. He had searched long and hard, read hundreds of textbooks and papers on the subject, but had not found a solution. Somehow the reaction had become ingrained in him. Just as he had been raised to serve, just as he found it second nature to run toward the battle not from it, so he had been programmed to fear the flames. While the basis for his fear was rational—flames burned, that was a fact—even when they were under complete control, in a fireplace or a pit at a camp, he could not overcome the notion that the control was illusory. He had been happy to move into Beth's townhouse back when she had suggested it, not because it was modern and convenient and cozy, but because it had no fireplace and an electric stovetop.

Flynn fought himself. This was not the time and not the place. He had always been adept at suppressing emotion and fear, compartmentalizing it while the job needed to be done and dealing with it later. He would take a bottle of bourbon and his thoughts into a private place and let the smell of the liquor pervade his senses. It had been his father's drink, and the scent of it brought forth his father's memory and that of his family, and of their deaths. And then the flames would come and he would see the hotel in Abu Dhabi, smoke and flames. And then he would see another house, the family who had slept while their house burned as Flynn lay passed out in the barn, empty bourbon bottle by his side. He had not been responsible for any of those deaths, but he had not saved any of them either. The images came and went and so did all the other demons. And in the morning Flynn would pour the bottle of bourbon down the sink, his soul cleansed in a temporary kind of way, the flames defeated at least for that moment.

But he didn't have time for that now. The flames glowed from the farmhouse where both Beth and Hutton were sure to be. Flynn closed his eyes and bit down hard on his lip until he drew blood. The acrid taste on his tongue, anything to distract his mind. He tried to slow his breathing, but his heart rate refused to yield. The panic cared nothing for his predicament. Then he thought about Beth, brought into a world that she had no understanding of. He had tried to find a new place, a family away from all that he had known before, and for a fleeting time he had believed he had outrun his past. But he had been wrong. A man cannot outrun his past. Wherever he goes, his past goes with him.

Flynn opened his eyes. There was no fighting the panic. There was no suppressing the flames. There was only forward momentum, taking head-on that which would defeat him. The action that should create real panic—going into battle—never had. He had been afraid during battle, but that wasn't the same thing. Not by a long shot. So he stood. He licked the blood from his split lip. And he turned toward the flames.

There was now a perimeter of light right around the tires. It was a basic military strategy. Build a stronghold with a wide perimeter. Easy to defend. Hard to attack. And it made your enemies come to you. It was a tactic used since prehistory. It was the basic idea of castles and fortresses. Flynn figured the enemies would be somewhere within the tire fort, waiting.

There was really only one major drawback to the tactic. Supply. Even a well-provisioned stronghold couldn't last forever without supplies from outside. Eventually food or ammunition or raw materials ran out. Or often just patience. It took a lot of willpower to sit tight under sustained attack. Sometimes the willpower was there. Flynn had studied the siege of Candia in Crete. Those guys had held out for twenty-one years. But Flynn figured the tire fort was somewhat less resilient. It was designed for confrontation, not siege. He preferred to sneak up in the darkness and take them out, but he had neither the weapons nor the advantage for such an approach. Hutton was down there. Beth too. He'd spent a lot of time hunting terrorists. He knew the tactics. And one of their preferred tactics was to use human shields.

Unlike the shields, Flynn was Teflon. The B-team had abducted Beth because they weren't capable of kidnapping him and they couldn't kill him. The A-team had arrived at the house in Katonah with plenty of firepower, but none of it had been aimed at him. He thought about his approach. They were drawing him out, but he needed to do some drawing out of his own. Sneaking around in the dark wouldn't work. He had learned playing football at school in Belgium that sometimes it paid to use the flanks and cross the ball into the box. And sometimes it paid to just run straight at the defense.

It was time to run straight.

He didn't drive fast. There was no stealth involved. No surprise. They would see the headlights well ahead of time, and he couldn't drive the dark road without them. Even if he could, they would hear the throaty roar of the Yukon's eight cylinders before they ever saw the headlights. So he took his time. He headed back down across the hill, following the fence line. Then he turned a hard left and moved onto the smoother road. He rounded the bend and saw the firelight ahead. It looked like a campground. But there were no campers gazing lazily into the flames, marshmallows on sticks, camp songs sung to the stars.

Flynn pulled into the driveway and felt the crunch of the gravel under the tires. His headlights swept across the scene. What he saw was good and bad. Good, because he saw both Beth and Hutton, and they were both alive. Bad, because they had each been tied to one of the turrets of truck tires. Beth was fixed to a turret on the left of his field of view, on the side of the tire fort that opened up to the gravel turnaround area and the large barn. Hutton was similarly fixed but on the opposite side, close to the house. Flynn sat in the Yukon and considered his moves. There were many. Too many. He would need to narrow his options.

He stopped with the Yukon blocking the driveway and turned the engine off. Left the headlights illuminating the two women and the tire fort between them. Opened the door and stepped onto the gravel and closed the door, nice and easy. His Glock was held down by his left thigh, away from the light.

He stepped forward. Flynn's body was split in half by the sharp light coming from the Yukon. His left side in darkness, his right in full light. He felt the warmth of the fires. The flicker of the flames was lost in the arc of bright headlights. Beth's head was twisted away as if the headlights were flames themselves. She slowly turned back around. And Flynn saw the message on her face.

Terror. She was white with fear. Her hands were fixed behind her. Lengths of oily rubber had been wound around her and the large truck tires. He could see tears on her cheeks, but she made no sound. Hutton was tied to her turret of tires in a similar fashion. But her face was different. It was tight across her jaw. Angry. Perhaps angry at herself for getting caught, or angry at Flynn for involving her at all. Unlike Beth, Hutton had tape across her mouth. Clearly she had something to say, and her captors didn't care to hear it. Her eyes connected with Flynn's. She blinked. Hard. Twice. Then she waited a few seconds and repeated the move. Two blinks. *Two enemies.*

One of the enemies appeared. Flynn recognized the scrappy hair and puffy features of Cameron Dennison. Her mouth was fixed somewhere between a snarl and a smirk. She stepped out of the shadows behind Hutton. Flynn pulled his Glock high and aimed it at Cameron's head. The smirk stayed plastered on her face.

"You should drop that," she said. Her speech was slow and deliberate.

"You think?"

She nodded and edged backward. The fire from the drum near her lit the side of Hutton's face. And showed the handgun aimed at her temple. Hutton flinched and Cameron scowled but didn't move the gun. Hutton hadn't been playing nice. It was impossible to say for sure, but it was probably her own weapon pointed at her head. She wouldn't like that. Bureau types had a thing about losing their weapons.

Flynn didn't alter his aim. "You shoot her, you're dead."

"You think?" she said, mocking him. "You're pretty far away. You might miss. I won't."

It was a reasonable point. He was about twenty yards from Cameron. A yard was close enough to a meter to count, and he shot ninety-five percent at twenty-five meters. But that was without distraction or pressure, at tin cans in the desert or targets at the range. And now was not the time to discover the five percent. He didn't fire. But he didn't drop his sights either.

"Nice operation you got going here," he said. "Almost looks law-abiding."

"You think?"

"Not like you at all."

"You got a big mouth."

"Let me guess, you put less tread on to make your rubber go further."

"Some folks is cheap."

"And what about these ones?" He nodded at the tire fort. "They're past even being retread."

She smiled. It wasn't an endearing grin. "The dealers charge customers a recycling fee. But some don't go to the expense of using the official dump."

"What do you do with them?"

The smile grew. She nodded at the drum in front of her. One half of her face was lit by the headlights. The other side glowed in the firelight.

"I burn 'em."

"So not too law-abiding."

"You need to drop your gun. I ain't gonna ask you again."

Flynn looked at Hutton. She closed her eyes slowly, then opened them. No, she was saying. Don't give up your weapon. But she didn't know. Didn't know about the plan B, or the plan C. She didn't know that in being drawn out himself, he was actually drawing someone else out. And he was Teflon. They weren't going to shoot.

So he dropped his aim. Lowered his Glock to his side.

"Toss it down," Cameron spat.

He threw the Glock onto the gravel, in the glow of the headlights. About six feet away. Then objective one was met.

Cameron removed the gun from Hutton's ear and pointed it at Flynn.

"Now what?" Flynn asked.

A voice came from the darkness. Slurred, like a drunken sailor.

"Now you pay."

Flynn watched the second person appear from behind Beth. Just as he planned. But the person he saw wasn't what he expected.

He was emaciated, like a prisoner of war. The jacket and trousers he wore hung from his frame. His face was pink, like fresh skin after a scab had fallen off. New but stretched tight across his cheekbones. But the skin ran in contours across his face like a topographical map of the very mountain ranges they were standing in. It was as if a million years of rainfall had run across him, wearing his face down like a riverbed. He had one eyebrow, and no eyelashes. He had no hair on the left half of his skull. Just a wide arc of pink skin. And Flynn saw why his speech was slurred. His lips were fused tight across his mouth, hard like the skin on the sole of a foot. It didn't flex and form the words the right way. Like talking after getting punched in the mouth. Flynn looked hard at the pink man.

"Take a good look," the man said. He nodded, fast like a spasm, "Even the bogeyman can't hide forever."

And Flynn clenched his jaw. He knew who it was, and who it was told him what it meant. It meant that he had drawn out the wrong guy.

It was Ox Dennison.

CHAPTER THIRTY

Ox nodded again, as if he had trouble with the motor control of his head. Despite that, he pressed a handgun into Beth's chest steadily enough.

"I dreamed a this day. For four years. E'ry night I dreamed a this." He nodded more.

"They told me you were dead," said Flynn.

"Told me the same a you." He laughed, but it sounded like he was choking.

Flynn said, "You shot me."

"And you me."

"And then you tried to burn the evidence. Doesn't look like that went very well."

"Shut it!" he yelled. Then he coughed like a cat spitting a fur ball. Except without lips, he couldn't spit a yard. He gathered himself and looked up at Flynn.

"Six years. They made me stay in that hellhole for six years. The army packed up and left. And I was still there. Looking for traces of you."

"At least you got the medical attention you needed. They did a good job."

Ox screamed, but the sound only made it halfway out. He shook his head savagely.

"Do you know what Iraq was like after the US pulled out?" He shook his head. "But we found you." He choked on another laugh. "And now it's my turn."

"What do you want, Ox? You want to hurt me?" Flynn spread his arms. "Go ahead. Hurt me."

Ox wobbled his head, up and down, side to side.

"Oh, I wanna hurt you. But I can't kill you. I kill you, they kill me."

"Who is *they*?"

Ox said nothing.

"Who are they, Ox? Where are they?"

Ox nodded again. "They are the air you breathe. They are e'rywhere, but they are invisible."

"You said it. Even the bogeyman can't hide forever, Ox."

Dennison grunted. "They can. And they want what you got. So I can't kill you." He nodded as if trying to force his lips to bend into a smile. He failed and gave up. "But I can hurt you."

He held up his gun again and pressed it into Beth's breast. She tried to squirm beneath her bonds, but it was effort without reward.

"I hear you fell in love." Ox hacked another cough. "Bad move." He lifted the gun up to Beth's ear. At twenty-five meters, the old Ox would have been about a fifty-fifty proposition to hit a human-sized target with a handgun. But even the new disfigured Ox was close to a certainty with the muzzle held to Beth's head.

Beth turned away. Closed her eyes. It was reflex, but it didn't help. Mortality rates for gunshots to the side of the head were ninety-eight percent. Mainly because side-to-side shots saw the bullet travel through both hemispheres of the brain. That was usually a terminal event. Front to back had the best chance of survival, about five percent, because there was a chance the bullet would only hit one hemisphere, and maybe only the frontal lobe. Quality of life was rarely very high regardless. But to Flynn's knowledge there were zero documented cases of a human being shot in the brain stem and surviving. The brain stem was made of three sections, starting with the medulla oblongata at the base of the skull, which became the spinal cord at the top of the spine. Right where the muzzle of Ox's gun ended up.

Flynn's world moved slow. Like his feet and his muscles and his brain were stuck in cement. He turned and pushed off and dove into the darkness as if it was him that was being shot. One moment he was visible and then next he was gone, into the darkness. He flew above the ground for what felt like forever. Waiting for the sound of the gunshot. Then he hit the gravel hard. His momentum slid him forward like a runner trying to steal second base. Gravel flew into the undercarriage of the old sedan that sat on cinderblocks. His slide was stopped by his shoulder crashing into the rear block. He reached out in the darkness. Still waiting for the sound. Reaching, grabbing at loose gravel. For the Heckler and Koch MP5K he had left there. Plan B.

But plan B failed. He pulled himself half under the car and spread his reach and dug at the ground. But there was no gun to be found. He stopped moving and tried to control his breathing. He could hear the sound of a cat choking.

He slowly pushed himself out from under the car and got up on his knees. The sound was Ox Dennison. He was doubled over. Maybe he was laughing. It sounded painful. Flynn cast his eyes on Beth. Still tied to the tires but alive. Ox collected himself and pushed on his thighs to stand as if his muscles weren't strong enough to lift his birdlike frame. He stepped back to the turret of tires and reached down beside Beth.

"Looking for this?" he said, holding up the MP5K. He nodded, like a version of a satisfied smile. "I saw it all."

"How?" asked Flynn, but he already knew the answer.

"Seven generations Dennisons been in this county."

"The storm shelter, behind the barn," said Flynn, standing up. "It's not the entrance, it's the exit."

"You is a smart boy. Just not smart enough."

"Your family had a still, right? But not in the barn. In the woods."

Dennison nodded. He pointed his gun out into the darkness over Flynn's shoulder. "You had a gone another hundred feet up the hill, you might a seen it. Now, step into the light where I can see you."

Flynn thought it through as he moved nice and slow. An old still up on the hillside, a tunnel dug over generations. That explained how they had gotten behind him and taken Beth. It explained how Ox knew about the MP5K he had hidden. Flynn stepped into the arc of the headlights, as he had been before. Half in, half out.

"Now, where were we?" Ox took a step toward Beth and lifted his gun to her head. This time he pushed it hard into the side. Improving her chances by two percent.

Flynn glanced out of the side of his eye at Hutton. She was looking at Beth. Frowning, Not from fear. She was tied up, a gun to her own head, and still she was working the problem of how to save Beth. Bureau types. They didn't give up. Flynn looked at Cameron. She was looking at her brother, face impassive, like he was watching football on the TV and she had become bored of it.

Then Flynn looked into the darkness beside her. At the capped oil drum beside the farmhouse. Plan C. He tensed, ready for the starter's gun in his head. He calculated the distance. Twenty yards. Close to twenty meters but not close enough. 18.2 meters. And from a standing start to a full sprint, that was about fourteen strides. With the leap, he calculated twelve. About three seconds. He readied himself. Then he saw Cameron turn.

She eased the gun away from Hutton's ear and looked away. Away from the imminent action, away from her brother. Past the farmhouse. Up the hill and into the darkness. Into the ether. And Flynn stood down. Let his body relax. He focused his attention on Ox. On Beth.

"Any last words, lover boy?"

Flynn said, "You're a dead man."

Ox nodded his head in his facsimile of a smile and turned his focus to Beth.

And his head exploded in a mess of brain matter and pink skin.

CHAPTER THIRTY-ONE

A ROUND FROM A SNIPER RIFLE CAN TRAVEL AT SPEEDS more than twice the speed of sound. The supersonic rounds give off a sound of their own, the snap of the sonic boom, but the round can even outpace that. Unless the distance is great, however, in practical terms, the two events are almost simultaneous to an observer close to the target. Or the target itself.

So Ox Dennison might have heard the sound of the sniper rifle, but his brain would not have had time to process the sound before his head exploded into an atomic mist.

The force of the round drove his body backward, and the last part of him to hit the gravel was his feet. The round landed half a mile into the field beyond. Beth closed her eyes, which was good, as she might have caught any number of bloodborne diseases from Dennison as his plasma splattered across her face. It was then she started making noise. Frantic screaming filled the air. Cameron Dennison turned to see her brother hit the ground and then spun back toward the direction from which the shot had come. Hutton looked amazed at the result of intense kinetic energy exerted on a human head. Flynn stood still. He thought about making a play for his Glock, which lay in the gravel in front of him, but he wasn't sure what the field of view was for the sniper, or whether his Teflon status extended that far.

He fought the desire to run to Beth. To console her, to wipe her eyes and tell her it would all be okay. Right then he was consoled by the fact that she was still alive. And if they were still alive that minute, they could be for the next. He stood at a casual attention, weight distributed evenly across both feet, ready to go one way or the other. But he went neither way. He just waited.

To draw out the fifth man.

It took some time, but eventually he heard the footsteps on the gravel. A consistent cadence, the sound of someone who knew how to walk with maximum efficiency and minimum effort. Someone who had learned to march. He watched the sniper appear from the other side of the Yukon, the tendril-like shape of the sniper rifle held at ease across his arms. He was in battle dress, an older version of the US Army's camouflage uniform. The woodland pattern, a design that had been made largely superfluous when the US military's battles had become desert-bound.

The team leader stopped short of the headlight beam and surveyed the landscape. He wasn't tall, but he wasn't short. He was a little older and had grown out his mustache into a scraggly beard. But he had the same broad shoulders, the same puffed chest. He wore the quiet confidence of a man doing exactly what he was best at. Flynn knew the look. A lot of guys in the Legion wore that look. Many wore it right up until the point that they crashed out, unable to take the conditions, or the solitude from family and friends, or the marching.

Flynn had known him as Steve White, his Legion name. But he recalled their last meeting, in Iraq. White had become a private security contractor and his name was Neil McConnell.

The pieces fell into place for Flynn. Two sides of the same coin. Amateur and professional. Dennison and his small-time grifting, finding himself in the middle of something way above his pay grade; and a professional unit, sent in to clean up the mess.

THE BROAD SCOTSMAN looked across the lit space at Ox Dennison's remains lying in the gravel. Then Cameron Dennison stepped forward. Dropped her handgun from Hutton's ear. It looked like she was going to pop McConnell in the side of the head. But McConnell didn't flinch.

Cameron said, "You didn't say you were going to blow his head off."

McConnell kept his eyes on Ox's body.

"What did you tell me you wanted?" he asked in his heavy Scottish brogue.

"Money?"

"Apart from the money."

"The farm?"

McConnell nodded. "The farm. This glorious farm. And when your parents died intestate, who did the court give the farm to?"

"What's intestate?"

McConnell huffed. "Without a will."

"You know who. Oxnard."

"And why did the court do that?"

"They thought I killed my parents."

"No. They knew you killed ya parents, lass. Lucky for you another court deemed you too young to be tried as an adult. So Ox got the farm. So sad. But then Ox disappeared in Iraq. And what did the court say?"

"They said the Army had him listed as MIA, not KIA. They said I had to wait until the Army changed its status or at least seven years."

"Because?"

"Because there was no—what did they call it? Tangible proof of death."

McConnell turned to Cameron. His voice remained low and steady. "There's your tangible proof. Now shut up."

He stepped into the light and across in front of Flynn. Picked up Flynn's Glock and looked at it like it was a dinosaur bone in an archeological dig.

"Glock," he said. "You went Austrian. I figured you would stick with the Italians."

"A gun is a gun."

McConnell suppressed a mirthless chuckle. "You always were so damn pragmatic. And so wrong. Take this fine weapon, for example." He tapped the sniper rifle in his arms. Flynn recognized it as an AS50 rifle produced in Britain by Accuracy International. It was designed for a 12.7×99mm NATO round, otherwise known as the .50 Browning machine gun cartridge. The BMG round had been in play since 1921, but the version that the military favored today bore little resemblance to the original. Flynn had heard they now incorporated microprocessors and steering vanes to adjust trajectory midflight, although he had never seen such a round in action.

McConnell continued. "This fine weapon is a work of art."

"The Barrett is more accurate."

McConnell shook his head. "You know that's not true. And at my level it's more about the quality of the round than the rifle. I can hit a coconut at fifteen hundred meters."

"And a human head."

McConnell nodded. "That was considerably closer."

"How far was the shot in Iraq?"

He frowned. "Iraq?"

"The suicide bomber that came for me and Hutton. That shot wasn't one of your men. That was you."

"Oh, that guy. You got me. But that was only about three hundred meters."

"In the dark."

McConnell shrugged, as if talk of his sniper skills embarrassed him.

"And you just happened to be there," said Flynn.

"Of course not. We were following you."

"What about the bombers' families? You did that too."

"We had to clean up Dennison's mess. He wanted to fix the problem. Make himself the big man. But he was shite. He thought he'd earn brownie points if he killed you. But my orders were to keep you alive. Because at that point they figured your death would attract too much attention."

"But the women and children at Dennison's safe house?"

"Casualties of war."

"They were little kids."

"Little kids grow to become men. And in that part of the world, they don't forget a damned thing. They remember who done them wrong. They remember for a thousand years. Better that they not grow up."

"That's cold."

McConnell shrugged. "You're no angel, remember."

Flynn remembered plenty. The ghosts visited often. But he had never put a double tap into a child.

McConnell stepped backward away from Flynn. As he moved, the light cascading over him lessened, until he reached the edge of the tire fort, where it became a soft glow. He looked at Beth. She was hanging limply from her bindings, her wind and strength gone. McConnell studied her for moment.

"A pretty one."

Flynn wanted him talking. "Where's your team?"

McConnell kept his eyes on Beth. "You did a good job on them, back at the house."

"They made mistakes."

"They made one. Those electric shock guns. We should have just shot you in the legs."

"Four guys, that's all you've got?"

McConnell nodded and looked at Flynn. "Don't be stupid. Don't go thinking that you've almost won. I had four guys because I didn't call for backup. I wanted you for myself. You did something with their shipment. They blamed me, even though it was this muppet that lost it." He turned and spat on Ox Dennison's body. "And I needed to clean it up."

"You should have come for me. You shouldn't have involved Beth."

"I didn't. That was Dennison. You don't get it, do you? They are everywhere. They were in your pretty girl's law offices. They heard her use your stupid phrase about the bogeyman. You shouldnae have a catchphrase, Flynn. Makes you famous."

"They can't have operatives everywhere, McConnell. The name of the organization would be everywhere."

"It is everywhere, you dullard. You call it what you want. Government. Big business. The church." McConnell smiled through his rough beard. "They have a billion eyes and ears. The minions working for them don't even know they're doing it. Take your girlie's clients. They think they're bankers. But everything they say is recorded and run through a super computer, searching for key phrases. Homeland security departments look for words like *attack* or *bomb*. But the same programs look for phrases like yours. And after all these years, they found one. So they called me back from the Middle East to check it out. But old Dennison here had his own little network and got wind of it. We were both in Iraq, so he called his sister from over there. Got the jump on me." He looked at the body in the gravel. "Not again. Now I right this, and I get my life back."

"You get your life back from whom?"

McConnell smiled. "You don't give up, do you?"

"Who's in charge?"

"You can't fix this one, Fontaine. Or Flynn, is it now? They are the system. And you can't beat the system."

"I can beat anybody."

"That's cocky, especially for you."

"I'm motivated."

"No. You're not. And that's the problem."

McConnell stuck Flynn's gun in the utility belt of his uniform and bent down next to the nearest burning drum. There was a small five-gallon gasoline canister sitting near the base. The fuel that the Dennisons used to start their fires. McConnell unscrewed the cap and then picked up the canister. He adjusted the strap on his rifle so it was pointing in Flynn's direction.

"Time to choose, Flynn. One of these lassies is going to burn. I'm going to keep the other one until you bring the shipment to me. That's motivation. Now, you choose which one is which. Who burns?"

Beth found her second wind. She stood bolt upright against the tires as if backing away from McConnell and the can of gasoline. Her eyes were wide. Flynn looked to Hutton. She was looking at Cameron Dennison. Cameron had wandered next to the nearest burning drum, where the firelight lit her from below.

"Come on, Flynn. You were always the leader. The pick of the litter. So make your choice. Don't make me burn them both."

Flynn said nothing.

"You're going to kill them both, Flynn. Choose!" McConnell shouted the last order. Flynn knew he was testing the Scotsman's patience. He knew the man was generally a cool customer. But he also knew that his attention could waver. So Flynn waited. He tensed and cocked his left leg and looked at the muzzle on the rifle and glanced at the handgun that Cameron Dennison held by her side. Her mouth had formed a grin. It wasn't a look that would win any elections.

"Choose," screamed McConnell.

"I choose Beth." He looked at her. She was his link to a normal life. His chance at love and a future without the bloodshed of his past. And it was gone. Up in smoke, as the saying went. Her eyes were on him. Wide and beyond fear. What he saw was hatred.

McConnell nodded. "And you call me cold." He dumped the gasoline around the base of the tires Beth was tied to, splashing it around. Then he threw the can away into the fort and took a lighter from his belt. Flicked on a small flame.

And dropped it.

CHAPTER THIRTY-TWO

GASOLINE LIQUID BURNS. BUT GASOLINE VAPOR EXPLODES. So the base of the tire turret burst with a whoomp, pulsing flame outward. Not a long way, but enough. McConnell took a reflex step back to avoid the momentary burst. The muzzle of his rifle pointed out to his right, into the darkness beyond the sedan on cinderblocks. Not where Flynn was.

But Flynn was no longer where he had been either. McConnell's lighter was in midair, dropping toward the gasoline when he pushed away. He pumped his arms hard, pumped his legs harder. It was the advantage of a Legion career. All that marching made his legs strong. But marching was essentially an aerobic activity, which burned a lot of calories. It kept him lean and trim up top. Which made him fast. Not Olympic sprint fast. That was as much genetics as training. But faster than most. He was halfway through the arc of the headlights when the gasoline ignited and the flame burst from the base of the tires to which Beth was tied.

McConnell reflexed away from the flame. It was then he saw the movement. A flash across the bright lights. His momentum had taken his rifle out on a wide arc away from the field of light, and he had to arrest that momentum before he could bring it back again. It took half a second to slow the rifle, stop it out wide and start it moving back toward Flynn.

It was a half second Flynn used to leap up, like a runner in the steeplechase. Not like a hurdler. In the hurdles, the runner jumped over the barrier, but in the steeplechase he aimed to land on the barrier, to use it to propel him forward. Over some kind of obstacle, like a pool of water. But Flynn's obstacle wasn't water. And he wasn't planning on going over it.

He pushed off with his left foot, up into the air. It needed to be well timed, and it was. He knew the drum well. They were standard across the world, despite the different measurement conventions. In the US they were called fifty-five-gallon barrels, in British imperial measures forty-four-gallons drums, and in metric two hundred liters. For ease of transport and storage, the standard height was 33.5 inches, or 851 millimeters. Flynn knew from long practice that his best running box jump under fatigue was a meter high. That gave him 149 millimeters leeway. His right foot landed on the rimmed edge of the capped oil drum. His knee bent and took the impact and then extended in one fluid motion. He swung his left leg through its natural arc and onward, propelling himself farther forward and upward.

The first shot cracked from McConnell's rifle as Flynn pushed up from the top of the drum. But the rifle was just moving back across its arc, and the shot passed between the barn and the house and away into the dark mountains beyond. The second shot rang out as the rifle swept around and hit one of the headlights on the Yukon. Then McConnell swung the rifle around toward the oil drum.

Flynn launched himself up from the drum into the air. His arms were wide and high as if he were attempting to fly. His legs came up into a midair tuck like lifting the landing gear on an aircraft. He felt the heat from the next drum. It was open and flame spewed from it. He should have been filled with panic, his breathing uncontrollable. But he wasn't. He was doing what he had been raised to do. He was taking action. He was defending those that could not defend themselves, just as his father had. Flynn could only imagine what he must have looked like, flying through the air, arms splayed, legs tucked, lit by fire like a gargoyle burst to life. He flew over the top of the flame, over the second drum. As his momentum waned and gravity took hold and he descended toward earth, he pushed out with his legs.

The third shot flew behind Flynn and smacked into the side of the farmhouse. Flynn kicked out and twisted his body. It was like some strange karate move. Not a recommended tactic. He was going to land hard on the ground, and nine times out of ten he didn't want to be lying on the ground in any kind of fight, let alone a firefight. But this wasn't nine of ten. This was the tenth time.

He thrust his feet out and his boots connected with the dumbstruck face of Cameron Dennison. She had been watching the flame burst from around Beth's feet and turned to see Flynn launch through the night sky at her. His boots cracked into her chin and cheekbone and sent her flying backward into a mound of tires. Flynn twisted and braced and hit the ground with a shocking thud.

It hurt. But not enough to stop him moving. Maybe broken ribs. Something to check on later. Now he was on the ground but behind cover. He pushed up and dove for the side of the farmhouse. A fourth and fifth shot hit the drums between him and McConnell. One of the rounds hit the full drum, and as he landed by the house, Flynn heard the gasoline spilling through the hole. He had tested the drum on his earlier visit and knew it to be full, but unless McConnell was using incendiary rounds it was unlikely to explode from a rifle shot.

Flynn felt for the grass at the base of the farmhouse and

wrapped his hands around the shotgun he had taken from Cameron Dennison's armoire. He swung it around and got into a crouch and spent a second considering the order of his next moves. McConnell was firing. Cameron was down but probably not out. Hutton was tied up between him and McConnell.

And Beth was burning.

He moved as fast as he could while staying below the height of the oil drums. He swung the shotgun up and out. A shotgun didn't hit a pinpoint target like a bullet. It sprayed lead shot across a wide area. The further it traveled, the wider the spray got. And Beth was out there, somewhere near McConnell. So Flynn aimed out toward the sedan on cinderblocks and fired. He shot with the gun in one hand. The recoil on a Remington can knock an inexperienced shooter off their feet, if the weapon is not tucked tight into their shoulder and their feet are not splayed and planted firmly on the ground. Flynn expected the impact. He didn't hit the ground. But the recoil spun him around like an ice skater. He spun into the side of the tires that Hutton was tied to. But Hutton was not next in line.

"You're crazy, your woman's out here," screamed McConnell. He popped off three more rounds into the side of the house, and Flynn recognized the sound of a Glock. McConnell had emptied the five rounds in the box magazine attached to his AS50. Now he was using Flynn's handgun. But he didn't know exactly where Flynn was. Flynn pushed off the turret toward Cameron. She was on her back, dazed but trying to sit up. Flynn didn't know if she still had Hutton's firearm. He didn't ask. He swung the shotgun around to grab it by the barrel and fore-end and then drove it down into Cameron's face. Some newer rifles had a rubber pad attached to the stock to lessen the impact of the recoil. An original Remington was all wood. It made a sickening crack on impact. Nose and cheekbone splitting. He didn't wait to observe the result.

Flynn spun back around to Hutton and pulled the Glauca knife from his pocket. He flicked out the blade and held it high and slashed down hard. The blade was sharp and it had little trouble with the oily rubber tied around Hutton. He slashed again and again, hitting the tires behind as he did. Hutton saw what he was doing and pulled at her bonds. Another slash and another cut and Hutton pulled and the rubber snapped.

Hutton fell forward and instinctively rolled away from the enemy. Flynn grabbed her arms and dragged her behind the tire turret. He dropped the shotgun and pulled her up and held her in place against the tires with his hand in the middle of her back. Then he cut the bonds that held her hands behind her. He snapped up the shotgun and flipped the knife around in his hand so the handle faced her.

"Beth," he said.

Hutton nodded. She pressed against the tire turret and looked around toward Beth.

Flynn ran the other way.

CHAPTER THIRTY-THREE_

FLYNN RAN INTO THE TIRE FORT. IT WAS A DARK MAZE, A mix of neat stacks of truck tires ten feet tall and mounds of car tires that reached as high as the farmhouse. He ran for one of the mounds. It was not easy going. Any football player can recount their training days, working hard to lift their knees high into the air as they stepped in and out of tires placed on the grass. One misstep, one toe connecting with the lip of a tire, and that was it. Crash and burn.

It was like running up a sand hill. Lots of effort for little reward. But Flynn needed the high ground. Initially. He got about a third of the way up. Beth's screams rang around the farm. He didn't have time to get higher. It would have to do. From this height he could see the old sedan across the way, and the big barn. Fires burned in between and lit the ragged shapes of the tires like a vision of hell. He raised the shotgun to his shoulder and fired at the rear side of the turret Beth was fixed to. It was high and wide, spattering the turret with pellets. But it wasn't the shot that was important. It was the muzzle flash.

The burst of flame as the gunpowder exploded from the barrel was like a lighthouse beacon on a rocky shore. High and handsome and obvious as hell. Flynn didn't clamber down from his perch. He jumped. He hit the ground and rolled as three shots hit the mound of tires up high. Flynn rolled to his feet and ran back, farther into the maze of tires. He heard McConnell cry out.

"That's your two, Flynn. You idiot."

Flynn ran. McConnell was right. It was his two. Two barrels, two shots. But Flynn knew something McConnell didn't know. He had learned it from Ox. He'd learned it by scoping the farm from his own position up the hill among the pines. He knew what a position on the hill could see. And what couldn't be seen. Ox had seen him place the MP5K under the sedan on the cinderblocks from his position up on the hill. But he couldn't see the back side of the house. He couldn't see the side of the house next to the tires. Flynn hadn't seen that spot from his position up there. So neither had McConnell, who had clearly been watching from a position higher on the hill where he didn't have full visibility of the farm. He had taken the high position to watch Flynn while he was watching the farm. So he hadn't seen Flynn go in and out of the back of the house and hadn't seen him place the shotgun in the grass.

McConnell didn't know about the spare shells in his pocket.

Flynn ran. Then he stopped. Near the rear of the tire fort. He was surrounded by tires. He broke the shotgun open and pulled out the warm shell casings, blasted open at the end. He dropped the spent shells into the pocket on the right side of his coat and pulled out two fresh shells from the pocket on the left. Slipped them into the barrels and clicked the breech closed.

Now he had to move. He liked the odds of a shotgun in close quarters against a sniper rifle. The rifle was long and unwieldy. It wasn't for close action. But McConnell also had Flynn's Glock, which gave him a close-quarters option. Flynn's advantage would be in the middle distance. The shotgun was like a cheap camera. Point and shoot. No problems with accuracy. A spatter of shots far and wide. But that offered a disadvantage. He couldn't shoot in the general direction of Beth and Hutton. Not even roughly, not even a little. Too much risk. Because with luck they would be mobile. And if the tire fort was somewhat of a circle, he was right across the diameter from where Beth was tied up.

So he ran. Into the maze of tires. He had a plan. An illogical plan. Not a plan that would have passed muster by any military general in the history of the world. He was taking the low ground. McConnell was a sniper. Snipers loved the high ground. He would go for it. The highest ground available. The top of the mound of tires. It was a gamble. By Flynn and by McConnell. Flynn's gamble was becoming a fish in a barrel. McConnell's gamble was the climb.

Flynn found a pocket in the maze of tires. In another context it might be called a dead end. But he would be able to see McConnell coming from the front, and he could hear him coming across the top of the tires from behind. Most importantly, he would be shooting up and away from the farm and wherever Hutton bunkered down with Beth. He pushed in against the tires and waited. His eyes on the large mound. Sights fixed at the peak. McConnell's best option was to edge up the mound backward. Butt down, face out, rifle at the ready.

Flynn didn't look for McConnell. He looked for movement. Gave it over to the dinosaur part of his brain. The prehistoric instinct of a predator. And he saw it. A flicker, the slightest hint of movement as the sniper moved into place. Without the drum fires he would never have seen it. On the outer edge of his peripheral vision. Not on the tire mound at all. On the roof of the farmhouse. It was a good placement. McConnell could see the driveway and fort and the turnaround and the barn. Flynn trained his eyes on the spot and waited for them to adjust. No more movement. McConnell was better than that. Not the best, not even close. But certainly good enough to stay damn still once he was in place. Flynn waited and looked and saw. The muzzle of the rifle, low on its bipod mount. Behind it a shape, indistinct from the roof and the trees and the night sky beyond. But a shape that he knew to be McConnell. It wasn't rocket science. Sniper rifles didn't fire themselves.

McConnell wouldn't be using the scope. The field of view was too narrow, and he didn't have a spotter. Good snipers love their spotters. Because good spotters keep snipers alive. They are their eyes on everything that isn't the target. Without a spotter, a good sniper felt naked. It was a symbiotic relationship. But one McConnell didn't have.

McConnell was working on a couple of assumptions. All erroneous. He figured Flynn was hiding in the tires because he was out of ammunition. He figured Flynn would want to get the women out as priority one. He figured they would try to leave via the driveway, in their vehicle.

He was wrong. Flynn was armed. Flynn's priority wasn't Beth. It was McConnell. Because Flynn was confident Hutton would get Beth out. And he was equally confident that Hutton would not use the driveway.

Flynn stayed low. He got into a crawl and kept to the deep shadows within the tire fort. He had time. McConnell would wait. That was what snipers did best, even better than shooting. Lots of people can shoot. Not so many can wait. Perfectly still. For hours, or days, or weeks. Flynn crawled across the gravel. It bit into his elbows and knees and ankles. He slithered his way to the back side of the tires. Keeping hard up against the tires, he stood and edged to the point closest to the farmhouse. It was McConnell's weak point. In order to get maximum coverage of the turnaround and the driveway, he was on the slope of the roof angled down on the side. He was blind to the drop away on the other side, toward the field. And he was blind to the drop directly below.

Flynn took three fast light steps across the open space to the side of the house. Then he slipped the shotgun under the pine railing onto the back porch of the house. He climbed up the same way as he had earlier that day. Nice and slow. Minimum noise. He was glad he had surveilled the location earlier, not just for the fact that he now had a shotgun. He also knew the house. He took up the shotgun and stayed to the edge of the porch and moved to the wall of the house. Then on his toes he moved along the wall. The boards gave some, but they didn't creak and groan like they would in the middle of the porch. He reached the door and eased it open, just enough to slip inside.

The interior was dark. But Flynn knew the lay of the land. And he knew the floors would creak just as much in here as on the porch. Nothing to be done about it. He couldn't stick to the walls. There was too much furniture and the detritus of farm life. Magazine stands and floor lamps and wood for the fire. So he gave up silence and traded it in for speed.

He held the shotgun high and ran around the ratty sofa and made for the kitchen. The floors groaned and the walls shook. There was a transition between the floor in the main space and the floor in the kitchen. The toe of his boot hit it and he stopped on the mark. And fired into the ceiling. It was old plasterboard. Above it was a corrugated iron roof. The shot hit the ceiling and a torrent of plaster rained down. Flynn adjusted his aim slightly and fired his second shot. More plaster rain and the shot of pellets hitting sheet metal. And a grunt. A human grunt. Then the sounds of movement, like a giant raccoon scampering across the roof.

Flynn ran for the front door. He broke the shotgun open as he did. Pulled the two shells from the breech and stuffed them in his right pocket. Pulled out his last two shells and pushed them home and snapped the gun shut as he burst through the door. McConnell had jumped from the roof and hit the gravel and rolled. He was on his way up, breaking into a sprint. He ran toward the tires. He still held his sniper rifle. Snipers hated to lose their rifles. It was ingrained in them. Sniper rifles were very expensive, so armies trained their snipers not to lose them. It was good financial sense, but a bad move tactically. The weapon was long and unwieldy and put McConnell's motion all out of kilter. Over the course of a mile he would probably end up running in a circle. But he didn't get a mile.

Flynn splayed his feet across the front porch and tucked the Remington tight into his shoulder and lined up the iron sights. Then McConnell stopped running. Hit the brakes hard and skidded on the gravel. In one fluid move he discarded the rifle and spun around and dropped into a crouch and came up holding a handgun.

Flynn's Glock.

McConnell fired. He was a good shot. Not the best ever, but good. Under duress, with an elevated heart rate and blood pumping hard, he steadied a handgun and fired at a distance of about twenty yards. Ox Dennison would have been fifty-fifty to hit the house. Flynn would have been ninety-five percent to hit a target on the range.

McConnell's shot hit Flynn. His left triceps. His arm was up and angled, supporting the shotgun. McConnell's shot was slightly wide but took muscle with it. The pain stabbed at Flynn like an ice pick. He dropped back against the front of the house, grabbing at his arm. Blood ebbed into the fabric of his shirt. Some field medic somewhere would have grinned and called it a flesh wound. But Flynn had been shot before—through and through—in the chest. And this hurt more. But it wasn't gushing blood. It wouldn't kill him. Not today. He gritted his teeth and pushed away from the wall. McConnell was still out there. He had gotten his shot away.

But so had Flynn.

Flynn had his sights right on target. He knew he'd hit. He just didn't know how bad. He stepped down off the porch and crunched across the gravel. In the light of the fires and single remaining headlight, he saw the divot in the gravel, where McConnell's boots had bitten into the ground as he'd stopped and spun. But McConnell was not there. His sniper rifle lay where he had dropped it. Flynn's Glock lay nearby. Flynn picked it up and looked at the drag marks in the gravel.

McConnell had retreated to cover. Into the tire fort. He had dragged himself behind the turret Beth had been tied to. She was gone. McConnell was still there. He was using one arm to pull himself along the ground. The other arm didn't appear to function anymore.

"McConnell."

The Scotsman stopped. He lay motionless for a time, then he used his good arm to roll over. Flynn kept the shotgun aimed at him. McConnell was a mess. He had worn the shot all over. The bull's-eye was centered on his chest. His face was a bloody mess. One eye was a mass of red pulp. He was bleeding from a thousand holes. He was hit in the side of the neck and was choking on his own blood. He needed to sit up. He tried but couldn't do it with one arm. Flynn wasn't in a helping mood. He crouched by his old Legion brother.

"Who are they?"

McConnell gurgled.

"Who are they?"

McConnell spat blood. "They are your worst enemy. And your closest ally." He seemed to smile. It may have been a grimace. Flynn stood and looked down at McConnell. He thought about walking away. Then he thought about Ox

Dennison coming back from the dead. There would be no more coming back from the dead. Not for any of them. He looked at his Glock. It was the humane thing to do. One shot and McConnell was out of his misery. Flynn would do it for a dog. He aimed at McConnell's forehead and saw him brace his jaw.

Then Flynn pulled away. Dropped down again so he could hear McConnell's voice.

"Back in Iraq. My guy, Babar. Was that them or was that you?"

McConnell wheezed and gurgled. Bubbles of blood popped from his throat. And then he smiled. Through the ragged flesh of his face, he smiled.

"Babar the elephant man." McConnell coughed. "He cried like a baby."

Flynn stood. Aimed the Glock at McConnell again and watched him set his jaw once more. McConnell waited, and then frowned.

"Do it," he spat. "Do—"

He choked on the second word. It was his last. Flynn stood over him and waited. Until his chest stopped and the bubbles in his throat stopped popping and the blood stopped moving through his body.

Then Flynn walked away.

He moved slow, across the turnaround. To the Yukon. His daypack was inside. He removed his coat and wrapped duct tape around the wound in his arm. Duct tape was as good a field dressing as there was. But he made sure to put in on the outside of his shirt, because taking it off skin was a chore. He knew that for a fact.

He slipped his coat back on and walked across to the tire fort. To the side by the house. He found Cameron Dennison. She was not in good shape. The butt of the shotgun had really messed her up. Probably both cheekbones, definitely her nose.

She was only semiconscious. She was lying where she had fallen and sucking shallow breaths through her mouth.

Flynn found Hutton's Glock lying on the gravel a couple of feet away. He pocketed it and then crouched in front of Cameron. He didn't speak. He didn't ask her any questions. He just held the shotgun with the stock low and the barrel at Cameron's face, and he leaned back and turned away and pulled the trigger.

The sound was loud, but no louder than having the gun tucked into his shoulder. He wiped the trigger and the stock and then dropped the shotgun next to Cameron's body. He stood and turned away and looked around. For no reason, he thought of Rudyard Kipling. His poem, *If*.

If you can keep your head when all about you
Are losing theirs and blaming it on you ...

CHAPTER THIRTY-FOUR

FLYNN CALLED FOR HUTTON BUT GOT NO RESPONSE. He searched around the tires and looked out into the darkness of the fields. He walked through the barn, the machinery silent. He pushed out through the door partly hidden in the wall. As he stepped back outside, he saw it. The storm door, built into a cement collar in the ground. Not an entrance, but an exit. Except that now it lay open. Hutton had been in there, hidden, when Flynn had first visited the farm. Beth had been secreted away through the tunnels below it, from wherever the old Dennison family moonshine still was hidden.

He started up the Yukon. He backed out, and then had a thought and hit the gas and drove forward fast and turned toward the tire fort. Hit the drum full of gasoline at speed. The drum collapsed and gasoline spilled across the tires. Flynn pulled back and used the turnaround and pointed the one head-light down the driveway. Watched the rearview mirror as the gasoline spilled and sparks from the remaining fires descended gently into it and it burst to life. There was no explosion. Nothing so dramatic. Just the beginning of a long, slow burn.

His breathing remained steady, but he was under no illusion that this fire wouldn't also come back to haunt him later.

He drove up the road and hit the fence line he had used before, and bounced up the hill to where his lookout had been. Stopped behind the pines and cut the engine and called for Hutton. Waited and called again. Waited a whole minute and called again.

"Keep it down," she said from the darkness. Hutton was holding Beth up. Beth didn't appear hurt, but her motor skills were frazzled. Her brain had shut down. Flynn had seen it before. Fear can be truly debilitating. Flynn asked if she was alright, but she didn't respond. He helped her into the truck.

"Is she okay?" he asked Hutton.

"Physically, yes. Lucky rubber's a slow burn. The fumes would probably have gotten her before the flames did."

They drove back to the main road in silence. The lights were on in the diner. There was one car in the lot. The waitress's car. Flynn stopped and went inside. He wasn't sure if she would remember him. Her memory wasn't so good. But she looked up and offered him a nod. Then she frowned at his condition. He was covered in ash and gravel and dirt and sweat and blood. His trousers had holes at the knees and his coat was torn at the elbows.

"You're here late," Flynn said.

"I figured you'd be back. Or not."

"Thanks for waiting."

"Did you win?" she asked.

He nodded. "Can I get three bottles of water, and three slices of pie to go?"

She fished three bottles from a beverage fridge and put them on the counter. Then she put a single piece of pie into a container. Flynn said nothing. He patted his pockets for some money.

"On the house," she said.

He nodded again. "There's a big fire out there. At the Dennison place."

The waitress shrugged. "That was always the risk. All those tires."

FLYNN DROVE BACK to New York. He thought in passing about finding a hotel, for everyone to freshen up and maybe get some sleep. But a look in the rearview mirror told him Beth would not be sleeping. He drove on in silence. They arrived in Manhattan as the morning broke. Flynn left the Yukon in the garage below Hutton's building. She said she would take care of the truck. Hedstrom knew a guy who was good with that sort of thing. Beth washed up in the bathroom in Hutton's offices.

While Beth was cleaning up, Flynn took the downtown train to his bank. He went through the same process. He drank the espresso and waited for his box. When he was alone, he opened the secure box and returned the Glock he had taken from it. He returned the knife and the duct tape but kept the cash. He pulled out his old backpack and replaced it with the daypack the bank had given him on his last visit. Then he took out a Ziploc bag. *John Flynn* written on the front. He took a moment to look at the name. In the bag there was nothing more than documents. But those documents represented something. Or someone. Someone he had not had the chance to become as a young man, and had then been given a chance to become a decade later. Now he felt that chance had slipped away. He thought, perhaps, that it was someone he was not destined to ever become.

But he had come to a decision. He was not becoming someone else again. He was who he was—like everyone, the product of his experiences, good and bad. He opened the bag and took out the wallet, his ID, his passport. Slipped them into his pockets. He bore his mother's last name and his father's first, and that was how it should be. That was how he would go on.

He got back to find Beth sitting in Hutton's office. She looked better, more alive, but not complete. Flynn left her to her thoughts and found Hutton in her conference room.

"Is she okay?" Hutton asked.

"Alive," he said. "Otherwise, I don't know. You know how these things go. When you see the worst that people can do, it changes you."

Hutton nodded. "Are you okay?"

"Alive," he said. "How are you?"

She shrugged. "I didn't really learn anything about why I got forced out of the Bureau."

They stood in silence for a time, looking at each other.

"She'll understand, with time," said Hutton.

Flynn watched her. Hutton meant what she said, but he knew that understanding was not acceptance. Nothing would be the same. Dreams would come to Beth and she would deal with them or not. She might enlist professional help. But in the end, what happened in the mind was the sole domain of the landlord. No one could change you or fix you. They could set you on the path, but they couldn't climb inside and rearrange the furniture. He knew that he, too, would continue to face his demons, but he had had a lot more practice.

"What will you do?" Hutton asked.

"Work the problem."

"They're out there, aren't they?"

"It would seem."

"They won't give up."

"It's unlikely."

Hutton nodded. "If you need me . . ."

Flynn nodded and stepped to her and they wrapped their arms around each other for a moment. Then they separated and walked back to Hutton's office.

Hutton offered to drive them back to DC. He told her it wasn't necessary but he knew it was a futile argument. They retraced their steps back through Baltimore and down the parkway and into the capital. They drove mostly in silence. Hutton dropped them at the Watergate. She wished Beth well and Beth thanked her for saving her life. A simple thank you didn't seem to cover it, but there were no better words available. Hutton looked at Flynn across the hood of her car.

"Au revoir," he said.

Hutton smiled. "You said goodbye this time. That's real growth."

Flynn nodded. "I owe you."

Hutton shook her head, opened the door and slipped back into her car. The window on the passenger side buzzed down.

"Don't be a stranger," Hutton said, and then she drove away.

———

FLYNN AND BETH flew to San Francisco early the following morning. Beth had processed events enough to function but not enough to forget. On the flight she came up with the story she would tell her firm. There were likely criminal activities associated with the prospective client, and the firm would do well to stay well away from them. The partners would buy that and be thankful and give her a one-time grace for the expenses and unbillable hours.

When they got home to San Rafael, Flynn unloaded his backpack on their bed. Then he repacked it. He took everything he figured he'd need and nothing he didn't. He strapped it on his back. It felt like a second skin.

Beth didn't ask him to stay and he saw all he needed to in her eyes. She loved him, he knew that. But there were words stuck in her mind that would haunt her. Words she might learn to suppress but which would never be forgotten. McConnell had asked which woman should burn. And Flynn had said *Beth*. She would understand in time that he had chosen her for a reason—the best chance for her survival. Hutton was the better equipped to save them both, so Beth had to be the one McConnell was focused on. But logic would fight that battle and lose. Bridges had been burned. Her eyes would never again fall on him in the same way.

"They won't come again, if I'm not here," he said. He hoped it were true. The kidnapping had been Dennison's idea, and his side of the equation had been taken out. Flynn pressed a piece of paper into her hand. "But if there's ever any reason you think they have, use this. I'll come."

He kissed her as a tear ran down her cheek, and then turned and walked out onto the street. A cold morning in the Bay Area. There was a ring of cloud around Mount Tam, but otherwise a bright blue sky. A perfect day for leaving. A perfect day for marching.

Flynn settled the pack on his back and marched down past the Mission San Rafael. It was a good thirty-eight kilometers to Petaluma, staying off 101 where possible. He would be there before the businesses closed for the day. He'd rest up and then break east the next morning. Toward Sacramento and then Reno and then Utah and Colorado.

He'd keep marching until he came up with a reason to stop.

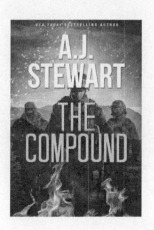

IF YOU ENJOYED THIS BOOK_

One of the most powerful things a reader can do is recommend a writer's work to a friend. So if you have friends you think will enjoy John Flynn, please tell them.

Your honest reviews help other readers discover John Flynn, so if you enjoyed this book and would like to spread the word, just take one minute to leave a short review. I'd be eternally grateful, and I hope new readers will be too.

ACKNOWLEDGMENTS_

Thanks to all my readers who send me feedback.

Thanks to the betas and early readers.

Thanks to Constance for the valuable feedback on character development and story. Your thoughts are gold.

Thanks to Eliza for the editing and Stacey for the proofing. Any remaining errors are mine.

ABOUT THE AUTHOR_

A.J. Stewart is the USA Today bestselling author of the John Flynn thriller series and the Miami Jones Florida mystery series.

He currently resides in Los Angeles with his two favorite people, his wife and son.

AJ is working on a screenplay that he never plans to produce, but it gives him something to talk about at parties in LA.

You can find AJ online at
www.ajstewartbooks.com

Made in the USA
Las Vegas, NV
13 March 2023

69000433R00194